MURDER
IN THE
RUE CHARTRES

THE CHANSE MACLEOD MYSTERIES
by Greg Herren

Murder in the Rue St. Ann
Murder in the Rue Dauphine

MURDER
IN THE
RUE CHARTRES

A CHANSE MACLEOD MYSTERY

GREG HERREN

alyson books
NEW YORK

Manufactured in the United States of America

This trade paperback original is published by Alyson Books
245 West 17th Street, New York, NY 10011
Distribution in the United Kingdom by Turnaround Publisher Services Ltd.
Unit 3, Olympia Trading Estate, Coburg Road, Wood Green
London N22 6TZ England

First Edition: November 2007

08 09 10 11 a 10 9 8 7 6 5 4 3 2

ISBN: 1-55583-966-5
ISBN-13: 978-1-55583-966-6

Library of Congress Cataloging-in-Publication data are on file.

Cover design by Victor Mingovits
Interior design by Jane Raese

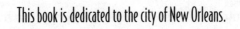

This book is dedicated to the city of New Orleans.

"I came out in the French Quarter years before
I came out in the Garden District."

from *Suddenly Last Summer* by Tennessee Williams

CHAPTER ONE

IT WAS SIX WEEKS before I returned to my broken city.

Usually when I drove home from the west, as soon as I crossed onto dry land again in Kenner, excitement would bubble up inside and I'd start to smile. *Almost home*, I'd think, and let out a sigh of relief. New Orleans was home for me, and I hated leaving for any reason. I'd never regretted moving there after graduating from LSU. It was the first place I'd ever felt at home, like I belonged. I'd hated the little town in east Texas where I'd grown up. All I could think about was getting old enough to escape. Baton Rouge for college had been merely a way station—it never occurred to me to permanently settle there. New Orleans was where I belonged, and I'd known that the first time I'd ever set foot in the city. It was a crazy quilt of eccentricities, frivolities, and irritations sweltering in the damp heat, a city where you could buy a drink at any time of day, a place where you could easily believe in magic. I couldn't imagine living anywhere else. Any time I'd taken a trip before, within a few days I'd get homesick and start counting the hours until it was time to come home.

But this time wasn't like the others. This time, I hadn't been able to come home, and had no idea how long it would be before I could. Now, I was nervous, my stomach clenched into knots, my palms sweating on the steering wheel as I sang along to Vicki Sue Robinson's "Turn the Beat Around" on the radio. It was everything I'd feared for the last few weeks when I thought about coming home, the anxiety building as the odometer clocked off another mile and I got closer to home.

It was *different*.

The most obvious thing was the lack of traffic. Even outside the airport, the traffic was usually heavy, sometimes slowing to a complete standstill. But other than a couple of military vehicles, a cement mixer, and a couple of dirty and tired looking sedans, I-10 was deserted. There was a film of dirt on everything as far as I could see, tinting my vision sepia. Huge trees lay toppled and debris was everywhere. Signs that used to advertise hotels, motels, restaurants, storage facilities, and pretty much any kind of business you could think of were now just poles, the signs gone except for the support skeleton. Buildings had been blown over, fences were wrecked and down, and almost everywhere I looked blue tarps hung on roofs, their edges lifting in the slight breeze. My breath started coming a little faster, my eyes filled, and I bit down on my lower lip as I focused back on the road.

No cars joined at the airport on-ramp, or the one at Williams Boulevard just beyond it. No planes were landing or taking off.

"Because we believe in rebuilding New Orleans, we here at—"

I jabbed a finger at the car stereo and Faith Hill's voice filled the car. I settled back into my seat. I was ready to be out of the car. It was just past four. I'd been on the road since seven and my back was starting to ache, my legs tightening up. No matter what I found when I got to my house, it would feel good just to get out of the car. My best friend Paige's apartment just a few blocks away was fine, and she'd been back as soon as power had been restored. She'd evacuated with other reporters from the *Times-Picayune* to Baton Rouge, and had been in and out of the city daily until she could return home. Her landline was still down, and cell phone service had been spotty since the storm for those with a 504 area code—sometimes you could get through; sometimes you couldn't. She'd gone by my apartment and given me a report within a few days after the disaster. The roof was still on, there was no mold, all my windows were intact, and most importantly, my neighborhood was not under water. She'd emptied out my refrigerator, opened some of the windows to get air circulating to help fight mold—and when the power came back on she'd turned the air conditioning on. I was luckier than most. The flood hadn't reached my house and the massive old oak in front of the house hadn't fallen. For me, it was just a matter of *when* I could come home, rather than what would I find when I finally did.

At least I had something to come back to. So many had nothing.

A few cars zoomed onto I-10 from the Causeway, and that was even stranger. No matter the time of day, the interchange between the two highways was always stop-and-go traffic. There was just no one in New Orleans, no one going in or out. I went around the corner just after the 610 split and headed for the underpass near Metairie Road, and that's when I saw that the mud line along the concrete walls was over my head. I choked back a sob and tried to fight the tears again. *Get a hold of yourself,* I thought. *It's going to get worse the further in you go. Be strong—you have to be strong.*

The huge red crawfish atop the Semolina's at Metairie Road was gone. Surely they hadn't taken it down—the wind must have blown it away. I swallowed and then couldn't help but smile a little. Maybe it had wound up in one of the cemeteries just beyond, wedged headfirst into a house of the dead. *Now THAT would be a really fun picture,* I thought, but then had the sobering thought that it also might have blown through someone's roof. But even that struck me as funny, in a gallows humor kind of way. How would you report that to your insurance company? "Um, a huge crawfish is embedded in my roof." It wasn't funny, really, but it was a distracting thought.

And then I went around the curve and saw the city skyline in the distance. It was immediately apparent to me, even at that distance, that the Superdome didn't look right.

I'd loved the Superdome. I played in two Sugar Bowls there when I was playing college football at LSU, to the roars of crowds wearing purple and gold, holding signs saying *Geaux Tigers* and other Louisiana-flavored slogans. After graduation, I'd cheered the Saints on through years of futility, shaking my head with everyone else as they blew another game, another season, and sank into the NFL cellar yet again, heading back to the beer vender in my black-and-gold jersey to drown my sorrows. I'd been to concerts there—U2, one of Cher's numerous farewell tours, and countless others. The odd oval shape just before the taller buildings of the Central Business District always brought a sense of joy to me, as another sign I was getting closer to home all those other times I'd driven back into the city. But now it meant something different, more than just another landmark of my homecoming. It was now a symbol of almost unimaginable misery and suffering, witnessed by the entire world—just as *New Orleans* itself meant tragedy, disaster and death instead of *let the good times roll*, good food, lots of drink, and Mardi Gras. As I sped closer, I could see that half the roof had been torn off by the wind.

Now, it resembled a half-peeled hard-boiled egg.

I took my eyes off it, instinctively readying myself for the interchange of I-90 West, I-10, and I-90 East, which all converged just before the St. Charles Avenue exit, with cars merging and trying to exit in the engineering nightmare of three or four on-ramps too close together for rational, safe merging. But there were no cars, even here. I didn't even have to touch my brakes once as I flew through and headed down the off-ramp. I stomped down a little too hard on the brakes once I realized the traffic light at the bottom was dark and a stop sign had been erected. It didn't matter. There was no traffic other than a station wagon crossing the intersection a block ahead. I glanced to my left and saw filthy cars, coated in mud, abandoned in the Mass Transit parking area under the elevated highway. There were hundreds of them, it seemed. I swallowed and drove ahead to St. Charles.

St. Charles during daylight weekday hours was always a hive of activity. The streets were crowded, the streetcars would be running, people would be walking along the sidewalks. There would be people in front of the Popeye's, cars in the drive-through at Wendy's, a full parking lot at Office Depot. The St. Charles Tavern was always full of people, as was the Voodoo BBQ on the opposite corner. Instead, all I could see were massive tree branches along the neutral ground and sidewalks. Some of the trees were denuded of branches and stood naked in the bright sunlight. Dirt, debris, and garbage were everywhere. Storefronts were boarded up. There were messages spray-painted on the plywood.

LOOTERS WILL BE SHOT ON SIGHT,
DON'T EVEN TRY IT.

WE ARE ARMED AND WILL SHOOT
ANYONE TRYING TO BREAK IN.

But then one on a carpet shop made me smile.

8/30 I AM HERE WITH A GUN, A MEAN DOG,
AND AN UGLY WOMAN.

9/2 STILL HERE, WOMAN LEFT YESTERDAY,
MAKING DOG GUMBO.

I turned down Euterpe, right past the darkened Burger King, and headed for Coliseum Square. There was no sign of life anywhere. The houses were empty, no cars in the driveways or parked in front. There were piles of roof tiles and garbage everywhere I looked. One of the huge oaks in the empty park was down, its massive gnarled roots stabbing at the sky. I turned onto Camp Street and pulled up in front of my house.

Paige had been right. There was debris all around the house, and some of it was roof tile. But the front windows appeared to be intact. The iron fence was leaning closer to the ground than it had been, and one of the huge branches that shaded the walk to the porch had been torn off, but there was no sign of it anywhere. It must have been carried off by the high winds. I got out of the car, lit a cigarette, and just stared at my house.

It had only been six weeks since I left. Six weeks that seemed like a lifetime.

The one litany that had gone through my mind the entire

time I was away was *I want to go home!* I'd been to several places in my wanderings since August 28, but everywhere I went, the places seemed different to me somehow, unreal in a strange way that made no sense. Maybe it was me that was different, I don't know. Those weeks had passed in a strange fog, days drifting into each other, one day after another in a monotonous surreal pastiche. I'd lost track of dates, even what day of the week it was. I was numb, and when I could feel something, it was sorrow and depression. I couldn't watch television after a certain point. I tried to read, focus on my work, but my mind just couldn't stay focused. I found myself searching message boards online, boiling with rage when reading ignorant posts by heartless bastards who claimed we got what we deserved for being so stupid as to live below sea level, or those who claimed it was God's punishment on New Orleans for her sins. The ignorance and cruelty of my fellow human beings had rarely surprised me before the disaster, but coming face to face with it in this instance, when we were all hurting beyond anything we could have imagined, consumed me with anger. But the rage felt good, because I'd begun to wonder if I'd ever be able to feel anything besides sorrow again—sorrow and guilt. I felt tremendous guilt for abandoning New Orleans, my city and home, to die by herself. Of course, there was nothing I could have done, but that didn't make the feeling any less real. I somehow felt like I'd betrayed the city I loved by not staying to die with her.

I'd taken enormous pride in the fact that I'd never evacuated before. I stayed for both Jorges and Ivan since I'd moved to New Orleans. In both cases the storms had turned to the east at the last moment, unleashing their fury elsewhere on the Gulf Coast. I'd never lost power, phone, or cable for either one of them. It hadn't even rained at my house during Jorges. I figured this one would do the same at first as the television started preaching death and destruction and the need to leave. While most people were stuck on the westbound lanes of I-10 on Saturday, I'd been calmly watching the doomsday forecasts on the Weather Channel. I went to the grocery store and stocked up on supplies—bottled water, canned goods, batteries, and candles, fighting my way through the panicked mobs in the store. But when I'd woken up that Sunday morning, turned on the television, and saw the size of the monster in the Gulf, in horror I realized that even if it turned east at the last minute, New Orleans was going to get hit, and hit hard. The size of the storm surge in the Gulf would surely overtop the levees along the river and the lake, and all those computer-generated models they'd been showing every year during hurricane season could possibly come true. Even as I sat staring at the Doppler images, Paige called and told me to get the fuck out of town as fast as I could. The terror in her voice was enough to erase any doubt that I had left. "We're going up to Baton Rouge," she said, her voice shaking with fear, "but man, you've got to go this time. And pray for the city." She hung up without giving me a chance to answer.

I packed in a daze, not knowing what to take or where I was going. Like the rest, I figured I'd go west and just get a room somewhere, maybe as far away as Houston. I don't really remember much of that morning; it passed in a haze as I rushed around the apartment looking for things like my birth certificate, my passport, the title to my car, and other things that would be hard to replace. I was in shock, and every once in a while I would break down crying. This was it, the Big One they'd been warning about for years, and it was possible I might not ever be able to come home. But I put those thoughts out of my head; New Orleans somehow always survived...and there was still a chance it might turn and spare the city its fury.

I wound up going to Dallas. I was throwing clothes into a suitcase when my phone rang.

"Chanse, this is Jude. I think you should come here."

I stopped, my hands full of black Calvin Klein underwear. "Really?"

"Yeah." Jude swallowed. "It doesn't have to mean anything. Really." He paused for a minute, waiting for me to answer. When I didn't respond, he said in a rush, "There's no sense in wasting money on a hotel room. Just come here."

"It makes sense," I said, putting the underwear into the suitcase, relieved to finally have some kind of plan. "Thanks, I appreciate it. It'll only be for a few days anyway."

"Yeah. Exactly." He sounded more relaxed, relieved. "You'd better get moving, okay? Call me from the road and let me know how you're doing, okay?"

It had probably cost him a lot to put himself out there. We'd reached a strange place in our relationship. Then again, our relationship had never exactly been normal to begin with. He'd been a friend and former sex partner of my boyfriend, Paul. We'd really come together after Paul had died a year ago. A few weeks after the funeral, he'd come to New Orleans for Halloween weekend, and we'd had dinner together at the Napoleon House. I hadn't wanted to go meet him, but finally figured it was better than just sitting around the house drinking vodka all night yet again. He was kind and sweet, and he could somehow, despite everything, make me laugh—and I'd almost forgotten what it felt like to laugh. We'd started talking on the telephone a couple of times a week. Paige warned me that it was a rebound thing, over and over again, like a broken record. "You're not ready for this, and you're going to wind up hurting him," she warned.

But I didn't care. Whenever I talked to Jude, I forgot. I was able to leave the misery and the loneliness and the pain behind and go to a different place. Not completely happy—there was always a sense of melancholy—but it was better than where I was. And it was infinitely better than the other ways I'd found, ways that involved way too much liquor and strangers with hard-muscled bodies with names I didn't want to learn or remember.

It had been almost a year now, and the last time Jude had come to New Orleans, he'd made it quite clear we needed to talk about things. We'd been coasting along quite well, but I knew at some point the ride was going to end unless we made a commitment of some sort. I tried to avoid the subject at all costs. I didn't want to talk about things. I knew I was being selfish and unfair to him, but I just didn't want things to develop any further just yet. I liked the distance between our two cities, and the lack of real seriousness the geography created. And while Jude was helping me to forget and move on, I didn't know that it was right that I should. The only way we could move forward would be for me to put Paul aside once and for all. And somehow, that didn't seem right to me.

And besides, I'd been a really shitty boyfriend to Paul.

Jude finally gave up, resigning himself to defeat, but there was a brittle quality to the weekend after that. And after I'd dropped him off at the airport—where we gave each other a listless, perfunctory kiss, I cursed myself for a fool. As he got out of the car, I fought down the urge to get out and go after him. Instead, I watched him walk into the airport and then drove off myself.

It seemed like a million years ago now. I put my cigarette out, took a deep breath, and walked through the gate into the front yard.

The house was a graceful old Victorian, painted fuchsia. It had been split into apartments; two side by side in the front, a large one that took up the back of the first floor, and two large ones upstairs. Mine was the one to the left. It ran alongside the driveway into the small parking lot in the back. I unlocked my door and stepped into the house.

It was cool inside. I always kept my apartment at about the temperature of a meat locker, and Paige had apparently turned it down to the level she knew I liked. The light in the kitchen was on. I looked up at the eighteen-foot high ceilings. No sign of mold up there or on the walls—she'd said there hadn't been, but I wanted to be sure for myself. I walked into the center room, which had been split into a hallway, bathroom, and small kitchen. There were dishes in the sink I'd left; there was mold on them. There were spores of mold in the coffee pot, which I'd left half full. But the walls and ceiling seemed okay in there as well, so I looked into the bathroom. The towel I'd hung to dry the morning I'd left for Texas was stiff but okay. I flushed the toilet to make sure it worked, and turned on the spigot in the sink. Everything was okay. I walked back to my bedroom.

It was strange. I wasn't sure what I'd been expecting, but the apartment was exactly the way I'd left it. It was almost like I'd just left to go to the grocery store or run errands, not been gone for six weeks. The bed was unmade and my laundry basket was overflowing. *That's right, I was going to go do the laundry on Monday,* I remembered, smiling at the memory.

That was before. Everything had changed in such a short period of time. Friday morning had been such a lovely day— hot and sunny and humid—typical of late August. I'd gotten up that morning, still a little distressed about not having heard from Jude since he'd gotten home. And a new client had called and fired me that morning.

Oh, yeah, that's right, I thought, and walked back into the living room to my desk. Sure enough, in the top left-hand drawer was a deposit slip and her retainer check for $2,500. She'd hired me on Wednesday, and I hadn't had the chance to get to the bank before she let me go.

I picked up the file I'd started for her, labeled VERLAINE, IRIS. I opened the file and took a look at the notes I'd written. Her business card was neatly paper-clipped to the inside. It was a thick, creamy-colored card, with her name in raised neat script on heavy vellum, and underneath in bold letters, *Vice President of Public Relations.* In the upper-right-hand corner was a multicolored logo featuring the prow of a freighter cutting through a breaking wave. In understated, slightly smaller letters underneath her title were the words VERLAINE SHIPPING COMPANY. On the bottom right, in the same understated font, were her office address, phone and fax numbers, and e-mail address: iverlaine@verlaineships. com.

I'd given her my card that day too.

I walked through the house, opening the windows as far up as they would go. It was a warm, sunny day. October was always beautiful in New Orleans, no humidity and sweet cool breezes that made the curtains dance. There was a thick layer of dust on everything in the apartment. I walked back out to the car, and marveled again at the almost absolute silence. I opened the trunk and got out the ice chest I'd bought at a Dallas Wal-Mart—almost everything in the car had come from Wal-Mart. It never entered my mind when I left that I wouldn't be back in a few days, so I'd packed haphazardly and only took enough clothes for four days. When the levees broke and it became horribly apparent to me I was going to be gone for a long while, I'd had to go buy clothes.

But even then, it never entered my mind I wouldn't ever be coming back. Relocating and not returning was never an option. New Orleans was my home; I'd lived there for almost eight years. With no offense to Dallas, I couldn't imagine relocating there and starting my business over again. Granted, it wouldn't have been that much of a struggle; my main source of income comes from working as a corporate security consultant for my landlady's company, Crown Oil. Crown Oil's corporate headquarters were in Tulsa, but they also had a skyscraper in Dallas. I could easily get office space there, but it wasn't what I wanted, where I could imagine staying for the rest of my life. No, no matter how bad it was, at some point I was returning to New Orleans. And with that in mind, I'd headed for Wal-Mart rather than Macy's or Dillard's or the Gap.

My closet was full of clothes, and so were my dresser and my armoire. I just needed some temporary stuff until I got back home, so why spend a lot of money? So, I drove over to the Wal-Mart and stocked up on cheap socks and underwear and T-shirts. I missed my clothes, my comfortable underwear, and was tired of wearing the cheap shorts and T-shirts. And when I was finally able to begin planning my return to New Orleans, another storm came in.

"It's okay." Jude said, as we watched the progress of Rita as she approached the Gulf Coast, and the mayor of New Orleans ordered everyone who had returned to leave again. "It won't affect New Orleans much, and you just need to stay here a few more days is all."

Jude refused to let me pay for anything, which made me feel like shit. He refused rent money, grocery money, any offer to take him out to dinner. He was always polite about it, but firm. "I won't hear of it," he would say as he unpacked groceries, leaving me standing there with a hundred-dollar bill crumpled in my hand. "I'd like to think if the situation were reversed, you'd help me the same way." Then he would bark out a bitter little laugh. "It's what friends do, right?"

And I would squirm in my smallness, wondering if I would indeed open my house and wallet to him, and hating myself for even harboring the doubt.

And even though Jude's bed was big and warm, and the feel of a warm body next to mine every night was a comfort, all I wanted was to be in my own bed, under my own roof, with my own clothes. The first night, I wasn't sure what to expect—although I was grateful Jude didn't put me in the spare room. We lay there, next to each other, the lights off, both of us awake.

Then Jude reached over and squeezed my hand. "It's going to be all right, you know," he said. "You'll get through this. New Orleans will get through this."

And I started to cry, and then he put his arms around me and held me tightly, kissing the top of my head while I sobbed, finally giving into the self-pity and misery I'd been holding off since Paul died. And then he was whispering to me, over and over again, "It's okay, it's okay, shhh, baby, it's okay."

No. I didn't deserve Jude.

And when I decided to come back, he had helped me load up my car. I put my arms around him and held him.

"This is goodbye, isn't it?" he asked.

"You deserve better than I can give you," I replied.

He bit his lower lip and nodded. "Good luck," he said, his voice shaking. "If you ever need me—"

I kissed his cheek, got in my car, and drove away.

There was a knock on my front door, startling me at first, but then I realized it had to be Paige.

She threw herself into my arms as soon as I opened the door, and I held onto her until her body stopped shaking and she was able to pull herself together. I wiped at my own eyes as she picked up a plastic bag. She shrugged. "I figured we could both use a drink." She pulled out a champagne bottle and popped the cork, aiming away from the house so the cork shot out into the middle of Camp Street. She poured herself a foamy plastic cup full, and then poured me one. "Salud," she said, tossing it all back in one gulp and erupting with a most unladylike burp. She sat down on the top step and waved at me to join her. I tossed back the champagne and sat as she refilled both cups.

"Christ," she said, lighting a cigarette. "Can you believe what a ghost town this is?" She shook her head. "Man."

"Yeah," I said, unable to think of anything else to say.

A camouflage-painted Hummer went by with a machine gun mounted on the front hood. A group of National Guardsmen, the oldest of whom couldn't have been more than twenty-three, rolled by. Solemnly, each one raised a stiff hand in acknowledgement, and Paige did the same back, all of them nodding.

"Nobody but nobody had better ever criticize the National Guard in my presence again, or the Coast Guard. Not if they want to live to see the morning," Paige said, taking a long drag on her cigarette. "Anyway, welcome home."

"Thanks for cleaning out the refrigerator," I replied, lighting my own cigarette.

"Yeah, well, I needed something to keep me busy besides work and dwelling on everything," she said, gesturing at her battered Toyota. "I went to Sav-a-Center and got you some things—soda, beer, you know, the essentials." She flashed a grin at me. "They're open, but only from ten to six, so re-member that—and our bank is open down there, and I went by Bodytech today and there was a sign up saying they're re-opening tomorrow, so you can work out and everything. And the Avenue Pub is open. We can go get a burger there later, if you want. They have really good burgers." She laughed. "I don't believe they ever closed, you know? They used char-coal and sold burgers. God, I love this city."

"How is it really? Here?"

"It's still New Orleans, but it's different." She lit another cigarette from the butt of the one she was smoking. "Nothing much is open, and what is, is on limited hours. There are help-wanted signs everywhere." She stared off at the park. "It's—it's—oh, hell, I don't know how to describe it, Chanse." She shrugged nonchalantly. "It's still New Orleans, though, that I can say. And I am so fucking glad to be here." She stabbed her cigarette out on the step. "So fucking glad to be here." Her lip trembled and her eyes filled again, but she snapped back out of it, standing up. "Well, let's get the cars unloaded, shall we?"

CHAPTER TWO

THERE USED TO BE two kinds of bars in New Orleans: the ones that have the big daiquiri machines and cater to the tourists; and the ones locals frequent, where they serve strong drinks, don't charge an arm and a leg for them, and have atmosphere that isn't manufactured. The Avenue Pub, on the corner of St. Charles and Polymnia, about a half block from Paige's apartment, is one of the latter. I wasn't a regular there, but stopped in every once in a while for a burger and fried cheese sticks. Most of the people who hung out there were working class, stopping in after work for a couple of drinks and staying longer than they probably should. Being gay, I always felt a little uncomfortable there. It wasn't like I had GAY tattooed on my forehead, but I never really felt able to completely relax in a straight bar environment. It was stupid—I never felt like I was in danger of being gay-bashed or anything there, but I always preferred to err on the side of caution. After Paige had moved down the street a few months before the storm, she'd fallen in love with the place and made it one of her preferred hangouts.

New Orleans wasn't the only thing different. Paige herself was different, in ways someone who didn't know her as well as I did might not notice. The changes were a little subtle, small, but they were definitely there. For example, she was chain-smoking, lighting one cigarette from the butt of another. She'd smoked from the time we'd first met, but I'd never seen her smoke this much—even when she was upset, even when she was drinking. Her mismatched eyes (one green, one blue) were bloodshot, and there were heavy, dark circles beneath them. Her reddish hair, usually streaked with blonde, looked unkempt, and about an inch of brown was showing at the roots. Her voice seemed a little higher in tone as well, as though she were on the verge of hysteria. Maybe I was just being hypersensitive, my own emotions on edge and raw. Maybe I also seemed different to her, changed in some ways that I wasn't aware of and only someone else could see. All I could feel, all I was aware of, was that dead sense of numbness to everything.

She parked me at a scarred table near the jukebox, which was silent. A silver-haired man in a dirty sports coat that had seen better days, a weathered-looking man of indeterminate age in paint-spattered coveralls, and a whipcord-thin black man in jeans and a flannel shirt sat at the bar. All the tables were empty other than the one I was sitting at. A pretty girl wearing glasses and with her thick, long, black hair pulled back into a braid was grilling hamburgers, while another girl, maybe in her mid-twenties with reddish-blonde hair, was pouring drinks with a heavy hand behind the bar. Paige came back with a glass of amber liquid and a sweating bottle of Bud Light, which she put down in front of me.

I looked at her glass. I had never seen her drink anything alcoholic besides red wine since we'd met in college. "What are you drinking?"

"I've developed a taste for whiskey. Sue me." She took a long drink before closing her eyes and pressing the glass to her forehead. "Damn, I'm getting another headache."

I didn't say anything. I couldn't think of anything to say.

"We're all a little crazy now." She shrugged. "That's something you're going to have to get used to, bud. The whole city has post-traumatic stress disorder. There's a big piece in tomorrow's paper about it."

"How late is this place open?" I started peeling the label off my bottle.

"Curfew's midnight." Paige lit another cigarette. "The soldiers take the curfew very seriously, too." She flicked ash into a plastic Budweiser ashtray. "If you're caught out after curfew, you spend the night in jail. You've been warned. Inside by midnight. Don't be calling me to bail your ass out if you break curfew."

"How are you doing, Paige?" On the rare occasions I'd been able to get her on her cell phone, we hadn't talked long. Her e-mails were even briefer. Just reports on my apartment, that she was okay, and not much else. "Are you really okay?"

"No, I'm most definitely not okay." She took another drink of her whiskey. "I don't know if I'll ever be okay again. It's horrible, Chanse. The things I've seen...the stories I've been told...what a fucking nightmare. And it doesn't seem to ever end...and what makes me the angriest is none of it had to happen. It didn't have to happen the way it did. I hope everyone in Washington, from the White House to the lowest paper pusher at Homeland Security and FEMA, suffer long painful deaths in agony, just the way they left New Orleans to die. I swear to God I would just as soon shoot Michael Chertoff's balls off as look at that son of a bitch. How that motherfucker can sleep at night is beyond me. It makes me want to believe there's a heaven and hell, you know? And the Ninth Ward, Lakeview..." she shuddered. "It's just awful out there, so dead...and sometimes I think I can still hear

people screaming. And the city just reeks of death and rot."
She shrugged. "The Xanax helps a lot, though. It evens me
out when I need it—but I seem to need it every fucking day.
And I take pills to sleep. That helps with the dreams."

"Should you drink when you're—"

"I don't fucking care," she snapped. "You don't know,
okay? The pills help but sometimes they're not enough, all
right? The whiskey helps. Sometimes it's the only thing that
does, okay?" She sighed. "Let's change the subject, okay?
The last thing I want to do your first day back is give you
chapter and verse of the tragedy that is Paige's life right
now, okay? I really hate talking about this, it just makes me
angry and then I have to take another pill or drink more or
both. I'm really glad to see you." She forced a smile that
looked terrible in its falseness. "What are you going to do to
keep busy now that you're back?"

"I don't know." I'd never really thought about it much. "I
was just so focused on coming home, I never thought that far
ahead."

"You need to find something to do—you can't just sit
around your apartment all day." She finished her glass.
"That's a one-way trip to the insane asylum, my friend." She
laughed. "I mean, look at me, for God's sake. I have a job to
go to everyday and I still need booze and pills to stay out of a
fucking straitjacket."

"Well, there's a lot of cleanup to be done around the
house outside." I shrugged. "That'll keep me busy for a
while."

"There you go—that's a good start." She stood up. "You
ready for another beer?"

I checked my bottle. It was half-full, so I chugged it down
and put the bottle down, belching as I did. "Yup."

She grinned. "That's the spirit." She walked over to the bar.

The door opened. I turned automatically, and felt a big grin creep over my face as Venus Casanova and Blaine Tujague walked in. Venus and Blaine were detectives with the NOPD; I'd met them when I put in my two years on the force out of college before going out on my own. Venus was a tall, muscular black woman with close-cropped hair. Her face was beautiful and ageless—she could be any age from thirty to sixty and no one could guess. She worked out regularly and was in great shape. A lot of guys on the force resented her—black and female, after all, is not a popular combination in any police department, no matter how much things had changed over the years—and called her a lesbian behind her back. I didn't think she was—I knew she'd been married and had two daughters, not that that meant anything. But whether she liked to sleep with men or women, Venus was a good cop.

Blaine was a handsome man about my age with blue eyes and curly black hair and a muscular body. He came from a wealthy, socially prominent family in Uptown, who'd been aghast when he joined the police force. He told me once he'd always wanted to be a cop, and when he was old enough, be became one. He lived with his partner, who was about twenty years older, in one of the big houses on the other side of Coliseum Square. We'd slept together a few times, and although Blaine insisted to me that he and his partner had an open relationship, I always got the feeling his partner hated me and was only nice to me because of Blaine. Blaine had a great sense of humor and was a lot of fun to be around. He always joked and teased, and his blue eyes always sparkled with humor. I waved at them, and they walked over to my table, pulling up chairs.

I stood and hugged them both. "When did you get back?" Blaine asked, after almost breaking a couple of my ribs.

"A few hours ago." I was grinning like an idiot, but couldn't help it. "Man, is it good to see you two." I meant it. I'd been unable to reach them any way other than e-mail since the storm.

The NOPD had taken a beating in the media in the wake of the storm. Some cops had turned criminal, others had abandoned the city, and in the chaos of the flood there had been no real command. But Blaine and Venus were both dedicated to their jobs, and I knew they'd neither looted nor stolen cars nor left the city. Both looked tired and haggard, though. The humorous sparkle I was used to seeing in Blaine's eyes wasn't there anymore. They'd both lost weight, and their eyes looked hollow with fatigue.

"Welcome home," Venus said as Paige put a glass of red wine in front of her and handed Blaine and me bottles of beer before sliding into her own chair. She lifted her glass. "Such as it is."

Her voice was bitter, and in that instant I remembered she had lived in New Orleans East, which wasn't there any more. "Venus, I'm sorry about—"

"Yeah, well, what can you do?" She shrugged. "Once the insurance settles up with me, I'll be fine. I was insured to the teeth." She took a sip of the wine. "If the fuckers ever do settle up."

"Are you going to rebuild?" I hated to ask. She'd probably been asked a million times.

"I don't know; there doesn't seem much point." She took a pack of cigarettes out of her purse and lit one. "Can't even decide until the government decides if they're going to let us. ... maybe it's time for a change and I should move." She sighed. "I don't need that big old house any more anyway. The girls are grown and on their own, and it was kind of lonely. I thought about selling before all of this happened, you know...should have moved beyond the thinking stage, I guess."

"She's staying in our slave quarter," Blaine said. "For as long as she likes."

"Now, white boy, how many times do I have to tell you not to call it that?" She flashed a ghost of the smile I remembered. "As long as you got a black woman living there, we're calling it a carriage house, remember?"

Blaine rolled his eyes at me. "See what I got to put up with? So, Chanse, what about you? Now that you're back, what are you going to do? You staying? Or are you going back to Dallas?"

"I'm staying." I wasn't in the mood to tell them about the breakup with Jude yet. And it felt good to say it out loud. New Orleans was home. "And I can keep busy, I'm sure. Was there a lot of damage to the shipyards and the port?"

"Some." Venus shook her head. "Why do you ask?"

"Just curious, is all." I laughed. "I was hired by Iris Verlaine to find her father a couple of days before the storm, and then she fired me on Friday morning—and was kind of rude about it. I figured it might be some karmic payback if their shipyard was destroyed."

"Iris Verlaine?" Venus asked, her voice strange.

I got a cold feeling in the pit of my stomach. "Yeah, that's what I said."

Blaine gave a weird laugh, and ran a hand through his curls. "Small fucking world, huh? The last case to drop into our lap was Iris Verlaine. She was shot and killed in her house the Friday night before the storm. We didn't really get much of a chance to look into it, what with the storm and everything on Saturday. And now I imagine the crime scene is destroyed. She lived in Lakeview."

"She's dead?" I could feel the hair on the back of my neck stand up. That was the last thing I was expecting to hear.

"Looked like a robbery—she came home and surprised them in the act, and they shot her," Venus replied. "Funny that should happen the same week she hired and fired a private eye, though. You say she wanted you to find her father?"

"Uh huh." I cast my mind back to that afternoon. She'd arrived punctually at twelve-thirty. At that time, Katrina was forming out in the Atlantic Ocean and looked like it would be heading across the southern tip of Florida on its way to the Gulf. We were all just starting to pay attention to the path, but it was still too early to panic about it. We'd already been hit by two small hurricanes—Cindy and Dennis—in July. Every time a storm forms in the Atlantic, we pay attention— a little. I had the Weather Channel playing on my big-screen TV, just to be on the safe side.

I'd opened the door. "Mr. MacLeod?" she'd asked, an eyebrow raised in a questioning manner, as though I wasn't what she was expecting.

She was a tall woman, probably around five-nine in her stocking feet, but she was wearing gray stiletto heels that added a few inches to her height. She was thin—almost too thin in that way some women get that looks unhealthy. She had a flat chest and almost non-existent hips. She was wearing all gray—skirt, jacket, and silk blouse, with a double strand of pearls knotted at her neck. The hand she extended for me to shake was bony and pale, with long, manicured nails. Her green eyes were almost too large for her narrow, angular face. Her lips were small, and her fine blonde hair was swept back into a tight chignon on top of her head. She appeared to be nervous, but then, most of my clients are when they show up for the first meeting.

I'd invited her in, asked her if she wanted coffee (which she declined), and offered her a seat. She'd sat down and crossed her legs, her eyes occasionally darting around my apartment, taking in my artwork, and judging it—the expression on her face clearly showing that she found my taste in art considerably lacking. "Would you mind shutting off the television?" she asked. Her voice was shaky and high-toned, almost like a little girl's. She'd gone to McGehee, I decided, and had probably been a Tri Delta at either Newcomb or Ole Miss. "Hurricanes bore me." She tilted her head to one side. "It's all anyone has been talking about all morning. No one seems able to get any work done." She folded her hands together in her lap. "Like talking about it will make it go somewhere else, the idiots."

I bit my lip to keep from grinning and obliged, picking up the remote and pressing the power button. "What can I do for you, Ms. Verlaine?" I gave her what I call my reassuring, I-can-solve-all-your-problems face.

She favored me with a little smile, which warmed her face up a bit. She was, I decided, pretty when she relaxed her face. "All business? I like that, Mr. MacLeod. What I want you to do for me is relatively simple, actually. I could probably have my assistant do it for me, but then Valerie is an incorrigible gossip—it would be all over the office by lunchtime—and I would prefer this to be my little secret for now, so can I count on your discretion?"

"Yes, Ms. Verlaine. Your secrets are safe with me."

"Good." She started twisting a diamond on her ring finger. "I'm getting married in the spring, and I would like for my father to give me away."

"Okay."

"The trick, Mr. MacLeod, is that I don't know my father, and I don't know where he is. I've never met him. He left my mother when she was pregnant with me, and no one has ever heard from him since." She said it in a rush, as if she'd been practicing at home in front of a mirror, to get it to sound just right. But then, she struck me as the kind of person who always prepared herself, so maybe she had.

"And how long has that been?"

The faint smile flashed again. "One should never ask a woman her age, Mr. MacLeod, as you well know, but as this is pertinent to the investigation, he disappeared in 1973."

I whistled. "Thirty-two years? You haven't heard anything from him in all that time?"

She nodded. "I realize that makes it harder."

"Why did you wait so long?"

She raised an eyebrow. "My mother died a few months ago. She was a rather, um, formidable woman. The mere mention of my father drove her into an insane rage, and when she was angry—" She shuddered at the memory. "Let's just say it wasn't possible while she was alive. But she's dead now, and I am getting married, and I've always been curious about my father. . . . My two older brothers barely remember him—I've asked them—and my grandfather just flatly refuses to discuss him." She made a little hopeless gesture with her hands. "So I have no recourse but to hire a private eye."

"He's never once tried to get in touch with you or your brothers?"

"He may have," she said grimly. "My mother was a very determined woman, Mr. MacLeod, to say the least. I don't even know what happened, why he left, but it was obvious from my mother's behavior that the separation wasn't her idea. Once he left, she erased him completely from our lives.

It wasn't until she died that I even knew what he looked like. All I knew was his name, which was on my birth certificate." She clicked open her briefcase and handed me a file folder. "Everything I know about my father is in that folder. There's a wedding picture that I found in with my mother's things, as well as his Social Security number. Their divorce decree is in there as well—she divorced him for desertion. She also had sole custody of us—her children. After the divorce, she petitioned the court to change our names—hers, my brothers', and mine—back to Verlaine."

"That's pretty extreme," I replied.

She raised an eyebrow. "As I said, my mother was a formidable woman. Are you interested in taking this case?"

I considered. Might as well be honest with her—that way it couldn't come back to bite me in the ass later. "After all this time, I can't promise that I'll find him—and you also have to take into consideration that—"

"He might be dead?" She seemed amused. "Yes, I have considered that. But in any case, Mr. MacLeod, I'd like to know one way or the other." She pulled out her checkbook and started writing me a check. "It's so horrible to just wonder."

"Ms. Verlaine—" I hesitated as I noticed the amount she was writing in. Usually, I give my clients a disclaimer. *People who disappear don't want to be found. Chances are if you think your spouse is cheating, he or she probably is.* But she also didn't strike me as being driven by sentiment. I didn't believe for one moment she wanted to have her father give her away at her wedding—not a father she'd never known. She wasn't looking for him to fill a void she'd felt most of her life. I sensed there was a further reason she was interested in finding him—something she wasn't telling me, nor was she likely to. But clients don't always tell me their true motivations, nor is having that information necessary for me to do my job. As long as their check clears, I don't care one way or the other.

She paused before signing the check. "Yes?"

"Nothing." I walked over to my computer and printed out my standard boilerplate contract, which I gave to her to sign. "How often would you like a report on my progress?"

"Weekly, if that would be okay with you." She paper-clipped a business card to her check. "You can reach me at any of these numbers—although I would prefer it if you would always try my cell phone first. Valerie answers my office line, and as I said, she is a gossip. And when the retainer runs out, I will decide then if I want you to continue." She stood, smoothing her skirt and extending her hand to me. "I look forward to hearing from you."

"I'll get started on Monday, if that's all right with you."

"That would be just fine, Mr. MacLeod."

She walked out of my apartment and got into a gray Mercedes convertible. I watched her drive off down Camp Street.

And she'd been killed later that same day.

"I guess I should just tear up the check," I said as the girl with the braid set down plastic takeout containers in front of us. I smiled at her before opening mine and squirting mustard and ketchup on my cheeseburger. I took a bite. It was amazing. There's no burger like a New Orleans bar burger.

"The Verlaine Shipping Offices are open," Paige said, dipping a steak fry into a puddle of ketchup. "Jack Devlin did a story on them the other day for the business section. The family never evacuated; they rode out the storm in the Garden District—I can get the address for you, if you'd like to stop by the house. Their offices are in the Entergy building on Poydras, if you'd rather do that. Let me know."

"Thanks," I said, focusing on my burger.

We ate the rest of the meal in relative silence. When we were finished eating we all walked out together. At Blaine's car, I hugged him again, and then turned to Venus.

"We get together for dinner and drinks pretty much every night here," Venus said as she hugged me back. "Hope you'll start joining us. It's good to see you again, MacLeod."

"I will whenever I can." I walked Paige home, and then headed home myself.

I opened one of the beers in the refrigerator, sat down on the couch, and turned on the television. It was only nine o'-clock, but there was nothing I wanted to watch. I turned it off, got a book, and got into bed. I read until I fell asleep.

I didn't dream, which was a blessing.

CHAPTER THREE

I USED TO HATE driving down Magazine Street in that time I was beginning to think of as simply *before*.

Magazine Street was an artery of the city that twisted from Canal Street all the way to Riverbend, following the course of the river, less than half a mile away from the protective levee at any point in its meanderings. It was one of those bizarre streets calculated to push a driver with out-of-state license plates over the edge rather quickly. It began as a one-way at Canal on the Uptown side, corresponding roughly to Decatur in the Quarter. Its path was pretty straight until it reached St. Andrew in the lower Garden District, where it suddenly and without warning changed into a two-way street for the rest of its narrow path. Magazine Street was lined almost its entire distance with shops of every shape, size, and nature, like A&P, Walgreens, coffee shops, thrift stores, antique shops, neighborhood bars, and upscale restaurants. It was potted and scarred, lined with parked cars, and always jammed with traffic. It always hummed with life and activity, which could be incredibly frustrating when you were in a hurry—and God forbid you got stuck behind a city bus. When I had to go uptown, I preferred to take Prytania, a few blocks away. It was more of a residential street, with fewer lights and a lot less traffic.

But after drinking a pot of coffee and getting dressed, I decided to take Magazine Street, just to see what it was like.

And almost immediately regretted the decision.

Few businesses were open. Most of them still had their show windows boarded up. There was a noticeable absence of both cars and pedestrians. The traffic light at Jackson wasn't working, and the National Guard had set up stop signs on small easels that were almost impossible to see. The Dunn and Sonnier Floral Shop at the corner had lost the wall facing Jackson Avenue, which had collapsed into a huge pile of dusty red bricks piled up on the sidewalk. There was a hand-painted sign atop the bricks, reading DO NOT RE-MOVE BRICKS. Like St. Charles, the sidewalks were covered with bagged garbage and piles of tree limbs. Some of the lampposts were bent into low angles over the street, and a telephone pole close to Washington Avenue looked like it was going to fall at the next gust of wind. It looked like one of those abandoned ghost towns in the old West. I'd always taken the vibrant life of the city for granted and regretted, as I passed closed business after closed business, all my bitching before about pedestrians and getting stuck in traffic.

I turned onto Fourth Street and parked in front of the address Paige had given me. Surrounding the entire property was a black iron fence, sunk into a retaining wall of cement, about a foot high. The house was huge, painted white with green shutters. It was about a three-story Victorian house, with a verandah that ran around the entire first floor. Some of the windows in the uppermost floor were still covered with plywood boards, and the shutters on the second floor were closed. The massive lawn was unkempt, as though it hadn't been mowed in weeks. There was another, unattached building in the rear. A driveway lined with a hedge on both sides led up to the house, and several expensive cars sat there. There was a big fountain in the center of the yard in front of the house, but it was completely dry. I stood there and looked at the house for a moment, and read the plaque mounted on the fence next to the gate. The house, like so many of the others in the neighborhood, was on the national registry of historic homes, and the plaque mentioned the architect who'd designed and built it for Henri Verlaine as a gift to his wife, Alais.

I'd never heard of the architect, but that didn't mean anything. I wasn't an expert on the history of New Orleans architecture.

I walked up to the gate and pushed the button. I stood there for a moment, watching the house. There was a flutter at the curtained windows beside the front door, and then the gate buzzed. I pushed it open and walked up the sidewalk.

As I reached the top of the steps, the front door opened to reveal a rather stout black woman in a maid's uniform. Her hair was shot through with gray, and her eyes were lined with red. I got a strong sense that she had a lot of inner strength. Her strong face was lined, but her eyes showed intelligence and wariness. She looked like one of those women who always dressed like a queen to go to church on Sunday and prayed regularly, yet had a strong bedrock of common sense at her core. "Yes?" she asked in a higher-pitched voice than I expected. She didn't smile.

"Um, is there a member of the family available?" I asked. I felt awkward under her stare, and found myself shifting my weight from foot to foot.

"Why?" Her facial expression didn't change, and I got the sense she was weighing my worth in her mind.

The question was inevitable, and I'd been racking my mind all morning to come up with the right answer. Garden District families rarely, if ever, answer their own doors, but at the same time I doubted the Verlaines wanted me telling their maid about Iris's business. Particularly when it was family business. My landlady, Barbara Castlemaine, lived a block over on Third Street, and no matter how many times she told me she considered her housekeeper "family," I never fully believed her. After all, it wasn't as if Barbara's housekeeper took meals with her, or was a guest at her parties. After an awkward silence, I finally said, "I worked for Iris Verlaine." I handed her one of my business cards, hoping that would do the trick.

Her face showed no change other than a slight twitch at the hinge of her jaw. She didn't even look at my card. Instead, she held the door open and gestured to a doorway to the right. "Wait in the parlor." She walked down the hallway and disappeared around a corner.

I walked in and sat down in an incredibly uncomfortable chair that was probably an antique. The room was large, with high ceilings and a massive chandelier that caught and reflected the sunlight coming through the big windows. There was a massive piano in one corner, its deeply polished wood gleaming, an oil painting over the fireplace, and several uncomfortable-looking chairs that matched the chair I was sitting in. The polished floor was partially covered by an old Oriental rug that was probably worth more than my car. There was no dust anywhere, no cobwebs on the chandelier. Eighty percent of the city might have been destroyed, but the Verlaine home was a well-kept museum. The air was stagnant, as though the windows hadn't been opened since the Second World War. The oil painting was from the 1800s, and from the stern look on the man's face, it probably was old

Henri Verlaine himself. He looked like the kind of man who would found a family fortune—mean and driven.

"Mr. MacLeod?"

I stood up and turned to shake hands with a man who looked to be in his early forties.

"Joshua Verlaine," he said. "I'm Iris's oldest brother."

His hair was that unnatural shade of black that comes from a bottle. There were lines on his reddish round face and dark circles under his eyes, reaching down almost to the middle of his nose. He was thin-lipped and his smile barely seemed to penetrate his heavy cheeks. There was a spot of dried blood on his upper lip, and he had missed a place shaving just to the right underside of his chin. His blue eyes were watery and bloodshot, and his hand soft and a little damp. He was low-waisted and big-bellied, so he looked top-heavy, his jeans crisply ironed blue pencils hanging down from a large inflated balloon covered with yellow cashmere. Under his cologne was a slight odor of stale liquor. "Have a seat," he said, gesturing me back into the uncomfortable chair. He himself sat down on the matching loveseat. He crossed one leg over the other. "So, Iris hired a private eye?" He ran a hand over his slick hair. "This was about Daddy, wasn't it?"

I didn't answer at first because I was trying to remember the last time I heard a man in his forties say *daddy*. I pulled her check from my shirt pocket and handed it over to him. I decided to ignore his question. "She hired me the Wednesday before the storm to do a job for her. Obviously, she no longer needs the job done. I wanted to return that." No sense in telling him she actually had fired me rather abruptly two days later by leaving a message on my machine.

He looked at the check. "You should have cashed it. I wondered what it was for when I went through her records, but we would have honored it." He barked out a laugh. "Most people would have, you know."

I shrugged. "I don't like taking people's money when I haven't earned it."

"An honest man, by God, in New Orleans!" He glanced at his watch. "Would you like a drink, Mr. MacLeod?"

Out of the corner of my eye I noticed the clock on the mantel read ten forty-five. "No, thank you," I said, standing up. "I should be going. I don't want to take up a lot of your time."

I'd taken a dislike to the place and wanted to get out so I could breathe again. The place didn't look lived in, not one thing slightly askew for the human touch of chaos that every home seems to have if you look carefully enough. I didn't much care for Joshua Verlaine, either. I'd known too many guys like him in my fraternity back at LSU—spoiled and privileged good ole boys who acted like your best friend so they could get close enough to stick the knife in your back at the first opportunity.

"Don't be absurd." He walked over to the side table and poured himself a very stiff bourbon on the rocks. "You sure you don't want something? Water?"

"I really should be going—"

"Where have you got to go?" he asked. He barked out that laugh again. "Welcome to post-Katrina New Orleans. None of us have anywhere to be." He took a swig from the glass. "Now sit down and tell me why Iris hired you. It *was* Daddy, wasn't it?"

I swallowed. Much as I hated to admit it, he was right. I didn't have anywhere to go, except to drive around the city and look some more—or go home and watch mindless hours of television. It wasn't like the phone was going to ring. Neither prospect was any more appealing than spending more time in the Verlaine mausoleum. I considered my options for a moment, and then I sat back down. "I'll have a glass of ice water then, if you don't mind."

He handed me the glass before he sat back down on the divan. "Iris had a thing about Daddy. I guess it was because she never knew him, and of course by the time she was born Mother had erased him from our lives completely."

"I take it the divorce was unpleasant?"

He laughed again and took another drink. "The divorce was pleasant because he was long gone by the time Mother went to court. One day, he was just gone. Darrin and I had no idea what happened. . . . I mean, they always say the kids know, no matter how much you try to hide it from them, when there's trouble between their parents, but hell, it took me and Darrin totally by surprise. Gone, poof, never heard from again." He snapped his fingers and finished his drink. "Mother got rid of every picture of him, and Grandpa, well, basically he forbade us from talking about him or mentioning him to her ever again."

"She didn't explain why?" I sipped my water. "That seems rather odd."

"Mother never explained anything." He put his glass down. "If it was unpleasant, there was no need to talk about it. That's just the way she was, bless her heart—he was gone and that was the end of it in her mind. Grandpa, though, took me and Darrin—that's my younger brother—aside a few days after the pictures disappeared and told us that Daddy had left us because he didn't want to be married to our mother anymore. Mother was upset, and didn't want to talk about it, so we weren't to say anything to her about him anymore. He didn't know if we would ever see Daddy anymore, but he thought Daddy was never coming back." He laughed again, a little bitterly. "I could tell Grandpa wasn't one bit sorry Daddy was gone. He never liked Daddy much, we could all tell that. You didn't have to be a private eye to figure that out."

"How old were you?" I felt myself softening a bit toward him. There was pain in his voice and etched on his face, even after all this time. And he obviously had loved his sister. Maybe I'd been too quick to judge.

"I was ten, I think, ten or eleven. Mother was still pregnant with Iris, and I'm a little under eleven years older than her. . . . I really don't remember much about that time." He shrugged. "School was out, so it was sometime in the summer."

If my father had disappeared when I was ten, I'd have led the cheers. "Were you close to your father?"

"I have good memories of him, if that's what you mean. I was upset when he was gone. Darrin was about six, so Grandpa told me I had to help him be strong ... and besides, you know, boys don't cry." He looked down at his hands. "But yeah, I missed him. He was a painter, you know? He used to let me play with his paints and make my own paintings." He laughed again. "Mine were terrible. I'd certainly not inherited his talent." He shook his head. "To this day, I don't understand how he could just take off like that, never see us again. I'm divorced myself, but I see my kids every chance I get. What kind of man does that to his kids? No matter how big a bitch Mother might have been, he could have tried to see us." He bit his lower lip. "But you know, Mother changed after Daddy left. She was never a real warm woman, but afterward. . . ." He scratched his head. "It was like she forgot how to laugh."

"And Iris?" I prompted him. I was trying to imagine what it would have been like for her.

He blew out a sigh. "It bugged her that he left, that she never knew him. A lot. I mean, for Darrin and me, well, at least we got a chance to know our dad. She never did ... and well, I don't know. I'd say to her she was better off than we were because she didn't know him at all, so she didn't miss him, if you know what I mean." He shook his head. "She never said anything to Mother, of course. But she used to talk to me about it from time to time. I'd tell her to just let it go—if he wanted to see us he knew where we were—but every once in a while, she'd start thinking about it again. It was her particular little craziness, and after she started planning her wedding, I knew it was going to come up again." His eyes got wet. "And now, of course, she's dead. . . . We haven't even been able to have a memorial service, you know?" He looked away from me. "I mean, can you imagine? The police came by late that Friday night; I had to go identify her body—and then the next day we had to get ready for the fucking hurricane."

I tried to imagine what it would be like. I speak to my sister about once or twice a year. We exchange half-hearted Christmas cards and call each other on our birthdays—awkward phone calls out of obligation, with a lot of silence while we try to think of things to say. We didn't have much in common when we were kids; we have even less now. We'd both put Cottonwood Wells and the trailer park firmly in the past, and we never spoke about our parents. I don't know if she ever talks to them or not, but if she does, she never says anything about it to me. I've never even told her that I'm gay, but I'm pretty sure she's figured it out. She's one of those Super Moms now, driving all over Houston in her SUV, taking her kids to this practice and that class and running errands, a cup of latte in the cup-holder and a cell phone in one hand. But even so, it would be a shock to find out she was dead, murdered, from the police, and before you even got a chance to grieve, a massive hurricane was heading for your home. "I'm sorry," I said, and I meant it.

"And of course, the days after when the city was being looted and we didn't have power, all we could do was sit around and drink everything in the wine cellar and think about Iris, wonder what happened to her, where her body wound up—they were keeping her for the coroner, whenever that was going to happen, and by then we'd have the Bultman Funeral Home take care of everything ... but then the fucking storm came." He got up and poured himself another glass of bourbon. "And now all we get is a runaround. I know damned well they don't know where she is. I think the morgue flooded, and her body sat around in that fucking water for weeks, that's what I think happened, and no one has the goddamned balls to tell us." He sat back down. "What the fuck do they think, we're going to sue them? Like they were going to evacuate bodies out when they couldn't evacuate people out of the city? Jesus fucking Christ."

I didn't have the slightest idea how to answer that and was wishing I'd just left when I'd had the chance. Over the years, I've noticed that sometimes a private eye winds up being a bit of a therapist, which made me wish I'd paid more attention in my Psych class back at LSU. But sometimes people don't want you to say anything—they just want you to listen, no matter how uncomfortable you are with what they are saying. They're not looking for an answer to what's eating them alive, they just want to get it all out of their system. And Joshua Verlaine didn't seem to have anyone he could talk to about any of this. I wondered what the younger brother, Darrin, was like.

Sounded to me like the whole family was fucked up.

"You know something?" He finished the second glass in a

single gulp. "You stay right here." He weaved a little bit as he walked out of the room, and I heard his footsteps going up the stairs.

Get out of here, I told myself, and glanced out the doorway. I saw the maid standing there, her lips pursed. When our eyes met, she shook her head and moved down the hallway out of sight. I looked around the room again, and started studying the portrait over the fireplace. It was from the mid-1800s, judging by the style of the clothes and the stern look on the subject's face. There was absolutely no resemblance between the man and Joshua Verlaine, but then the bloodline had undoubtedly been diluted enough over the years. He looked tough, the kind of man who would shake your hand and then fuck you over at the first opportunity if it benefited him in the slightest way. I stared at him and wondered how he would have handled the storm and its aftermath. With piss and vinegar, and an eye to turning a profit out of it. Those, I thought, were the men who built this country. It couldn't have easy being either married to him or one of his children.

Joshua came back in clutching a checkbook, and gave me a half-smile. "Mean-looking bastard, isn't he? That's the great Henri Verlaine, to whom we owe everything."

He sat down on the divan again, leaning forward to make out a check. He tore it out and handed it to me. "There. Take this."

It was for ten thousand dollars. "Um—" I stared down at it.

"I want you to find Daddy." He waved his hand. "Iris wanted him found, for whatever the hell reason she did, and you know something? I'd kind of like to see the bastard myself. I've got a few questions for dear old Dad."

"You're hiring me." It's really never a good idea to make a business deal with someone a little the worse for alcohol. "You're sure you want to do this?"

He sat up straighter. "Mr. MacLeod," he said in an almost regal tone, one he undoubtedly used with the house's staff, "I may not be able to legally operate an automobile in my current state, but I am certainly not intoxicated enough to have my mental faculties impaired. Yes. I am hiring you."

I wasn't sure I wanted to work for Joshua Verlaine. He'd probably sober up and stop payment on the check, and regret spilling the family secrets to me. But then again, what else did I have to do? And I was starting to like him—well, at least feel sorry for him. "You realize that it's highly likely that he's not alive," I said, realizing I was telling him the same thing I told Iris. "And the trail, even if he is alive, is pretty cold."

But it was what she wanted. She hired you. He just wants you to finish the job—for a lot more money, that wretched little voice inside my head whispered. *And it's not like you have anything else to do anyway. Stop trying to talk him out of hiring you. You could stand to have something to keep you occupied, or you could end up on pills and drinking a lot. He's just trying to honor his sister's last wish—he can't bury her or do any of the things you do when someone you love dies. How would you feel if it was Paul? If you had no idea what happened to his body and you couldn't get an answer from anyone as to what happened to it?*

That was all it took for me to make up my mind. If nothing else, it would make him feel better. Maybe he'd sober up and change his mind. He was entitled to that, and it wouldn't be the first—or the last—time a client fired me.

I reached over and shook his hand. "Mr. Verlaine, you've got a deal." I rose. "I'll report back to you weekly, if that's okay with you."

He waved his hand. "That's fine, whatever you think is best." He reached into his wallet and handed me a business card. "Call me on my cell phone." He grinned at me. "You probably think I'm going to sober up and change my mind, right?"

"The thought has crossed my mind."

"Well, that's not something you have to worry about." He walked me to the front door of the house.

"You changing your mind?"

He laughed. "No, you don't have to worry about me sobering up. That's not going to happen any time soon. Not as long as there's liquor in this house—and that's one thing we always have in supply."

The front door closed behind me.

CHAPTER FOUR

I DECIDED TO DRIVE up Magazine Street a little farther after leaving the Verlaine mausoleum and see if my gym had opened back up.

Bodytech was located on the corner of Magazine and Louisiana. I'd been working out there ever since it opened four years earlier. I'd known the owner, Allen Johnson, for years before he'd opened up the place. He'd been a trainer at my old gym before he went out on his own. Bodytech was a great space. It was a lot bigger than the old gym in Canal Place where I'd used to work out, brighter and airier and not as cramped. I'd fallen in love with the place when Allen had his grand opening and had switched almost immediately. I also liked that it was the only gay-owned and -operated gym in the city. The clientele was an interesting mix of Uptown gay men and straight women, with some straight men showing up every now and then. The place was always packed in the mornings, at lunchtime, and after five. I prefer to work out in the off times because I hate to wait for a machine I want to use; plus it's not quite as distracting when the place is emptied out. Allen always played the latest glitterball dance remixes over the gym's state-of-the-art sound system, which got you pumped up and energized to hit the weights a little bit harder than listening to Billy Idol's "Mony Mony" for the ten-thousandth time or some heavy metal thrash garbage like other gyms played. Besides, I'd always had a bit of a crush on Allen. Joining his gym gave me the chance to get to know him better. It seemed like he was always there when I came in for my mid-morning workouts, and we'd always shoot the shit for a little while before I hit the weights. Allen lived with his longtime partner, Greg Buchmaier, in the old Buchmaier mansion on St. Charles Avenue further uptown, closer to the campuses of Tulane and Loyola Universities and Audubon Park. Allen was a good guy, if not the brightest, and he always knew all the local gay gossip. I could always count on Allen to give me the scoop on any gay man or gay couple in town—I guess running a gym makes you privy to all kinds of information. He still worked as a trainer, and he told me once over a protein shake that being a trainer was kind of like being a therapist. "You wouldn't believe the shit people tell me," he said, rolling his eyes and grinning at me, "and it's not like we have any kind of client-trainer confidentiality thing. I'm always afraid I'm going to be subpoenaed to testify in a divorce case or something. Could you imagine?"

I don't know what I was expecting, but I didn't expect to see Allen's white Lexus in the parking lot and the neon OPEN sign in the big front window lit up. It was such an unexpected moment, a slight semblance of normality in a crazy world where normal no longer existed, that I just slammed on the brakes and swung the car into the parking lot. Fortunately, there was absolutely no traffic on Magazine Street. *Before,* such a sudden move would have caused a massive accident and backed traffic up in both directions for miles. I put the car in the spot next to the Lexus and walked through the front door.

Even though the air conditioning was on and it was cool inside, there was a faint musty smell to the place. Other than that, it was like stepping into a time machine and going back to the last time I'd worked out. All the machines sparkled and shone in the lights, the mirrors that lined the walls were spotless, and Allen himself was behind the front counter, resting his thick arms on it. A huge grin spread across his face when he saw me. He's only about five-nine, with dark blond hair he'd recently started buzzing off to hide the fact it was thinning—which was a really hot look for him. I knew he was in his early forties, but he could easily pass for his late twenties. There were no bags under his eyes and no tell-tale lines emanating from his eyes or the corners of his mouth. His chipmunk-like cheeks were deeply dimpled, his gray eyes almond-shaped but wide open and cheery, and his body showed the years of hard work he'd put into it. Veins bulged in his forearms and his biceps. His tight black tank top with BODYTECH in red lettering across his chest fit like a glove. His thickly muscled legs were hidden beneath a pair of black sweatpants with a white stripe running up each side.

"Chanse!" He came out from behind the counter and gave me a big hug, squeezing long and hard. "When did you get back?" He stepped away from me, still smiling.

"Yesterday, actually," I replied, finding myself grinning back at him.

"I got back last week—I wanted to get the place back open as soon as possible." He scratched his head. "How'd you come out? The house okay?"

I nodded. "Yeah, I was lucky. I guess the floodwaters stopped a couple of blocks away from Camp Street, and the roof held on. Paige got back to town right after and emptied my refrigerator. How'd you do?"

"Yeah, we did okay, besides the refrigerator." He made a face. "I got a new one on the way down from Baton Rouge. But we did lose one of the oak trees in the yard. Went down right through the gazebo. Lucky—if it went the other way, it would have gone right through the living room." He shuddered. "That would have been a disaster—I don't even like to think about that." He went back around the counter and opened the glass-fronted cool case. "You want a protein drink? On the house, as my first post-Katrina customer." He smiled at me again. "Damn, it's good to see you."

I took it from him with a grin. Strawberry, my favorite. Allen knew his customers well. "Thanks. Greg back too?" I opened it and took a swig.

He shook his head. "He's in Atlanta, running the company from the store there." Buchmaier Jewels was one of the oldest jewelry stores in New Orleans, with a flagship store on Canal Street and branches scattered all over the city. Greg had expanded the company and opened stores in Dallas, Houston, and Atlanta. The new stores had required Greg to travel a lot more than Allen would have liked.

"When's he coming back?" I finished the drink and tossed it into the trash.

A dark look crossed Allen's face. "Good question." His eyes narrowed. "He thinks we should move to Atlanta." His face reddened and his jaw clenched. His hands balled into fists. "Yeah, easy for him. Everything I own is tied up in this place, you know? And he says, 'Let's just move to Atlanta.' He wants to sell the house, close the stores here, just move on. I know everyone thinks he gave me the money to open this place, but I didn't take a goddamned dime from him, thank you very much, and I'm not about to start being the rich Mrs. Buchmaier because a fucking hurricane came through New Orleans." He spread his hands. "He's never kept me, and he's never going to. If I have to live in this fucking gym, I will."

"Wow," I said. Not exactly the most profound thing, but I couldn't think of what else to say. The Buchmaiers had been in New Orleans since the early 1800s, when they'd left what was then Bavaria and opened their first store. The family had been one of the backbones of the New Orleans Jewish community ever since. "What about Ruth?" Ruth was Greg's sister. She worked for the Vieux Carre Commission. "Is she going to leave too?"

"They're in Houston, got the kids enrolled in school there, but they're planning on coming back. She's furious with Greg for even considering it." He laughed. "She calls me every day to tell me how much she hates being in Houston." He ran his hand over his buzzed hair and gave me a grin. "I don't know, maybe it's time to be single again."

"How long have you guys been together?"

"Almost eighteen years." He shrugged. "Our anniversary is in November."

"Really?" I knew the story—everyone did, really. It started when Greg hired Allen to be his personal trainer, and they'd both been attracted to each other, but neither ever acted on it. Greg went from a once-a-week client to a three-times-a-week client before he finally, after a few months, got up the nerve to go ahead and ask Allen out on a date. They'd dated for a few months before Allen moved into the big house on St. Charles. They were practically an institution in New Orleans—the Nelson-Buchmaiers, Greg-and-Allen, Allen-and-Greg. They raised money for every gay charity in New Orleans, opening up the big house and having parties for the Human Rights Campaign, the NO/AIDS Task Force, the Lesbian and Gay Community Center, and many Democratic Party candidates for public office. I'd been to many a fundraiser at their place, as well as other parties they'd thrown just for fun. I couldn't wrap my mind around the notion of them breaking up. They were one of those couples I always envied, used as a reference point in my own mind to show that yes, gay couples can indeed make it work and stay together.

Allen shrugged. "I'm staying in the house until he sells it, although I probably should start looking for an apartment. If you hear of one, let me know, okay? But that's not going to be easy. So many people are looking for a place to live—and I hear the rents are all being jacked up." He looked down at his hands and sighed. "Maybe I am crazy. Maybe I should just pack it all in and move to Atlanta with him. I don't know. But I'm not ready to give up, you know? I mean, leave New Orleans? Give up all my hard work? It just doesn't seem right, Chanse. Sure, it's going to be hard, but if everyone just gives up and doesn't want to do the work—I mean, I can't imagine a world without New Orleans, let alone not living here. I can understand people with kids staying away because they've got to go to school, but shit. You're back to stay, aren't you?"

"Yeah. I guess. I don't know. Probably." I hadn't really thought about it much. The whole time I was away, all I'd wanted to do was come home. It never occurred to me to think about moving away. Besides, where would I go?

Growing up in Cottonwood Wells in east Texas, about 50 miles from Houston, had been hellish for me. The town was small, about twenty-five thousand people, and heavily Baptist and Church of Christ. My dad had worked in the oil fields and we'd lived in a trailer on the wrong side of town. When I was a kid, all I wanted to do was grow up and get the fuck out of there as fast as I could. The football scholarship to LSU had been a lifesaver. I left and never looked back. I didn't discover New Orleans until after my freshmen football season ended. I'd gotten in my car one night and driven down I-10 to the French Quarter. For a small-town kid like me from a Bible-thumping county, the French Quarter had been mysterious and magical, a small piece of decadent heaven on earth. I'd walked around, gawking like the big kid I was, and somehow managed to find my way to the gay bars down Bourbon Street by St. Ann. The first time I walked into the Bourbon Pub, I couldn't believe my eyes. There were gay men everywhere I looked, of all shapes and sizes. The place was packed, and I couldn't help but grin. It was like being in a candy store. "I'll take one of everything," I thought as I worked my way up to the bar, where a sexy young bartender in a tight black T-shirt with the sleeves cut off winked at me and said, "What'll you have, sexy?"—somehow managing to make himself heard over the remix of a Mariah Carey hit that was playing at ear-bleed levels. I got a bottle of Bud Light, delighted that the cute bartender didn't card me, and stood in a corner just staring at everyone with a big stupid grin on my face. A muscular guy about thirty, wearing a tight black tank top and a pair of white jeans cut off just below the curve of his ass, introduced himself to me as Jay and bought me another beer. After about an hour I found myself walking back to his apartment on Royal Street. He was the first man I'd ever been with. He'd given me my first blow job, my first experience with gay sex, and for a nineteen-year-old, I'd thought I'd surely died and gone to heaven. And when I'd walked back to my car in the morning as the sun came up in the east, I made up my mind right then and there I was moving to New Orleans as soon as I graduated. New Orleans was home for me, and over the next four years I came down to the city whenever I could. I'd slept with Jay a few more times, met other guys, had a lot of sex, discovered the back room of Rawhide, where I could get my dick sucked if I'd struck out in the bars, and even found the bathhouse down on Toulouse Street, where for twenty bucks I could get a bed for the night and wander the halls with a towel wrapped around my waist and find someone to fuck if I wanted to—well, several people to fuck. And when I'd graduated, I got a job with the New Orleans Police Department, got a small little apartment in a slave quarter behind a huge mansion painted coral on Dumaine Street, and made New Orleans my home once and for all.

"No," I told Allen, "I'm staying. There's nowhere else I want to be."

Allen smiled back at me. "Good." He clapped me on the shoulder. "That's the spirit."

Somehow, having said it out loud made me feel better. "All right, man, I need to get to the Sav-a-Center before it closes. I'll come back in soon and work out. What hours you going to be open?"

Allen shrugged. "I'm opening from ten to eight. I don't have anywhere else to be."

"All right." I gave him a hug, and he held on to me tightly. "It's good to see you, man."

"Don't be a stranger." Allen winked at me. I winked back and headed outside.

The Sav-a-Center was at the corner of Tchoupitoulas and Napoleon, and the parking lot was packed. I pushed my cart around for a while, trying to figure out what to buy, and was surprised to notice little things. They were out of charcoal, ice trays, and strange little things like that—the cleaning products aisle was pretty much picked clean, for example—but there were plenty of food choices. I spent about two hundred dollars and headed home.

I was in the middle of stir-frying some vegetables for beef

lo mein about an hour later, a Fleetwood Mac CD blaring on my stereo, when someone knocked on my front door. I checked through the blinds and opened the door. "Hey, Venus. Where's Blaine?"

"He's off today." She looked tired, just as she had the previous night. She came in, plopped down on the couch, and lit a cigarette. "I'm going off duty myself, but I'm not ready to head back to the carriage house just yet. Mind if I have a drink?"

I checked my liquor cabinet and found an unopened bottle of Grey Goose vodka. "I don't have any mixer," I called back to her, turning the burner off and moving the wok off the eye.

"Vodka's fine. Just ice, if you have any."

I plopped a couple of cubes in the glass, made myself a Kahlua and cream, and carried the two drinks back into the living room. She took a healthy swig from hers. "Thanks, bud. That's good."

"So what brings you by? I mean, not that you can't just stop by whenever you want—you're always welcome, you know that—but..."

She gave me a look. "Ah, you know me too well, MacLeod." She reached into her bag and handed me a manila envelope. "Thought you might want to take a look at this."

"What is it?" I put it down on the coffee table. It was thick and sealed with tape.

"Look, I don't know what you're planning to do with yourself these days, but I figure you gotta do something, right? Or go nuts, like the rest of us, and what with all the post-traumatic stress shit and everyone popping pills like M&M's. . . . I talked to my boss and he agreed that it would be okay to let you have this." She took another drink. "Look, my crime scene for the Verlaine murder is all fucked to shit. I drove out there this morning, just to be sure, and yeah, Iris's house took at least ten feet of water. And it's not like I've got the time—or Blaine has the time—to do anything about it. You're kind of involved in a way, since she hired you. . . . I don't know if that has anything to do with her being killed or not, but you never know."

I looked at the envelope. "So this is ..."

"Copies of our notes, files, crime scene photos, everything we've got." She dug into her purse and pulled out a folded piece of paper and handed it to me. I unfolded it. It was on NOPD letterhead and was signed by the police superintendent himself. I scanned it. Basically, it was a letter authorizing me, as an official consultant to the New Orleans Police Department, to enter Iris' property as well as conduct my own investigation into the murder. "That," she nodded at the paper in my hand, "will get you into the neighborhood without any trouble, and will keep you from being arrested if you get caught on the property. You're not on payroll, but you're officially investigating the crime at the request of the New Orleans Police Department. You just need to keep me informed of what's going on. You can't break any laws or procedures to get evidence—anything you might dig up has to hold up in court, but you know all about that from your days on the force—and if you need me to open any doors for you, just call me and I'll take care of it all."

"Wow. This is kind of unusual." Usually Venus was all over my ass for getting mixed up in criminal investigations and warning me off.

"Desperate times call for desperate measures. Consider yourself deputized." She finished the drink and held it up for me. I got the bottle, filled her glass, and left it on the coffee table. "I hate loose ends, you know that. It just doesn't seem right to me that we just forget about that woman. Someone killed her ... and even if the killer evacuated and is thousands of miles away, she deserves better, you know? It's not right. It's just not right." She took another swig of vodka.

"So, I gather you don't think she was really killed because she walked in on a robbery." I tasted my own drink. It wasn't bad. Jude drank Kahlua, which was why I had some in the house. I generally preferred something stronger, but I didn't feel like anesthetizing myself. At least not yet—maybe later.

"That's what the killer wanted us to think." Venus shrugged. "Messed the place up a bit, but he didn't take her purse. She had all her credit cards, and about four hundred bucks in cash in her wallet. Sure, maybe he freaked after he killed her and just got the fuck out of there, but it didn't sit right with me. She was dead, no one was coming, no one knew she was there—and the alarm had been deactivated. Someone knew the alarm code, or she let her killer into the house. Now why would she let a burglar—or any stranger—into the house? And when she got home, if the alarm was off, wouldn't that have sent her right back out of the house?"

"Maybe she forgot to activate it," I suggested. "That morning, when she left." As a security consultant, I knew that often happened. People would get in a rush, running late, and wouldn't think to set the alarm as they ran out. And even if they did remember to set it—particularly in the morning, when most are still foggy with sleep and not quite awake—when they came home and found the alarm wasn't set, they just assumed they forgot.

"Security company records show the alarm was turned off at seven-thirty that night, by someone who knew the alarm code." Venus took another drink. "So either she did it, or someone else who knew it did." She set the glass down and refilled it. "I think the killer went there specifically to kill her. It had nothing to do with a robbery or anything like that. Someone wanted Iris Verlaine dead. I can't prove it, and I don't have any evidence to back me up. Call it a gut instinct, a hunch, whatever. But that was not an interrupted robbery. It wasn't a break-in." She sighed, and polished off her new drink. "But who the fuck knows now?" She put the glass down and stood up. "All right. I'll leave you to it. But you know how you get a gut feeling when you see a crime scene? This one just didn't feel right." She weaved a little bit, and the words were a little slurred.

"So you think her death might have something to do with her trying to find her father?"

"You like coincidences?" She threw her arms up in the air dramatically. "I sure as fuck don't."

"No. No, I don't," I replied. "Her brother is paying me to keep looking."

Her eyebrow went up. "Better keep an eye on him or something bad might happen to him." She barked out a laugh. "Listen to me. Like something bad didn't happen to all of us." She rubbed her eyes. "Christ, what a fucking mess, huh? You gonna stay?"

I shrugged. "New Orleans is home."

She clenched a fist and punched it into the palm of her other hand. "That's what I keep telling myself. This is home. I've lived here my whole life—grew up in the Lower Ninth. The house I grew up in is gone. The house where I raised my girls is gone. I don't want to live in that carriage house the rest of my life, but where am I going to live? Sometimes I think I should just pick a place and move. I'm close to retiring. Maybe I should just pack it all in, take early retirement, move close to one of my daughters. I'm going to be a grand-mother someday. Might be nice to watch those kids grow up. And this isn't a city for the living anymore. It's a city for the dead."

The door closed behind her.

CHAPTER FIVE

I DECIDED NOT TO MEET PAIGE and the rest at the Avenue Pub that night.

I just wanted to be alone. I needed some time to myself, to think and put my house in order. It was something that was way overdue.

After Venus left, I made myself another drink. So what if it was only four in the afternoon? That kind of thing didn't matter anymore—not that it ever had in New Orleans. I added a healthy dose of Grey Goose to my second Kahlua and cream, took a drink—the vodka added the perfect bite to the drink—and got my bag of pot out of my suitcase. I sat back down on the couch and rolled a joint. I took the joint and the drink out to the front porch and sat down on the stoop. A city bus rolled by, completely empty other than the driver. There was a refrigerator out on the curb on the other side of the park, so someone else had come back—there were also lights on in the house and a car parked at the curb. There were piles of full garbage bags around the refrigerator, and written in black magic marker on the refrigerator's door was *Fix Everything My Ass,* with the letters *FEMA* circled. The entire thing was taped shut with black duct tape. It made me smile a bit as I lit the joint and took a hit. That, I figured, was the spirit of New Orleans—a defiant *fuck you* to the federal government written on a ruined appliance. I looked out at the park and took a sip of my drink.

It never entered my mind until talking to Allen and Venus that New Orleans wouldn't be rebuilt, that everyone wouldn't come home, that everyone wouldn't stay. I was so wrapped up in my own misery I hadn't paid any attention to anything other than myself. I was a selfish bastard. Sure, things were bad—the only way things could be worse was if the entire city had been destroyed, but that hadn't happened. Most of the city might be gone, but parts of it remained, including my neighborhood. Sure, driving Uptown had been unsettling, but there had been signs of life reemerging from the strange hibernation the city seemed to be in. The fresh produce in the Sav-a-Center and its full parking lot and the reopening of Bodytech were signs that the city would slowly come back to life. Several other businesses had been open, or had signs up proudly announcing that they were planning to reopen as soon as possible. It wasn't completely hopeless. Let the federal government bitch and argue about whether to fund the rebuilding process—New Orleans would do it, with or without their help. This disaster had been mind-boggling, but the city had never bowed down and given up before—not in the face of yellow fever epidemics that killed half the population, not in the face of the horrible river flood of 1927, or Hurricane Betsy, or any of the other countless horrors since the French landed back in 1718.

As long as there were people who loved New Orleans, there would always be hope.

Hope. That was something I'd had a short supply of for a long time. Since Paul died, in fact. I'd kind of been sleepwalking through my life ever since the funeral. I'd been smoking too much pot, drinking too much. I'd fallen into the relationship with Jude for all the wrong reasons—to put the pain aside while I found release in his arms, and now I'd hurt him. "Who the hell are you kidding, Chanse?" I said out loud, taking another hit and holding the smoke in till it burst from my lungs in an explosive hacking cough. I took another swig of my drink to cool my burning throat. "You've been walking around under a dark cloud your entire fucking life."

In a moment of clarity, probably enhanced by the pot and the liquor, I knew I was on to something. I took another drink. "You're nothing but a big fucking downer. And you wonder why people leave you? Why everyone heads for the hills the first chance they get? What do you have to offer anyone other than misery?"

So many people were worse off than I was. So many people had lost everything, had been caught in unfathomable suffering in the city for days without food and water. People had been trapped on rooftops waiting for rescue for days, begging for help, praying. People had died—and no one was really sure how many. People were missing. And here I sat, on my front porch, with liquor and a joint. My apartment was intact. I hadn't lost anything. Katrina had taken nothing from me. The storm and the flood had just driven me away from home for a while, but I had a home to come to and I was back. My possessions were still there. My apartment was no different than the day I'd left. Hell, Paige had even saved my goddamned refrigerator by cleaning it out before the food rotted and ruined it.

I was fucking lucky. I hadn't had to go to a shelter. I wasn't waiting for a FEMA trailer.

Allen might lose his relationship after eighteen years, and his home as well, if Greg decided to sell it. Venus had lost everything, her entire life—possessions, mementoes, photographs—and the house she'd invested in was now worth nothing.

And here I was, with my life pretty intact and feeling sorry for myself, playing "poor poor pitiful me."

What a load of bullshit.

And it was about goddamned time I was grateful for what I had.

I'd been a shitty boyfriend to Paul—that was true. I hadn't even allowed myself to realize how much I loved him, how much I needed him, until he was lying in a hospital bed in a coma being kept alive by machines. No, I kept him at arm's length, throwing away happiness with both hands, and I'd been too goddamned stupid to realize I was doing it. And for what? Because my first love had walked out on me in college and I was afraid of getting hurt again? Well, that plan sure the fuck had worked out well for me, hadn't it?

I'd done the same thing with Jude.

Paul would hate what I'd become. Paul would hate how I treated Jude.

"You need to move on," Paul's mother, Fee, had told me the last time I'd gone to Albuquerque to visit Paul's grave. She had a thick Irish accent, being from County Cork. She was a short woman, with ivory-colored skin and black hair shot through with gray. But despite her petite size, she ruled her brood of much larger sons with an iron fist. Her husband, Ian, was also a large man, but there was no question which one of them ran the Maxwell family or the family business, an Irish pub always filled with music and laughter. I hadn't met her until Paul was in the hospital, and she and the entire Maxwell family had flown in. Each and every one of them had treated me like a member of the family, something I'd neither expected nor deserved. After he died I had spent

both Thanksgiving and Christmas in Albuquerque with them, and even with Paul gone, his parents and his siblings still called, still e-mailed, still treated me like I was a Maxwell.

It was an amazing feeling, to be part of a family for the first time in my life.

We'd stood, Fee and I, in the cemetery, our arms around each other, looking down at the beautiful marble headstone with Paul's name, the dates of his birth and his death, and "Heaven called another angel, only too soon" carved into its smooth face. "I am worried about you, son." She looked up at me, her green eyes that Paul had inherited concerned and lined with worry. "You need to move on."

I loved that she called me son. "I can't, Fee, I can't."

"Do you think any son of mine would want you to be miserable and lonely for the rest of your life?" Fee pulled away from me, the twinkle in her eyes belying the severity of her words. "That wasn't my son, that isn't any of my children. I didn't raise them that way. Paul would want you to be happy. And Paul would not want you to blame yourself for what happened to him, Chanse. He wasn't that way, and you know it. Things happen for a reason, and it's not always for us to know why. For whatever reason, this is how God wanted it to be. It was his time to go, Chanse, and there's nothing you could have done to change that. God will have His own way."

I knew she was right, but somehow I couldn't make that empty feeling go away. The guilt was too much for me to just walk away from.

"Do you honestly think Paul would blame you?" She shook her head. "If he'd lived, do you think he would have walked away from you and blamed you for everything that had happened, for his almost dying? It wasn't your fault, Chanse. You have to realize that. It was not your fault. And

Paul would have never blamed you. Of course not! He loved you, Chanse, and your happiness was the most important thing to him. And I'll tell you something else, mister. You are not honoring his memory by treating Jude the way you are." She pointed her index finger at me. *"He loved Jude too. Jude was important to him, just as you were, and he would be happy that the two of you have found each other. Has it ever occurred to you, in all your self-pity and misery, that maybe Jude was the one you were meant to be with all along? That Paul came into your life simply as a means to bring the two of you together?"*

"That's impossible." I shook my head. "That can't be true."

"You don't know the mind of God."

And with that, she turned on her heel and walked back to where we'd parked her car.

I'd flown back home the next day, and that following weekend was when Jude came, when I'd screwed everything up. And then came the bitch Katrina.

I walked back inside and looked up at the print on my fireplace. It was a black-and-white full-sized print of Paul, naked, from the back. It was a gorgeous photograph, with impressive lines, and the use of shadow to create the illusion of life was stunning. He was standing against a brick wall, his back to the camera, both of his arms stretched out over his head, every muscle in his back rippling and flowing. It showed all his strength, yet at the same time the way his head was turned somehow gave the sense of vulnerability, of gentleness, of a kind heart. The photographer had somehow managed to capture, on film, exactly who he was, his beautiful soul. It was a masterpiece, and had hung in Paul's apartment. Fee had given it to me when we'd cleaned out his apartment, before we'd gone to Albuquerque for the funeral.

"Are you doing okay, son?" Fee asked as I stared at the framed image. She had her hair tied up in a scarf, and a smudge of dust marred her cheek. She was taping shut a box of clothes we were having taken over to the Bridge House store.

I'd managed to pick out a few things of Paul's that I wanted to keep—a watch he loved, a necklace he always wore, a couple of his favorite shirts, a blue wool blanket he had bought in Mexico that was the most comfortable blanket I'd ever slept beneath in my life, and a few photographs—and had already placed them in the car.

"I'd like to keep this, if you don't mind, or want it," I said, looking at the small mole just above the left butt cheek. I'd always loved that mole, the one blemish on an almost completely perfect body, the flaw that made him even more beautiful.

"Lord, Chanse, like I'm going to be hanging a naked picture of one of me boys in my house?" She roared with laughter. "Yes, I think he'd want you to have that, of course he would." She came over and put her arm around my waist. "But are you doing okay, Chanse?"

"I'll be fine." That was my mantra, the thing I said whenever anyone—a Maxwell, Paige, Blaine, Venus, any of the people who knew what I'd lost—asked me how I was. I didn't want to talk about it. I wanted to deal with it, to get through my pain, by myself. I always had, and I wasn't used to the notion of sharing emotions and feelings with other people. Wasn't that the fatal flaw in my relationship with Paul? My inability to let go, to break down the reserve I'd built in my childhood to keep other people out?

"I don't think you're fine." Fee shrugged. "But if you aren't ready to talk to me, to get it out, that's fine too. Just be careful, son."

"*Careful?*"

"*Sometimes when you try to handle enormous pain by yourself, all you do is keep the wound fresh rather than letting it scab over and heal.*" *She gestured to the print.* "*If your purpose in keeping that is to look at it and keep picking the scab off, then I'll keep it, thank you very much. That isn't healthy, it isn't right, and it isn't what my Paul would have wanted. You're family, now, whether you like it or not, and we Maxwells always say what we think.*"

"*That isn't what I'll do with it. I promise.*"

"*All right, then.*" *She climbed up on a stool and took it down, handing it to me, her green eyes dancing. She pointed a finger at me.* "*But if I ever find out you're talking to it, or pretending you can communicate with him through it, I'll come back here and take me scissors to it, until all that's left is confetti, and I will burn it, do you understand me?*" *She put her arm around me.* "*You're one of us, now, and you will always be. The fact we've lost him will never change that, you hear? You are one of us now ... and there will always be a place at our table, there will always be a room for you in our house. And the good Lord help you if you ever forget that.*"

I looked at the picture, and for the first time, I broke my promise to Fee.

I sat down on the couch. "Paul, I'm so sorry about everything. I miss you so much, wish I could do everything all over again." I rubbed my eyes.

"*I love you, Chanse,*" *Paul had said to me that last Sunday morning we were together. We'd slept late, having stayed up really late watching a tearjerker movie starring Susan Sarandon, and then making love before drifting off to sleep in each other's arms. I'd gotten up and made coffee, bringing* him a cup to wake him up. He flashed his blue eyes at me, his sensual thick lips spreading in a delighted, sleepy smile.

"Oh, you're just saying that because I brought you coffee," I teased as I slid underneath the covers and pressed up against his warm body.

"Don't be so dismissive." He snuggled up against me. "I love the fact that you woke me up with a cup of coffee because you knew that would make me happy." He took another big drink from the massive mug I'd gotten for him. His coffee addiction was intense. He said it came from having to get up so many mornings at four for flights when he'd been a flight attendant, and he could drink an entire pot of coffee by himself every morning. He got me to start buying a higher grade of beans and grinding the coffee myself rather than buying it in a jar. He got me to start filtering the water for the coffee so it would be free of impurities and taste better. He taught me to clean the coffee maker once a month with white vinegar so the coffee would taste pure. He would drink a normal-sized cup of coffee in two gulps, so when I saw the huge mug at a coffee shop in Uptown, I bought it as a joke. But in typical Paul fashion, he loved it and always brought it with him when he spent the night, telling me he couldn't drink coffee out of anything else now that I'd given him the perfect coffee mug. It was beige with a black fleur-de-lis on each side, and written under the symbol on both sides were the words, "New Orleans—we take coffee seriously."

"This is so nice, don't you think?" he asked. "I love sleeping in and spending the morning in bed."

"Yeah, it's a great way to waste the morning." I put my arms around him and put my head on his shoulder.

He set the mug on the nightstand and kissed my cheek. "Spending lazy time with someone you love is never a waste, Chanse. Love is never a waste of time."

I smiled, even laughed a little bit.

Love is never a waste of time.

I sent a mental apology to Fee for breaking my word to her and talking to the picture.

I could never make things right with Paul, but Fee was right. The way I could honor his memory was by becoming a better person, by letting go of the past and living a good life.

That was his legacy to me.

I poured myself another drink and raised my glass to the print of Paul. "If there's a heaven, or somehow you're watching me, or can hear me, thank you, Paul."

I walked back into the kitchen to finish making my dinner.

CHAPTER SIX

I WOKE UP FEELING INVIGORATED and alive. It was almost as though the breakthrough I'd had last night had changed my perception of everything, as if heavy weights I'd been carrying around my neck had finally broken free.

I felt like I could conquer the world.

I went through my usual morning ritual of drinking an entire pot of coffee and checking my e-mails. I was hoping Jude might have sent me one rather than calling me back—after all, it's much easier to tell someone to go to hell electronically than in person—but there was nothing in my inbox other than hot stock tips, penile implant ads, and requests for assistance from someone in Nigeria who apparently wanted my bank information so he could put a couple of hundred million dollars in there. I shook my head in amusement at the notion of how many people would probably leap at this opportunity, not realizing it was a scam until their identities were stolen and their bank accounts wiped out. I thought about sending Jude an e-mail, and finally decided against it. I'd just call him again later—he couldn't duck my calls forever.

And if he did somehow manage to avoid me, I might just show up at his door one evening.

I turned off the computer and opened the envelope Venus had left for me. I started going through her notes. As I expected, Venus was very thorough and pretty much had checked out everything in the house. There had been no sign of forced entry, and as she'd mentioned, the alarm system had been deactivated with the code, which meant Iris had done it or the killer had known the code. The killer had to be someone she knew fairly well. The downstairs hadn't looked as though it had been searched or gone through in any way; the DVD player, a computer, and other portable electronic equipment—the kind of stuff that is easy to unload and relatively untraceable—hadn't been touched. Even the liquor arranged on the bar was untouched—and the inventory of bottles Venus had scribbled down was all good, expensive stuff. Iris obviously never stooped to cheap liquor.

I took out the photos and started paging through them. Crime scene photographs are always unpleasant to look at. I'd seen a lot of death when I was on the force, but it's never something you really get used to, and the photographs show death in all its stark ugliness. Iris lay flat on her back in a puddle of blood, her lifeless eyes open and staring up. She was wearing the same outfit she'd worn to her meeting with me earlier the day she was killed, and my mind went into a "disconnect" mode. You have to erect a barrier in your mind and dismiss the victim as a person, think of the corpse as a "thing," something not quite human. The bullet had torn a huge hole in the front of her gray silk blouse, which was drenched in blood. There was a look of surprise still on her face, frozen there until the mortician could do something about it. At some point, she'd taken her hair down before she was shot. Her hair was spread around her head, and some of it was saturated from sitting in the puddle of blood. Her purse sat on the nightstand, unopened. The carpet she was lying on was a beige shag style, and as I took in the other room details, I realized that the room was tastefully decorated. It looked like the bedroom of a woman with money to burn, and she'd apparently spared no expense in her determination to have a sophisticated yet comfortable bedroom.

The purse bothered me, as it had Venus. How had it ended up sitting on the nightstand? If she'd come home during a burglary, how had she managed to get into her bedroom and put her purse down on the nightstand before being surprised? Had the burglar somehow followed her in? There was no sign of forced entry. On the floor beside the nightstand I could see her briefcase, also untouched. Had the burglar been upstairs, and she'd come up and been surprised in the bedroom? Then he'd shot her, and fled? And how had the burglar gotten into the house beforehand if the alarm was still set?

No, it looked to me as though someone had come expressly to her house to kill her.

It was the only thing that made any sense. But even with the flood damage, I'd have to go take a look. It would help me get a sense of things. I showered and dressed, putting on a white T-shirt and a pair of jeans. The "safety kit" I'd assembled before returning was still in the trunk of the car—plastic gloves, Purel, bottled water, and surgical masks—so I was ready to deal with anything in Iris's wrecked house. I also made sure my gun was loaded—no telling what I might find out there. I doubted the killer would be around, but even with the National Guard in town, there wasn't much point in risking running into looters. I got into my car and headed out to Lakeview.

There still weren't many signs of life in the city, but at least the Central Business District looked to be fairly intact, other than all the windows blown out of the Hyatt Hotel by the Superdome. Out of habit, I took O'Keefe, which eventually joins up with Rampart about a block uptown from Canal Street. None of the traffic lights were working, and there were no other cars out and about. I crossed Canal and couldn't help but smile as I drove up Rampart Street.

In the days after the storm blew through and the water from the breeched levees filled the city, a lot of fundamentalist Christians had claimed that God had destroyed New Orleans for "her sins and her acceptance and tolerance of gays." The fact that Southern Decadence, the big gay Labor Day weekend celebration, had been scheduled for the weekend after Katrina also played a part in the statements by those ministers who claimed to have a direct line to God. The Thursday before, I'd driven down to the Quarter to get a haircut, and city workers had been hanging rainbow banners from the streetlights on Rampart, as they do every year for Decadence.

The rainbow banners were still there. Katrina hadn't blown them down!

"Take that, you sanctimonious fuckwads," I said out loud, a broad grin spreading over my face. I turned onto Esplanade and drove past some guys picking up trash on the neutral ground. They waved as I drove past, and I waved back. The city was getting cleaned up; there was no debris anywhere along Esplanade Avenue, and the beautiful old houses looked intact. I glanced down the streets of the Quarter as I drove past, and other than garbage bags and the ubiquitous refrigerators, it looked intact and clean. My heart sang with joy, The French Quarter had always been the heart of the city, and its survival seemed a good sign to me. If we'd lost the Quarter. . . . It would be hard to imagine the city without its beating heart. There was no traffic at all on

Elysian Fields, and the light at St. Claude was out—those ubiquitous stop signs placed at every corner.

My good mood started to fade as I drove along Elysian Fields. It had never been a pretty drive: the blocks between St. Claude and the I-10 on-ramp had always been relatively poor and not kept up as well as the neighborhoods I was more familiar with. The silence was oppressive, and I turned the car stereo up louder. Brother Martin High School looked desolate. The closer I got to the lake, the more depressing it got. The houses all along Elysian Fields had those horrible spray-painted X's on them, and the farther along I got, the more I started seeing the water lines stained onto the sides of the houses. The street itself was caked with dirt left behind when the water receded. No traffic lights were working; no businesses open. It was a dead zone. I felt a sob welling up inside me and I fought it back down.

My own evacuation had taken me down Elysian Fields; that was the last time I'd been down the street. I'd headed that way to try to avoid backed-up traffic on I-10 that Sunday before Katrina had come ashore, getting on the highway at the Elysian Fields on-ramp. As I drove along, I remembered the anxiety I'd felt, and why I'd decided to take the eastern route out of the city, rather than heading west through Baton Rouge. I'd turned on the TV after packing up the car, and every single newscaster on every single news station had been advising late evacuees to head east and then north. "It's taking eight hours to get to Baton Rouge"— what was usually an hour-and-a-half drive—"so head east, then turn north when you get outside the city. The highway is clear going east! Head east!" I'd gotten out my map, decided to head east on I-10, swing west on I-12 at Slidell on the other side of the lake, and catch 55 north through Jackson, Mississippi, then cut over toward Dallas.

It had been a huge mistake—which I didn't realize until I was actually on the highway.

The traffic was bumper to bumper and crawling along. The westbound lanes were bare and empty. Every so often, I would see someone climb out of a car and get bottled water out of the trunk. Once in a while, I'd see a car on the shoulder, with people out walking dogs or wandering off into the bushes to relieve themselves. I kept glancing at my watch, anxiety growing within me with each passing minute. I couldn't help but feel that at the rate the traffic was moving, we weren't all going to get out in time. The radio kept broadcasting doom and gloom—and despite the fact we weren't moving at all, the broadcasters kept insisting to everyone they head "east" to avoid the congestion heading west. Every so often, they'd talk to a member of their crew on a cell phone, stuck heading west between New Orleans and Baton Rouge. As the hours passed, I began to get really annoyed. Why didn't they have anyone out actually reporting what was going on eastbound out of the city? But I was also amazed at how well behaved everyone on the highway was, all united in a grim single purpose. I breathed a sigh of relief when I finally reached the twin spans across Lake Pontchartrain, but the traffic was still moving at a snail's pace. And when I was out over the lake, it started raining just as one of the broadcasters stated, "The outer bands are starting to reach New Orleans," and my heart skipped a beat. I couldn't imagine anything more frightening than being trapped on the twin spans as a hurricane roared ashore.

It took eight hours to get to Slidell, but I was able to relax once I was off the bridge. (After the hurricane, when we were safely ensconced on Jude's couch, CNN showed an aerial view of how the storm had blown the twin spans apart. I said to Jude, "That's the bridge I took out of the city," and he started crying.) Once there, I couldn't go west on I-12; it was closed off by state troopers. So I headed north to Hattiesburg on 59, then cut over to Jackson. I'd left my apartment at ten in the morning, got to Jackson finally at ten that night, and kept heading west. The entire time I was absolutely terrified. The news reports on the radio were frightening. Katrina was such a huge storm with such intense power, it was undoubtedly going to be felt as far north as Jackson—and the weather people kept saying, "This storm's intensity may not dissipate before it reaches Tennessee!" So, I kept going, afraid to stop for anything other than gas and coffee and to use the bathroom. I couldn't eat. I sped through the night, and didn't breathe a sigh of relief until I crossed the Mississippi River back into Louisiana from Vicksburg and kept going. I'd gotten to Jude's house in Dallas twenty-six hours after I left New Orleans, all the while listening to the reports of the destruction the storm was causing, not just to New Orleans but all over the Gulf Coast. The reports had been so hopeful and positive when I got to Jude's—"New Orleans has dodged a bullet!" Wind damage was all; the storm had taken an eastern jog as it came ashore. I got out of my car, collapsed onto Jude's living room floor, and slept, relieved and thinking I would be able to head back home in just a few days.

It wasn't until I woke up that evening that I found out the levees were breached and the city was filling with water. I wouldn't be going home any time soon.

I fought back tears as I turned onto Robert E. Lee. The University of New Orleans campus was a wasteland, and the horror only got worse the farther into Lakeview I got. I finally found the street that Iris Verlaine's home was on, and turned onto it.

There was nothing alive out there. The grass was dead and brown. Trees were down, and the ones that were standing were covered in dried mud over my head on their trunks. There were no leaves. Everything just looked dead, and the entire neighborhood stank. In some houses there were piles of garbage in the yard, and everywhere there were dead dirty cars, with dried mud at least an inch thick on them.

I'd never spent a lot of time in Lakeview. I'd pretty much kept to my neighborhood, except when I had to for a case— and I wasn't really familiar with the rest of the city and its multitude of neighborhoods. For me, the city boundaries had been Elysian Fields in the Marigny, St. Charles Avenue through Uptown, the river, and then Audubon Park on the other side. I'd always known there was a vast city of diverse neighborhoods out there, but I never really ventured beyond my area of town. I'd been to Lakeview a few times in my seven years in the city: it was a beautiful neighborhood of gorgeous and expensive homes, lovely emerald-green well-kept lawns, thriving businesses, and main streets crowded with cars.

Now it was just—well, dead.

Iris Verlaine's house was on what used to be a quiet side street, and as I pulled up to the curb in front of it, I shook my head. Her house, pre-storm, had probably been worth a minimum of half a million dollars; now it wasn't worth a dime. It was a big house, probably three or four bedrooms from the size of it, with a driveway leading to a garage behind. There was a dirty fountain in the front yard, with a statue of what looked to be Aquarius in the center of it. It was filled with disgusting brown water with a film on the top of it. I got out the safety kit and made my way to the front walk.

The front door was off its hinges and lying down in the dirty foyer. I wasn't sure if the house had been looted or not, but the spray-paint symbol showed no pets found, nor corpses. I called out a greeting before stepping over the front door and entering the house. There was no answer, and immediately I was greeted by the smell, a smorgasbord of scent that made my stomach clench. Every drop of coffee I'd consumed that morning came right up in a spray into a dead flowerbed.

I went back out into the yard and took deep breaths, hoping for the nausea to clear. I rinsed my mouth out with a bottle of water and smeared Vicks VapoRub over my nostrils—it made my eyes water, but I couldn't smell anything else. I then placed one of the surgical masks over my nose and mouth and slipped rubber gloves onto my hands. I went back to the front of the house, but paused. Instead, I decided to go look in the garage windows—and sure enough, there was her car, covered in grime.

Hell, no, it hadn't been a burglary. Surely someone inside the house would have heard her pull into the driveway.

I headed back to the front door, and stepped into the wreckage of Iris Verlaine's home. As I walked across the mucky foyer tiles, my shoes stuck to them, and some of them even pulled free from the floor. I looked down at the muck on my shoes and realized I was going to have to throw them away—I didn't even want to get back into the car with them on. The carpet was black and squished under my feet. The floodwaters had tossed her furniture around like toys. The sofa was on its side, coated in grime. A recliner rested on top of it somehow. Tables and other chairs and bric-a-brac were thrown about as if there had been an earthquake. The walls themselves were coated with grime. I could see the mold and mildew streaking on the ceiling and through some of the grime on the walls. Beyond the living room, in the kitchen, I could see the refrigerator lying on its side, the door open, flies and coffin fleas buzzing around. Paintings and photographs were scattered all over the floor, their glass coverings cracked; the images beneath the broken glass no longer recognizable through the mildew and the filth. The sideboard, which she must have used as her bar, was tilted on its side, its doors hanging open, and I could see the grimy liquor bottles the killer hadn't touched. Some of them were broken; undoubtedly that was a part of the overpowering smell.

I found the curved staircase and squished my way up. About halfway to the second floor, the carpet was dry; the water hadn't gotten that high, and although the wall along the staircase was covered with black mold all the way to the ceiling, I could see that the hallway walls of the second floor were completely clear. As I kept walking up, the contrast was startling. By the time I reached the second floor, it was as though I had entered a completely different world. On the second floor, everything was fine, the way it had been before August 29. The walls were painted in soothing pastels; the carpet was the expensive-looking beige shag style that I'd noted in the crime scene photos, and black-and-white photographs lined the hallways. There was a room with a washer and dryer just across from the staircase, and when I looked in, everything was in its place: cleaning materials lined up neatly on their shelf, a box of Tide powder next to a bottle of Downy and one of bleach, next to them an open box of dryer sheets. I opened the dryer door, and there was a pair of women's jeans and a couple of T-shirts sitting in there, a crumpled dryer sheet on top of them. She'd probably thrown them in the dryer that morning before she left for work, and they'd been sitting there ever since.

The upstairs was frozen in time, like Miss Havisham's wedding banquet. The wall clock was stopped at 3:37, which was probably when the power had gone out in Lakeview that morning as the storm started moving in. I took a deep breath and headed for one of the bedroom doorways.

Iris Verlaine's house had only two bedroom suites, one at each end of the hallway. One was obviously a guest room; it was devoid of any signs that anyone had ever lived there. The bed was made and the closet was empty, other than some plastic hangers. I opened some of the drawers in the chest opposite the bed, but there was nothing inside any of them. I moved down the hall to the other bedroom suite, and sure enough, it was where she'd spent the last few moments of her life. There was a dark brownish stain on the rug and the chalk outline of where her body had fallen with the bullet. On her dresser were framed photographs—I recognized Joshua and assumed the man on her other side was Darrin, the other brother. There was a photograph of a severe-looking older woman who must have been her mother, and a studio photograph of a really old man who could only be her grandfather. I opened the closet doors and was struck in the face with the smell of mildew. All the ruined clothes looked expensive, though. I closed it back and walked over to her desk. There was still fingerprint dust all over. I started opening drawers and going through everything but found nothing—it looked to be primarily her bills and her bank statements. Iris was organized; every credit card had its own file folder, where she stored the bills by date; on each one was written in red ink the date she paid the bill, the amount she'd paid, and the check number. In every instance, she paid her credit cards on a monthly basis in full. She'd had American Express, several different versions of Visa and Mastercard, Discover, Shell, Amoco and Exxon, and every department store credit card you could think of. There were file folders for her bank statements, investment accounts, you name it—I leafed through them, not sure what I was looking for.

There was nothing that would be of interest to me, as far as I could tell. I got a plastic garbage bag out of her bathroom and began filling it with her records so I could go through them more thoroughly later. You never know what you might find in someone's financial records. It's boring work, but it has to be done.

But in the center drawer of the desk, the one that held her stationary and her pens, there was an unlabeled file folder. Venus and Blaine had left it behind, no doubt, because there was no reason for them to take it—her briefcase and purse had gone with them—but I opened it. The only thing inside of it was an 8-by-10 black-and-white photograph of a handsome man and an incredibly beautiful woman. It looked as though it had been taken at a party; the hairstyles were years out of date. It had to be from the 1970s, given his feathered and layered hair and the size of the lapels on his tuxedo. She, too, had what we in New Orleans tend to now call "big Texas hair"—lacquered to within an inch of its life and teased and gigantic, and her makeup was thickly applied. Her cleavage was also prominently on display in her low-cut dress—and it was rather impressive. Her skin looked creamy and smooth, and her eyes were almond-shaped and cat-like underneath the thick mascara caked on her eyelashes.

"The higher the hair, the closer to God," I thought with a laugh as I took a closer look.

They were both laughing with an amazingly carefree look on their faces, each holding a drink in their free hands. I could barely make out a place card on the table behind them. . . . I looked closer. REX 1972.

I turned it over.

Written on the back, in Iris's carefully measured handwriting, were the words, *Dad and Aunt Cathy?*

And just below that, underlined twice: *Chartres Street?*

CHAPTER SEVEN

MY CELL PHONE RANG just as I was getting ready to walk out my front door to meet everyone at the Avenue Pub.

I'd smoked a little pot when I'd gotten back from Lakeview. Paige had mentioned that everyone in New Orleans was suffering from post-traumatic stress disorder, but I'd thought she was exaggerating, as she is prone to do from time to time. Now that I'd somehow managed to shake off the numbness and depression, I thought I was on top of the world. But on the way home, it had come over me without warning. Maybe it was the enormity of the wreckage I'd seen out there—I vaguely remembered starting to feel a little overwhelmed on my way out there—but I thought I'd successfully fought that off. I'd also been relatively fine while going through Iris's house—but on the way back to my neighborhood it hit me with the full force of an almost complete emotional breakdown. It started as I passed under I-10 on Elysian Fields—my hands started to shake on the steering wheel. The harder I gripped it, the worse they shook. Before long my entire body was trembling, and I was having difficulty catching my breath. My eyes began watering, and all I could think was *oh my God oh my God oh my God* over and over again. My mind began racing, heading down into a deep dark space. It was horrible. I was aware of it and unable to stop it. The car started swerving a bit, and I slowed down to a crawl, and I finally managed to pull over into the deserted parking lot of an abandoned Exxon station. I sat there for a few moments, listening to my heart pound while I tried to focus on breathing normally. I cleared my head and focused on the breathing, closing my eyes. *In and out, nice and slow, nice and steady, that's it, just breathe, in and out, in and out.* I don't know how long I sat there, trying to get a grip on myself, but it eventually started to pass, leaving me breathing hard and still shaking a little, completely drenched in sweat. I managed to get the car back home, and once I was safely inside my house I loaded my pipe and took a couple of hits. That seemed to help take the edge off, and I decided it might not be a bad idea to meet Paige and everyone over at the Avenue Pub for a drink or two—or three, or however many felt right.

It was fucking scary as hell.

I glanced at the phone and didn't recognize the number. The caller ID just said NEW ORLEANS. I generally don't answer numbers that aren't familiar to me, but I was in a good mood and chances are it was a wrong number, so I answered, "Chanse MacLeod."

"Please hold," a woman's voice said, and for a few seconds I listened to hold music—a horrendous Muzak version of something that sounded vaguely Andrew Lloyd Webberish—and was just about to hang up when a raspy, whispery voice said, "Mr. MacLeod?"

"This is Chanse MacLeod." Now I was getting annoyed. I'd reached the Prytania corner, and if this call wasn't over pretty soon, I was going to hang up before entering the Avenue Pub. "Who is this?"

"Percy Verlaine," the voice replied, sounding like he was having trouble breathing.

I stopped dead in my tracks. Percy Verlaine? Iris's grandfather? Why the hell was he calling me? "Yes? What can I do for you, Mr. Verlaine?"

"Are you free tomorrow at noon?" he asked, pausing between each word as though forming the words caused him pain.

"Perhaps."

"Please come to my home for lunch. There are some matters we need to discuss." And the phone went dead.

Now I was annoyed. First of all, I hadn't said I was free. Second of all, what on earth did we have to discuss? Unless he had some information about his missing son-in-law. Joshua Verlaine must have told him I was continuing the investigation Iris had started. That kind of worried me a little—if Iris had indeed been killed because she was looking for her father, that didn't bode well for Joshua. After viewing the remains of the crime scene, I was relatively certain Iris's death hadn't been a random burglary. I couldn't make any sense of why, though—unless, of course, her father hadn't disappeared but been murdered himself—and what did that note on the back of the picture mean? Chartres Street?

Maybe Percy Verlaine had some answers for me.

I made a mental note to myself to find out if Iris's fiancée was back in town yet, and I needed to talk to Darrin Verlaine as well.

But as I crossed the street, I saw Blaine and Venus enter the Pub, and I remembered that Percy Verlaine was very rich. I've dealt with a lot of rich people in my line of work, and one thing they all have in common is an incredible self-absorption. Of course you're free when they need to see you.

They don't mean anything by it; it's just what they are used to. Rich people are terribly spoiled, and the privilege that comes with their wealth doesn't help in that regard. My landlady, Barbara Castlemaine, was like that too—she inherited Crown Oil from her husband. Of course, she was also my biggest client, and I was her security consultant, and Crown Oil not only paid the bills but was going to be my retirement as well, so I was *always* available when Barbara needed me for anything. And Percy Verlaine owned Verlaine Shipping outright—no stockholders, no board of directors to answer to—so he'd been making people jump when he snapped his fingers his entire life. And curiosity would eventually win out over my irritation. What did he want, and what information would he have to share with me?

"Percy Verlaine is a world-class grade-A bastard," Paige said when I mentioned the phone call. Our burgers had already come—they were out of French fries so we had to make do with small bags of Zapp's Cajun Crawtator potato chips—when I brought his name up, after listening to their recaps of their days. "He'd sell his mother to make a buck."

"Maybe, but he donates a lot of money to charity," Blaine replied. The Tujagues were an old-line New Orleans society family. They weren't in the same financial league as the Verlaines, but Blaine's father belonged to both Comus and Rex, and his mother was one of those women who are always raising money for this charity or that charity. "All Mom has to do is call him up and he writes a big check for whatever she wants."

"Buying his way into heaven." Venus looked tired, even more tired than she had the day before. She swung her head to look at me, and I noticed her eyes were rimmed with red. "What did you do today, besides get a call from the great and terrible Oz?"

"I went out to Lakeview." They all recoiled and looked away from me. "Yeah, I know, but I wanted to see Iris's place and take a look around."

"You should go down to the Lower Ninth Ward." Paige took another bite from her burger. "Lakeview is bad, but it's nothing compared to what you'll see down there." She put her burger down. "Everyone in this country needs to go down there and see what it looks like for themselves. Not on television, but in person." She shuddered. "I swear, you can still sometimes hear the people screaming for help." She reached for her second glass of Jack Daniels and downed half of it. She raised her glass. "Here's to you, Mr. President and your asshole cronies, may you all fucking burn in hell for eternity."

"Hear, hear." Venus raised her own glass. "Here's to FEMA and the Army Corps of Engineers. May the ghosts of your victims haunt your dreams for the rest of your life."

I decided to change the subject before the conversation turned into what apparently was becoming *the* conversation in town—how much we all hated the federal government and the Army Corps of Engineers. "So, Paige, why don't you like Percy Verlaine? How do you know him?"

She finished her glass and signaled for another. Her eyes were starting to get a little glassy. "Percy? I dated one of the grandsons for a little while. Not long, maybe once or twice." She shrugged. "Darrin. Man, was he a lousy lay. But the second date was a dinner at the big house in the Garden District. Oh my God. What a fucking nightmare. The old man wheezing with his oxygen mask ... and he looks old as Methuse—Methus—whatever the hell that guy's name was. The old one. Anyway, his eyes—mean as a snake. It was just me, Percy's daughter—Margot, that was her name—and some friend of hers, me and Darrin. None of the others were there. I don't know why Darrin took me to that, thought that was a good idea. Maybe he figured having me meet the family was a way to chase me away—although I could have told him the bad sex was much more likely to get me to dump his bony ass. Anyway, what was I talking about? Oh, yeah, the old man. Man, what a bastard. All he did was just sit there and belittle Darrin, his mother—but she was a cold bitch, that one was—and it was like that all through the whole lousy fucking meal. Just horrible, I kept drinking, gulping glass after glass of wine and praying for the last fucking course to come—and then finally, the old man looks at me and says, 'I hope you're enjoying that wine, Ms. Tourneur, it costs $75 a bottle, and you've drunk about $200 worth already.' I just looked at him and said, 'You got ripped off then, because it tastes like it should have cost about twelve bucks.'"

"You said that to Percy Verlaine?" Blaine's eyes about popped out of his head. "What did he do?"

"He laughed and said to help myself, he liked my style." Paige accepted a fresh glass of Jack Daniels from the bartender and laughed. "Needless to say, I never went out with Darrin Verlaine again. That whole fucking family is a major creep show." She shuddered.

"Why didn't you tell me you'd dated Darrin Verlaine?" I asked.

She shrugged. "What single straight man in this town haven't I dated? Although it's my studied opinion that Darrin Verlaine isn't straight by a long shot. Not 100 percent straight, anyway."

"I'm heading home." Venus stood up. She put a twenty down on the table. "I'm tired and—"

"Venus hates it when we speculate on people's sex lives." Paige hiccupped. "Probly cuz everyone thinks she's a lesbian."

"You're drunk, Paige," Venus said, more tired than angry. "And I'm tired—it's been a long day. Good night."

Blaine pulled a twenty out of his wallet, laid it on the table, and they walked outside. I could see them through the window. Venus had her face in her hands and her shoulders were shaking. Blaine put his arms around her and gave her a long hug. Paige turned and followed my eyes. She looked back at me, her face flushed. "I'm drunk and I'm a bitch." She started crying.

I slid around the table and put my arm around her. She sobbed for a few moments into my shoulder, blubbering apology after apology, and then things started pouring out of her. "I'm such a horrible person, such a horrible person."

I held her. "No, shhh, no you're not. You're just drunk, that's all."

"Oh yes, Chanse, I am a horrible person. You have no idea just how horrible I am." She buried her face in her hands. "Sometimes I wonder if this is all my fault?"

"What?"

She threw an arm out. "This, all of this, Chanse. What happened here."

"Paige—" I sat there for a moment, trying to think of the right thing to say. "It was the goddamned weather. No one has any control over the weather, Paige, and hurricanes don't happen to punish people. That's just crazy talk."

"When all those preachers were talking about how God was punishing New Orleans for her sins..." Her voice trailed off.

"Paige." I cupped her chin in my hand and turned her so she was looking me in the eye. "That's nonsense, and you know it. They don't know what the hell they're talking about. And if that's how their God behaves, the kind of thing their God is capable of, well, then *fuck* their God. He isn't my God, and he isn't your God, either. Those guys are cracked, insane, and you know that as well as I do." I tried to make a joke. "Surely if they had a direct line to God, He'd tell them to do something about their hair."

She laughed, then hiccupped, and then turned away from me. "I've never told you anything about me, you know."

"So we're even. You don't know anything about me."

"I grew up in the Lower Ninth Ward, you know." She looked into her glass. "What they used to call the Holy Cross District, on Caffin Avenue. My mother was a drunk, you know. She drank in the morning before she'd go to work. She was a functioning alkie. No one she worked with even knew she drank, but at night she'd be so drunk she'd fall out of her chair and just pass out on the floor. I used to have to put her to bed, clean up her puke."

"My mother drank too."

"It sucks, doesn't it?"

"Yeah." My mother's weakness was gin. She always smelled of sour gin. As soon as my father left for work in the morning, she'd get the gin bottle out from under the kitchen sink and fill a coffee cup with gin. By the time my brother, my sister, and I were ready to leave for school, she was weaving and hardly able to stand up. Our trailer was always dirty, because she was too drunk to clean, which would then send my father into a rage and they would scream at each other for hours, throwing things and calling each other nasty names. As soon as we were old enough, my sister and I started cleaning the house when we got home to try to keep the peace. Mom would sit in her reclining chair watching *The Edge of Night* and *Donahue* while we dusted and vacuumed and washed the dishes.

"Mom would go out to bars every night," Paige went on. "My dad left when she was pregnant with me—hell, for all I know they were never married; it wouldn't surprise me—and so she would go out looking for men to buy her drinks and tell her she was pretty. It was so pathetic; even when I was a little girl I thought it was pathetic. I would hear her come in at night with whoever Mr. Goodbar for the night was, and lay there in bed, listening to them, swearing that when I grew up I was going to be different from her. I wasn't going to be like her." She picked up the glass and toasted me with it. "And look at me! I'm just like her."

"No, you aren't," I replied. "You've been through a hard time, is all, and there's nothing wrong with having some drinks to dull the pain, Paige. It's not a crime."

"But you don't know the worst." She stopped and threw the rest of the liquor down her throat. She belched and gave me a look. "When I was thirteen one of her men raped me."

It was as though time suddenly stood still. I no longer heard the television set, or the music someone was playing on the jukebox. It was like the entire bar had frozen in time. I couldn't have heard that right; I couldn't have.

The fading sunlight coming through the window lit up her face. Her lower lip was trembling, but her jaw was set, her eyes clear and dry.

"She passed out," Paige went on. "I think she was barely conscious when she came home, but I remember hearing her fall to the floor in the living room. I got out of my bed—I was in my nightgown—and I walked out to see if she was okay, to see what was going on. He was standing there in the living room, looking down at her. I could see she was fine—I was used to her passing out by then, you see—and then he looked up and saw me. And he got this big smile on his face. 'What do we have here?' he said. I'll never forget his face as long as I live. He was a big guy, about your size actually, and he had a fleur-de-lis tattooed on his right bicep, and a bleeding sacred heart tattoo on his left forearm. He was wearing a white wife-beater shirt, and there were food stains on it. He was wearing jeans and boots … and he started walking toward me. He grabbed me and tore my nightgown off of me, and he just raped me."

I didn't know what to say, so I just held her tighter.

"He was gone when she finally came to, me lying there on the floor in my ripped nightgown, and she didn't believe me." She laughed bitterly. "She didn't fucking believe me— and what was worse, she couldn't even remember his name. She accused me of seducing him, if you can believe that. My own fucking bitch drunk of a mother."

"Paige, I'm so sorry." I'd known her for almost ten years, and I'd never had any idea what had happened to her. She didn't like to talk about her past; she didn't like to talk about her mother. I knew her mother called her from time to time, and whenever she talked to her, it upset her and required a lot of pot to forget about it. "Why didn't you ever tell me any of this before?"

"It's my cross to bear." Her eyes swam with tears. "It's probably why I can't ever seem to make anything work with any guy I ever date, you know."

"That wasn't your fault, Paige." I kissed the top of her head.

"Oh, I know that, Chanse. That wasn't my sin. My sin—" She bit her lip.

"You don't have to tell me if you don't want to."

She raised her chin. "My sin was the abortion." And then she broke down and wept, her entire body shaking with sobs. "That motherfucker got me pregnant. . . ."

I kept holding her, my mind reeling, murmuring over and over again that it wasn't her fault, that there was nothing she could do, and Katrina had not been sent by God to punish her for that. After a few minutes, she pushed me away and wiped her face with a napkin, smearing her makeup all over it.

I watched her as she somehow managed to pull herself together. "Well, I must look a wreck." She rose. "Will you walk me home?"

At her gate, she gave me a big hug. "Thanks, Chanse, you know—talking about that, finally telling someone—it helped a little bit." She gave me her crooked grin. "Sorry to dump that on you."

"Are you going to be okay?" I asked. "Do you want me to stay over?"

She stroked my cheek. "No, I'm fine. I'll just go in and take a Xanax and sleep like a baby." She hiccupped again. "I think I need to switch back to wine." She opened her purse and handed me a little vial of pills. "There's five Xanaxes in there." She winked at me. "You never know when you might need them."

"I don't want to take your—"

"Trust me, I have plenty." She shrugged. "And trust me, the longer you're back, the more you'll need them."

She shut the gate behind her, and I watched her walk back to the carriage house. Once she opened the door, she gave me a little wave, and then she was inside.

Maybe, I thought as I took a deep breath and started walking home, getting my own Xanax prescription wasn't a bad idea.

Everyone was on the verge of a nervous breakdown, it seemed.

The meltdown I'd had in the car on the way back from Lakeview had been pretty scary.

Just focus on what you're doing, and keep working, I told myself as I crossed Coliseum Square, digging out my keys. *If you keep your mind occupied, you won't have the time or energy to have these kinds of meltdowns.*

Once inside my apartment, I sat down on the couch with a notebook. I always make lists when I'm working on a case—I don't trust my memory enough not to do so. I wrote down everything I knew so far, and everything I needed to find out. I made a list of people to interview, notes to make some computer searches on Michael Mercereau's family—Iris had to have some relatives on her father's side.

I got up and stretched.

Yes, move forward, don't take the time to stop and think.

That was the only way to get through all of this.

I went to bed and fell asleep within seconds.

CHAPTER EIGHT

I WOKE UP AROUND THREE in the morning from one of the worst nightmares I'd ever had. My hair was soaked and plastered to my scalp. My skin—and the sheets too—were drenched in sweat. I sat there for a moment in the dark, waiting for my heart to stop pounding and my entire body to stop trembling and relax. The images were so vivid, so real. ... I turned on the nightstand lamp and sat there for a moment before reaching a trembling hand out for a cigarette. I breathed in the soothing nicotine, closing my eyes and letting calm wash over me. I stubbed it out when it was burned about halfway down to the butt, and got out of bed. I went into the bathroom, turned on the shower, and stood under the hot spray for a few minutes, letting the water soak into my tense muscles, and then toweled off, got a soda, and went into the living room. The pipe was sitting where I'd left it after getting home from Paige's, and I took a long, slow hit, hoping it would help.

Before the storm, I'd had bad dreams from time to time. After I'd killed a man a year or so earlier, I'd relived that horror at night, waking up screaming and drenched in sweat—but I'd had Paul to hold me and calm me down, to get me through it. The nightmares I'd endured after Paul's death had been bad as well. After a few months of being nightmare-free, the dreams had come back after the evacuation and the breaking of the levees, but this one was, hands down, the worst I'd ever had. This dream had been so *real*, more real than any other dream I'd ever had. Back when I was staying in Dallas with Jude, the nightmares had never been New Orleans–related: they had Paul as the common theme. It was like the disaster had triggered the synapse in my brain controlling the Paul dreams. But I'd never dreamed about the horror that had befallen New Orleans. That horror I'd watched on television day after day, and those horrible images had haunted my waking hours. No, when I'd gone to sleep, it had been Paul who'd haunted my dreams.

Maybe it was because of what Paige had told me—maybe that had triggered the nightmare. I took another hit from the pipe and leaned back against the sofa. The pain Paige had been carrying around locked inside her head for all those years—it was no wonder she was popping pills now like M&M's and guzzling whiskey. I couldn't help but wonder if she'd always been suffering, or if the flood had somehow washed away her own internal defense mechanisms, releasing memories she'd locked away for years.

The pot was helping. I could feel my body relaxing, my heart rate slowing to normal.

I'd dreamed I was in a house I didn't recognize. Paige, Venus, Blaine, and I were all sitting on the floor, around a hurricane lamp and its eerie yellowish glow. Outside the storm was hitting—that horrible howling roar, the crashing of debris as it slammed against the building, the sound of trees blowing down and smashing through things as they landed. Blaine kept moaning over and over, "Why didn't we leave? Why didn't we leave?" None of us answered him; we were holding hands. Venus was squeezing my right hand so hard I thought my hand was going to break, and on my other side, Paige was crying softly and praying under her breath. And then the storm was over and the sun came out, shining through the windows. Everything seemed to be fine. The power was out, but we had water and more than enough food to last us for however long we needed. We all got up and walked outside, and marveled at the tree branches, the debris, and whatever else had changed since we'd gone inside to ride it out. We were joking and laughing, hugging, and giving each other high-fives . . . and then Paige got a puzzled look on her face. "That's odd," she'd said, and we'd all turned to look. The street was filling up with water.

"Where's the water coming from?" Blaine asked—and then in the distance we heard a loud crash and roar.

And then the water started rising, faster and faster. "Get inside!" Venus screamed, and I slammed the door behind us. I stood in the window as they ran upstairs, and the water was submerging cars, climbing and swirling up to porch level.

"Come on!" I heard Paige scream, and then water was coming over the threshold.

I ran up the stairs to the second floor, and the angry swirling water came after us. "We've got to get on the roof!" Blaine screamed, grabbing an ax. Venus pulled on a rope and the trapdoor to the attic opened, a folding wooden ladder unfurling. Blaine went up first, then Venus, and then I followed. Paige came behind me and then I heard her scream. I turned to look, and I saw her being carried away in the angry brown water, and I tried to reach for her. But she was gone . . . *she can't swim,* I thought, and started screaming for her. The water kept rising and I felt the house shift and move, and then it was washing away, floating until it smashed into another house and came apart. Venus screamed, and I tried to grab for Venus but couldn't get there in time and she was gone, her head going under. "Blaine!" I screamed, and I couldn't see him anywhere, and the water was at my knees. I grabbed the ax and started swinging it at the roof. I hacked my way out, and climbed out. The sun was shining, and I could see the house we'd slammed into, and then the roof began to tilt, and I leaped onto the other house's room. "Blaine!" I shouted, and then I saw him floating facedown beside the house and I started screaming.

And that's when I woke up.

Jesus *fucking* Christ. I reached for the pipe again, and took another hit. *Calm down, it was just a dream,* I told myself.

My heart had started racing again, and I could feel my mind starting to spiral off. I couldn't stop it, and that was the worst part. I *knew* I was thinking crazy thoughts, but I couldn't make them stop, I couldn't get my brain to rewire itself and think calmly. There would be another hurricane and we wouldn't be able to get out this time. This would be it, it would come up the river, what was left of the city would be destroyed when the river levees collapsed and we'd all die. . . . I fumbled for the pill bottle Paige had given me, grabbed a Xanax, and washed it down with Coke. I took another hit off the pipe and sat back, letting my mind race until suddenly. . . .

It was over. It was like a curtain of calm had dropped over me. The panic was gone, my heart stopped racing, and everything was just—fine.

"Wow," I said aloud.

Paige was right. Xanax was a wonder drug.

I walked back into the bedroom and stripped the damp sheets off the bed. I got some fresh ones out of the linen closet and remade the bed, humming the whole time. Wow. I lay back down, staring at the ceiling. Everything would be fine.

"So that's what an anxiety attack feels like," I thought, shuddering a little at the memory. It was astonishing what a difference the drug had made. I made a note to myself to get my own prescription as soon as I could.

And finally, I fell asleep again.

I woke up feeling incredibly rested and relaxed—like the nightmare and the following attack had never happened. I took a shower while I brewed a pot of coffee and signed on while drinking my first cup. Might as well take advantage of this energy, I figured. Time to start looking for the missing dad—if Iris had been murdered because she wanted to locate her father, maybe I could find some kind of hint as to who didn't want him found by finding out what actually did happen to him. I went to a website for licensed private eyes and keyed in a search for his Social Security number. His last known address was the house on Third Street; no address—nothing of any kind—after 1973. I cruised around on a number of different sites. He hadn't filed an income tax return, either state or federal, under that Social Security number since 1972. He had never applied for a new Social Security number, either. There was absolutely no trace of him out there past June 1973.

There were only two possibilities: he'd either left the country, or he'd died. In fact, the last time his Social Security number appeared anywhere was in the court records when Margot Verlaine divorced him for desertion in 1980.

And although it was possible he'd left the country, I thought it unlikely. If Michael Mercereau had left the country for good, it was unlikely Iris had been killed because she wanted to find him—and like Venus, I distrusted coincidences. So, not only was it more likely that he was dead, it was also likely he hadn't died of natural causes. It was the only thing that made sense.

I pulled out the envelope I'd found in Iris's bedroom and slipped out the photograph of Michael Mercereau and "Aunt" Cathy. I went to a few search engines and typed his name in, but all that came up were links to websites with mentions of a couple of Michael Mercereaus who were obviously too young to be the one I was looking for—one was a baseball coach in Georgia, another a real estate agent in Montana, and the third a college professor in Utah. I did a search for Cathy Verlaine, then Cathy Mercereau, but those were both useless as well—nothing came up on either name.

So, the question was, who the hell was Aunt Cathy?

Might as well ask the old man when I went over there.

I arrived at the Verlaine house promptly at noon, and was buzzed in the gate. The front door opened as I climbed the steps, but instead of the black woman who'd greeted me the last time, a white woman in her late fifties stood in the doorway. Her steel-gray hair was pulled away from her face in a rather severe French braid that was a little unflattering, but her face was round and pink. Her eyes were wide and brown, and she was wearing a pair of gold-rimmed glasses, a pair of gray slacks, and a blue silk blouse with a scarf knotted at the neck. She smelled faintly of Elizabeth Taylor's White Diamonds perfume—Paige always wears it. She was smiling. She looked pleasant and friendly and was still relatively attractive, even if a little thick in the waist and hips. "Mr. MacLeod? You're right on time." She extended a ring-free, blue-veined hand for me to shake. "I'm Emily Hunter, Mr. Verlaine's personal assistant. He's waiting for you in the solarium. You'll have lunch there. I hope you aren't allergic or have any aversions to seafood?"

"No, Ms. Hunter."

"It's *Miss* Hunter. Good. Mr. Verlaine always likes to have shrimp Creole for lunch on Wednesdays, and he sticks to his schedule. There will be a salad and shrimp bisque first, then the main course, and bread pudding for dessert." She gave a slight nod. "Does that sound all right?"

"Sounds good to me." I wasn't partial to shrimp Creole—while I like shrimp, this local specialty was made with a lot of tomatoes, and sometimes if made poorly it was more like tomato soup with shrimp floating in it—but I'd suck it up and eat it, if it meant getting some information out of Percy Verlaine. He was the only one left who had really known Michael Mercereau. "Do you know why Mr. Verlaine wanted to see me?"

She gave me a very careful smile. "That's for Mr. Verlaine to tell you. This way, please. He's waiting—and he hates to be kept waiting."

She led me down a side hallway into a room that was all glass, and filled with gigantic plants of every kind—massive elephant ferns, orchids, roses, and banana trees, all in planters. The plants needed to be trimmed down; there was a sense of lush vegetation, kind of like a jungle gone wild. I recognized some Venus flytraps under glass just off to the left, their mouths open and hungry. The air was humid and damp, and I felt myself starting to sweat under my arms and on my forehead. The glass was tinted to keep out the direct glare of the sun, but it was still bright. There was a small wire table set up for lunch. Facing me was a shriveled old man in a wheelchair with an oxygen tank next to him. Just behind him was a thickly muscled man with his arms folded. His bare forearms were covered with brightly colored tattoos of a slightly Catholic persuasion—a sacred heart, a Blessed Mother, and some others I didn't recognize. He was almost as tall as me, but easily had thirty or forty pounds on me. Though thicker, he didn't seem fat at all. His hair was slicked back and the jet black color that comes from a bottle, like Joshua's. He had no expression on his face, but I could tell his nose had been broken more than once.

As I approached, the old man put a breath mask over his mouth and nose and sucked down some oxygen.

"Mr. MacLeod is here." She gave a slight bow, and walked out, her heels clicking on the stone floor. I heard the door shut behind her.

"Forgive me if I don't shake your hand," the gaspy voice from the telephone said as he placed the oxygen mask back down. "Germs. At my age, I can't take the risk. Please be seated."

"And you are?" I said to the man behind him.

"That's my bodyguard, Lenny Pousson." The old man waved a hand. "Pay him no mind."

I stuck my hand out. "Nice to meet you, Lenny."

Lenny stuck out a thick hairy paw that seemed to envelope my hand completely. "Nice to meetcha," he said in a thick yat accent. "I watched you play in the Sugar Bowl a coupla times." His mouth twitched at the corners in what probably was supposed to pass as a smile.

"Sure you want to shake hands with a fag, Lenny?" the old man wheezed. "Aren't you afraid you might catch something?"

Lenny's face froze and he pulled his hand back as though burned. He refolded his arms and wiped any expression off his face.

"I didn't come here to be insulted," I said, keeping my voice even.

"My apologies." Percy Verlaine gave me a nasty smile. "I like to yank Lenny's chain from time to time. Please be seated."

I sat down and took a good look at him. His head was completely devoid of hair, and his scalp gleamed in the sunlight. His skin was thin as paper, so I could see almost every vein in his face and neck. He was wearing a white linen suit, complete with navy blue button-down shirt and a rather loud red-and-yellow tie. He looked as though he would blow away in a slight wind, but his watery blue eyes were small, hooded, and alert—and alive with malice. He rang a bell, and the black woman who'd opened the door for me the last time I'd been to the house placed a plate of salad in front of him and one in front of me. It was merely a heart of romaine sliced lengthwise, drenched in a raspberry vinaigrette, and covered in feta cheese and crushed walnuts. She poured me a glass of red wine and refilled his ice water from a metal pitcher and then disappeared without a word.

"Eat," the old man wheezed. "We'll talk after."

We ate in silence, him ringing the bell to signal the next course whenever we finished one plate. The salad was good, the bisque delicious, and it was easily the best shrimp Creole I'd ever tasted—not too much tomato and plenty of spices. The bread pudding was also heavenly, and then everything was all cleared away. He grabbed the mask, closed his eyes, and took in several deep breaths. He let the mask drop to his side, then opened the eyes slowly. I was reminded of a cobra.

"I don't know what my fool grandson was thinking, but I don't want you looking for my former son-in-law," he said quietly. "Nothing good will come of it."

"Your granddaughter wanted to find him before she got married." I shrugged. "I think he's just honoring her wishes, now that she's gone."

"Iris was a fool too," he hissed. "I told my daughter not to marry that trash, but she wouldn't listen to me. I knew he was only capable of begetting fools—and I was right. And he betrayed her, broke her heart." He waved his hand. "The best thing that ever happened to this family was the day Michael Mercereau walked out that front door and never came back."

"You'll need to take that up with your grandson." I shrugged. "He hired me, and until he tells me not to, I'm going to keep doing the job he hired me for."

"I'll double what he's paying you. Just tell him you can't find him." He gave me a vile smile. "That way you can make a nice tidy profit off the Verlaine family."

"Why don't you just talk to him yourself?"

He waved his hand again. "He won't listen, the more fool he. My grandchildren were all fools. Iris getting herself killed! Thank God Margot is safely in her grave. I told Iris not to move into that damn fool house, but she wanted to be independent, and Margot let her go ... the Verlaines have always lived in this house, safe and sound. I warned her."

"Was Margot your only child?"

"My wife and I had a son who was killed when he was sixteen. A car accident. Margot was all we had left." He closed his eyes. "Matthew was also a fool."

"Was Aunt Cathy Michael's sister?"

"Who told you about Cathy?" He looked down, and when he looked back up, there was a sly look to his eyes that I didn't like or trust.

"What happened to her?" I pressed on.

"Cathy Hollis is my wife's niece. Her parents died when she was very young, so we took her in, raised her as our own daughter." He shrugged. "Not that she was ever grateful for anything we gave her. She was wild. . . . She liked men, she liked to drink, and I suspect she took drugs. She liked to be looked at, have drinks bought for her—and she never cared if the man was married—or if the man was white." He shook his head. "She was out of control—she had a wild streak. She lost her mind a long time ago—the drink and drugs, no doubt had a part in it. But her own mother's family had a streak of madness in their bloodline. . . . There's no denying your blood, Mr. MacLeod."

"Is she still alive?"

"She's in a mental hospital somewhere in Mississippi. She's been there for a long time. I haven't seen her in years. Her mind is gone. She thinks she's a child again, and has for years." He shook his head, but his eyes gleamed. "We pay for her care, of course. All she ever did was drain our money off us like a siphon. Nothing was ever good enough for her, of course. She was nothing like Margot. Margot was a perfect daughter—completely obedient, did as she was told."

"Except for marrying Michael Mercereau."

"She learned from her mistakes. Cathy never did, and look where it got her!"

"I'd like to talk to Cathy. What hospital is she in?"

"I don't remember."

It was obvious he was lying—and he wasn't offering to have someone find out for me. If he was indeed paying her bills, there was a record somewhere.

But if he wouldn't tell me, it would be easy enough to find out.

I rose. "Thank you for lunch, Mr. Verlaine, but I need to be going now."

"Whatever Joshua is paying you, I will double it." He leaned forward. "Don't be a fool, Mr. MacLeod. Let the past stay buried. That's generally what's best to do. Why dredge up all that pain again? Michael Mercereau walked out of this house thirty-odd years ago and broke my daughter's heart— his children's hearts too. He never once tried to reach them, or talk to them. Do you think my daughter didn't try to find him? She hired detectives. They searched for him for years, and never found a trace of him." He shook his head again. "It's a waste of time and my grandson's money to keep looking for him now. If they couldn't find him back then, what makes you think you can find him now?"

"What's interesting to me," I said slowly, "is why you don't want me to look for him."

"Don't say I didn't warn you." He waved his hand. "Go."

I walked back out into the hallway and was heading for the front door when Joshua Verlaine stuck his head out of the drawing room door. He glanced around, and nodded toward the front door. Out on the porch, with the door shut, he whispered, "Heard you asking the old man about Aunt Cathy." He hiccupped, and I realized he was drunk again.

I nodded. "Were you eavesdropping?"

He winked at me. "Only way to find out what's going on around here, you know, is to listen." He shrugged. "Aunt Cathy was cool. She went away that same summer, you know. Lost her mind. She was always cool to us kids though."

"So?" I prodded him. "Where is she?"

"A place called St. Isabelle's. It's in Cortez, Mississippi, up near the Tennessee state line, on the way to Memphis. I'll call up there and give permission for you to see her." He gave me a brittle smile.

"Okay, I can find that place. You'll call this afternoon?" When he nodded, I stuck my hand out and shook his. It was sweaty. "Thanks, Joshua."

He closed his eyes, and when he opened them again, his eyes were glistening. "I loved Aunt Cathy. Besides Dad, she was the only adult around here who had any time for us kids. Mother couldn't be bothered, that was for sure. Cathy would play with me and Darrin. After Dad left, and she went away. . . ." His voice trailed off for a moment, and then he went on. "Grandpa was always hateful to Aunt Cathy. I don't know how she stood it around here, to be honest." He snorted, and mimicked Percy's raspy voice. "*It was probably the drink and the drugs.* Like being a part of this family wasn't enough to drive anyone to drink!" He hiccupped again. "I mean, look at me."

"I need to talk to your brother, too," I replied.

"I'll have him call you." He winked at me and started back toward the front door.

"And give Aunt Cathy my love."

The door shut behind him.

CHAPTER NINE

I WENT TO THE GYM after leaving the Verlaine house to work the creepy feelings out of my system. I couldn't even begin to imagine what it must have been like to grow up in that house under the thumb of that wretched old man. It was a wonder all the Verlaines hadn't wound up with Aunt Cathy in a mental hospital. Growing up in that trailer park in east Texas, sometimes I'd fantasized what it would be like to be the child of wealth and privilege, live in a mansion, and have more money than I knew what to do with. The creep show the Verlaine family was turning out to be made the lousy trailer park, a violent father, and an alcoholic mother look pretty damned good about now.

I worked out hard for a good hour. The gym was still pretty deserted, just Allen behind the counter and a couple of women on the stationary bicycles. I beat the hell out of my arms and shoulders, did about two hundred incline crunches, and did a good twenty minutes on a stair climber. There's something almost zen-like about a good workout. You can just focus completely on what you're doing and put everything else out of your mind. Before long, the rhythm of the repetitions puts you into an almost-trance state and nothing else seems to matter. I was still in that semi-trance when I headed for my car. I was almost out the door when I realized Allen had said something to me.

I came back in. "I'm sorry, what?"

Allen came around the corner of the counter and stood in front of me. His tongue flicked out and licked his upper lip. "Um, I, uh, I um asked you what you were doing for dinner tonight?" His face flushed bright crimson.

"Oh." Of all the things I might have thought he'd said, I wasn't expecting to hear that. It was from way out in left field. Was he asking me on a *date?* "Um, nothing, really. I mean, I meet some friends every evening for burgers and drinks at the Avenue Pub—kind of a standing date, but if I don't show, it won't be a big deal. Why?"

"I close up the gym at seven." He shifted his weight from one foot to the other. "And I'm sick of eating alone."

"You want me to have dinner with you?" Sometimes I amaze myself with how slow I can be on the uptake. That's me—master of urbane wit and putting someone else at their ease. Jesus, I can be a dork sometimes.

"You mind?"

"No. Of course not. I'd love to—it'll be nice." I glanced at my watch. It was almost three. "You want me to just meet you here at seven? Or meet you somewhere?"

"I can pick you up." He looked down at his shoes, his weight still going from one foot to the other. "If you'd rather..."

"I can just meet you here," I replied. "I have some work to do, and I can just swing by here. Is that cool?"

He nodded, and then he flashed his grin, the one that always made me think of a happy chipmunk, at me. "I'll see you then."

As I started my car, I wondered for a brief moment what I was getting myself into. I'd known Allen for years, ever since

I'd joined Bodytech. I'd been to parties at the big house on St. Charles Avenue, but Allen and I had never done anything together before. Oh, sure, on the rare occasion when we ran into each other at a bar during Mardi Gras or Southern Decadence or something, we'd hang out for a while, talk and joke and laugh, but nothing serious. I didn't really know him that well. He was a nice guy, attractive, had a great body, but I couldn't help but wonder. Was this a date of some sort?

Oh, good God, Chanse, get real and get over yourself, I admonished myself as I stopped at the intersection at Jackson. *He's lonely and bored. Can't anyone show any interest in you for something besides sex? And with everything he told you the other day that was going on with him and Greg, he probably just wants someone to talk to about things, a friendly ear. Will it kill you to be that for him?*

"But he and Greg are having problems, and do I really want to get in the middle of that?" I said out loud as I swung the car to the left at the St. Andrew junction, where Magazine turned into Camp Street. As I pulled into the driveway, I decided not to worry about it. It was just dinner, for God's sake.

I showered and got cleaned up before heading to my computer. I did a search for St. Isabelle's and found their website. It quickly disabused me of any perception that it was a mental hospital. St. Isabelle's was a "rest home," with supervision and a fully trained medical staff. As I browsed through the site, looking at pictures of the "living suites" and the grounds, the workout center, the dining hall, the swimming pool, I began to wonder a little bit about what exactly was wrong with Cathy Hollis. Percy Verlaine had been pretty clear that she was not in her right mind, but I didn't trust him. I glanced at my watch, and gave Paige a call, asking her to see what she could dig up in the paper's archives about Catherine and Michael Mercereau. I tried to dig up some stuff online about Catherine—now that I knew her actual last name but wasn't too surprised to come up with nothing.

"Okay," I said, leaning back in my chair and lighting a cigarette, "this isn't going anywhere." Solving a thirty-year-old disappearance wasn't going to be easy; I'd never thought it would be. The lack of information on Michael Mercereau anywhere online pretty much ruled out any possibility he was still alive; he'd vanished off the face of the earth. So, it seemed likely he'd been murdered. But why? Why would someone want to kill him? Obviously, Percy hated him, but why wait until 1973 to have it done? I wasn't getting far with the Verlaine family. The only ones who apparently knew anything were Percy—who wasn't about to say anything—and Cathy Hollis, who may or may not be insane.

I needed to come at it from a different direction. What about *his* family? I pulled out my old standby, the New Orleans phone book, and turned to New Orleans residential numbers. Sure enough, there were Mercereaus listed, but every single one of them had an address in the Lower Ninth Ward, and there was no one living down there now, not after the flood. There was no way of finding out where any of them had evacuated to, but I felt reasonably confident that not one of them was going to answer the phone. I found the printout I'd made of Michael Mercereau's address history. Sure enough, one of the listings had been for a Lucien Mercereau, at the same address where Michael had lived until he moved Uptown.

I leaned the phone book against the wall and started going through websites, keying in the names listed. Unfortunately, the only addresses and phone numbers the computer could find for them were the same as the ones in the phone book. I went to the Red Cross website's post-Katrina page and searched for them. If the Mercereaus had indeed gotten out of the city before the storm hit, they'd never bothered to register with the Red Cross. I doubted that all of them had been killed, so most likely, they had a place to go when they fled. I picked up the file Iris had given me and pulled out the birth certificate. *Lucien Mercereau* was listed as the father. I did a records search, and discovered there were two Mercereau children in addition to Michael: Jolene and Jules. I went to the address history website and typed in Jules Mercereau—he wasn't listed in the New Orleans phone book. His last known address, unfortunately, was in Chalmette—and Chalmette, like the Lower Ninth Ward it bordered, was gone.

With a sigh, I searched for Jolene Mercereau—and hit the motherlode. Jolene had married a man named Earl Mc-Connell in the early 1970s. Despite having moved around a bit, she was listed as living in Jackson, Mississippi, for the last seven years. I did a quick search and found a phone number for her. I got out my road map, and grinned to myself. Just as I thought—Jackson was on Highway 55 on the way to Memphis, and there was Cortez, just below the Tennessee state line, also on Highway 55.

I stubbed out my cigarette and grinned again. I could easily stop and see Jolene McConnell on my way up to see Catherine Hollis.

I lit another cigarette. Why had Iris never bothered to look up the rest of her father's family, and why had the family never bothered with their Verlaine relatives? It seemed more than a little odd. Of course, the old man had made it pretty plain he thought his daughter had married beneath her, and it was possible after the marriage failed he and Margot had purposely kept the kids from their Lower Ninth Ward roots. The Mercereaus might have wanted to keep the family ties alive, but a working-class family wouldn't have had a hell of a lot of recourse against a wealthy and powerful Garden District family—one of the wealthiest families in the city, for that matter.

Obviously, there was a lot more going on here than I could figure out by pure speculation.

I did a search on Iris Verlaine. The vast majority of the entries were links to www.nola.com, the *Times-Picayune*'s website. The first one was an engagement announcement from the social pages. I clicked on the link and found myself staring at a professional portrait of Iris and her fiancé, Phillip Shea. He was handsome, and looked a little younger than she. I scrutinized his face. He had thick lips, longish hair that curled at the ends, and clear eyes and skin. He was smiling at the camera, and his long lashes gave him a dewy-eyed look. He was so handsome he could almost be called pretty—a designation most straight men detested. His left arm circled Iris's waist, and she, too, smiled at the camera. But her smile, unlike his, seemed a little frozen and forced. It didn't reach her eyes. Her eyes looked uncomfortable, as though there were a million other things she'd rather be doing than posing with her fiancé for a picture in the paper. I printed it out and tacked it up on my corkboard. I tacked the picture of Michael and Catherine Hollis next to it, and then put the wedding picture of Michael and Margot up beside them. I leaned back and took a good hard look at all of them. Iris had no resemblance to her father at all. I could see a resemblance between him and Joshua Verlaine—in fact, Joshua could almost be a facial clone of his father—but Iris looked like neither one of her parents. Of course, that didn't have to mean anything—I didn't look like either of my parents, thank God, although my sister looked like our mother and my brother looked like our dad—but it made me curious. Maybe Michael had left Margot because he'd found out Iris wasn't his child?

Stick to the facts as you know them and stop speculating.

I looked closer at Margot. At first glance, in her wedding photo, with the long lace veil framing her face, she looked like any other happy bride, aglow with excitement on her big day. But closer inspection showed that her teeth were clenched; there was tension in her jaw, and again, her eyes looked cold, as though posing for the picture with her new husband was an ordeal for her. His face was alight with excitement—and looking closer didn't change that. But Margot … Margot was a different story.

My mother was, well, a rather formidable woman, I heard Iris saying again.

She sure looked the part. She didn't look like she could ever be happy.

I was startled out of my reverie by my cell phone ringing. I flipped it open and saw a local number, the caller ID reading VERLAINE SHIPPING. "Hello?"

"Mr. MacLeod?" The voice was soft and feminine.

"Yes?"

"Josh Verlaine suggested that I get in touch with you. My name is Valerie Stratton; I worked—" She paused for a moment. "I worked for Iris Verlaine here at the company. I was her assistant. Although I can't imagine why he thought I should. I mean, I don't know what—" she broke off.

She sounded as if she was ready to start crying at any moment. "Thank you for calling. I'm sure this has all been rather difficult for you," I said, trying to make my own voice as calm and soothing as possible.

She sniffed a little, and I heard the unmistakable sound of her blowing her nose. "Excuse me, I'm sorry. It's just—well, I've been so overwhelmed. I didn't even know about Iris until I got back to the city, and now I have to figure out all this—oh, you don't care about any of this. When Josh suggested I call you, I thought, you know, I don't know what help I could be to you, but what the hell, I'll call and see, you know?" She gave a nervous giggle. "So, here I am."

"There's a couple of things you could help me with right now—but I'd really like to meet you in person." She seemed almost on the verge of hysteria, so it made sense to me to give her something to focus on.

"Oh. Okay. What can I do?"

"I need to know how to reach Phillip Shea. I'd like to talk to him. Did you know him well?"

"Oh, yes, I have his information right here in the Rolodex." I heard her flipping through it. "Here you go." She read off an address in Uptown, as well as two phone numbers. "That second number is his cell. I don't know if he's back in New Orleans yet or not, but these days who knows? I mean, I don't know if he left or. . . ." Her voice trailed off.

"Did Phillip and Iris seem happy together?" I asked as I scribbled the information down.

She sucked in some air, and let it out with a slight whistle. "Well, that's a good question, Mr. MacLeod. You know, I've been working with—oh, I guess I mean I worked with—Iris for almost five years. She didn't really talk much about her personal life, but you know, when you're an assistant you can't help but know things. I came to work for her right after she moved out to Lakeview, and I gathered her mother was not too happy about it—moving out of the house, I mean, and neither was Mr. Percy."

"Did you know her mother?"

"Not well, but you were asking about Phillip. Let me think, how can I put this?" She paused for a few moments, clicking her tongue. "The engagement came out of the blue.

I had no idea she was even dating Phillip. He never called here, she never mentioned him once, and then all of a sudden one day she's showing me a diamond ring."

"Did she seem happy?"

"Hmmm." She laughed. "I suppose I shouldn't be saying this, respect for the deceased and all, but she never seemed happy about anything. She rarely smiled, she never laughed … it was like she'd had her sense of humor surgically removed." She paused for a moment. "Her mother was like that too—you know, like she had a block of ice where her heart was supposed to be. I don't think I ever saw Margot smile, but then I only dealt with her here in the office about business things. She was a very hard woman. Iris, at least, was easy enough to work for."

"And what about Phillip Shea?"

"Such a nice man. Always sending her flowers and chocolates, he was always very sweet to me when he called. . . . I'd say he definitely was in love with her."

"Well, thank you, Valerie. I'm glad you called." I got out my date book. "I'm going out of town for a day, maybe two, but can I call you and set up lunch or coffee when I get back?"

"Sure. Let me give you my cell number." She recited it for me. "If I can be of any help to you, don't hesitate to call." She swallowed. "It's all so awful. . . ." She hung up the phone.

I looked at the address for Phillip Shea. It wasn't a Garden District address; it was on the wrong side of Louisiana Avenue, but it was pretty darned close. I looked at the clock on the wall. I had time to drive by and take a look on my way to meet Allen. I put on a pair of jeans and a yellow polo shirt, and headed back outside.

The lights were on at the address Valerie had given me. It wasn't a big house, but rather a Creole cottage. There was a white Lexus parked in the driveway. I slowed down as I drove past, but didn't stop. At least I was reasonably sure Phillip was in town. Someone was staying at his house.

I debated stopping, but after looking at my watch, decided it could wait until the next morning.

Allen was just locking up when I pulled into the parking lot at Bodytech. He'd changed from his tank top and shorts into a pair of jeans and a T-shirt. He smiled when I got out of the car. "Hey, bud."

"Hey," I said, and there was an awkward silence between us.

"You mind Louisiana Pizza Kitchen?" he asked finally. "The one in Riverbend is open."

"Fine with me."

We took his car. We didn't talk much as we drove up St. Charles Avenue, so I just looked out the window. Other than a few trees down and the huge pickup trucks parked all over the neutral ground, you wouldn't think anything had even happened. The Jewish Community Center at the corner of St. Charles and Jefferson had a huge FEMA RELIEF CENTER sign hanging on the front, but it was deserted, closed for the night. None of the stoplights uptown was working, either—apparently stoplights weren't working anywhere in New Orleans. The campuses of both Loyola and Tulane Universities were dark, and Audubon Park was a mass of black velvety silence. But when we reached the curve where St. Charles ends at Carrollton, there were cars and trucks parked all over the neutral ground.

Allen gestured with his head. "That pisses me off. All these relief workers parking all over the streetcar tracks. Don't they know they're tearing up the tracks?" He shook his head. "I mean, I appreciate the workers coming to help clean up and work and all, but they don't show any respect for the city at all. Every time I see that, I just want to take a baseball bat and bust out all their windows."

I didn't say anything as he parked, and we walked into the restaurant. I'd never eaten at this particular location but had enjoyed a couple of meals at the Louisiana Pizza Kitchen in the Quarter. Every table was taken, and people were three-deep at the bar. The hostess looked tired. "Two?" she asked.

We nodded, and Allen gave her his name, and we went back outside so I could have a cigarette. Allen just nodded okay when I made the request, which I appreciated. I kind of figured I'd get a lecture on the evils of smoking, him being a trainer and all, but he didn't say anything. A huge pickup truck, the kind with a back seat, pulled into a spot in the back of the lot, and a tired-looking family got out. The entire back of the truck was filled with boxes and mattresses, as if they'd grabbed everything they could out of their house. The father was holding a can of Pabst Blue Ribbon. The two kids couldn't have been older than six; the boy looked like he'd been crying. The girl looked dirty, had a thumb in her mouth, and was holding a baby doll by one arm. The father walked inside without even glancing at us. The mother got some wet wipes and started wiping the kids' faces down.

"I wanna go home, Mommy," the boy said, starting to sniffle again.

"I know, Joey," she said, pulling out a comb and trying to straighten his hair. "I do, too. But we can't. You saw what the house looked like. We have to stay with Grandma for a while."

"I DON'T WANNA!" he started wailing.

The dad came back outside, again walking past us without a look. "Darla, it's going to be about an hour wait. And why is he crying again?"

"Let's just get back on the road." She stood up. "Don't cry, Joey." She turned back to her husband. "Surely there will be something open on the road." She patted Joey on the head. "Maybe we could find a McDonald's. Would you like that, Joey?"

He sniffled. "Could I have a Happy Meal?"

"Of course you can, darlin'."

They all got back into the truck, and he backed up. Just before they pulled out onto Carrollton Avenue, I got a good look at her face. She, like Joey, was crying, but she wiped at her eyes and with a monumental effort, pulled herself back together. She gave Allen and I a sad little wave, and then they were gone, two red taillights disappearing into the darkness down Carrollton.

I don't think I will ever forget the look on her face.

"Breaks your heart, doesn't it?" Allen said, sitting down on a bench as I lit another cigarette. "It's the kids that get me the most, you know. I'm so glad I don't have any. How do you explain to a child what's happened? What about the teenagers? I mean, can you imagine being a senior in high school, and being all excited about finishing and getting out to college or whatever, and suddenly it's all taken away from you, you don't know when you're going to get back in school or graduate or anything. . . . Oh, hell, I don't know what the hell I am saying. It's bad for everyone."

The hostess opened the door. "Table for two?"

I ordered a margarita on the rocks with salt as soon as we sat down. It seemed like a tequila evening. Allen ordered a vodka martini. I looked around the room. Every table had at least one bottle of wine, and there were cocktail glasses too. Everyone was drinking, and drinking heavily.

We made small talk throughout the dinner, Allen talking about his plans for the gym, and I managed to relax as the drinks kept coming. The menu was one page, a computer printout with just a few choices. The tablecloth was paper, as were the napkins, and the silverware was plastic and came packaged in cellophane. But the food was good, and before I knew it, we were finished.

When we got back to the parking lot at Bodytech, Allen asked, "Would you mind if I came over? I really don't want to go back to that big empty house."

I was going to say no, but then I saw the look in his eyes and changed my mind. He just needs a friend, I told myself, and these days, we all could use whatever friends we could get. "Sure, Allen. We can have a drink or something. Just let me get my car."

CHAPTER TEN

ALLEN WAS GONE when I woke up in the morning.

It was almost nine; I'd slept later than I usually did. I used to always sleep late *before* unless I had a reason to get up early; since the levees broke I'd been getting up around seven every morning. I was kind of relieved that Allen was gone; the morning after—especially with a friend—can be really awkward, and I don't think all that clearly before I've put down a pot of coffee in my system. I washed my face and brushed my teeth before walking into the kitchen, the entire time wondering what the hell I'd been thinking. Had it been the drinks at the restaurant? No, that was too easy, and to be completely honest with myself, I hadn't been drunk. In my new way of thinking—my new sense of personal responsibility—I couldn't accept that, even if I had been drunk. I had to start owning up to my mistakes—and if liquor was the problem, maybe I'd have to think about giving that up. Maybe it was a mistake; then again, maybe it wasn't—it was too early to tell. There's nothing like a sexual encounter to ruin a perfectly good friendship, but I wasn't about to let that happen. If Allen had a problem with it, I'd deal with it then. As far as I was concerned, giving comfort to someone in pain, even if it was a sexual experience, couldn't be wrong. It would all work out all right in the end.

Everything always seemed to.

There was a note propped on the coffee maker. I had to move it to make the coffee, and once it was brewing, I opened and read it.

Chanse—

> *Thanks for being there for me last night. I really appreciate it, but I couldn't sleep, and decided it was probably best if I went back home. I didn't want to wake you ... see you at the gym later?*

> *Thanks,*
> *Allen*

It was nice of him to leave a note, I thought as I waited for the coffee to finish brewing. He could have just left, but then again, it wasn't like I wasn't going to run into him at the gym sometime. In the past, I probably would have just ignored him when I saw him again, or pretended like last night had never happened. That had been my old method of dealing with people I'd slept with. No, that wasn't fair. The truth was I never really knew how to act around someone I'd picked up in a bar when I saw them again, so I just always waited to see how they'd react to *me*. If they said "Hi," I'd talk to them. If they ignored me, I'd ignore them. It was a stupid way to behave, and actually kind of mean, now that I thought about it. I shook my head and wondered how many feelings my behavior had hurt over the years.

I filled a big mug with coffee and walked into the living room to check my e-mails. There was nothing new there other than the usual junk bullshit, so I logged off and sat down on the couch, grabbing my file on the Verlaine case.

The next thing to do was plan a trip up to see Cathy Hollis and arrange a meeting with Jolene McConnell on the way. Jackson was about two and a half hours north of New Orleans, and Cortez another two and a half hours from there. So, if I left New Orleans the next morning around seven, I could be in Jackson around nine-thirty—and even assuming I'd be speaking to Mrs. McConnell for about an hour, I could still be in Cortez before two in the afternoon. All in all, it could easily be accomplished in one day. I could be back in New Orleans before eight, given stops for gas, bathroom breaks, and dinner. Not bad.

I got my cell phone and dialed the number I had for Jolene. On the fourth ring, a machine picked up. I left my name and number, explaining that I was looking for her brother Michael, and hung up the phone.

I sat there for a moment thinking, and then thumbed through my speed-dial numbers, and called my landlady/employer, Barbara Castlemaine.

When I'd resigned from the New Orleans Police Department and given up my apartment in the French Quarter, I'd found the apartment on Camp Street, which had been my home ever since, through a property management company. The rent had originally been six hundred dollars a month, but within a week of moving in I'd gotten a call from the property owner, Barbara Castlemaine. She had a little problem she needed me to take care of for her—involving a pair of twin body builders from Thibodeaux, some rather explicit photographs, and a blackmailer—which I'd handled rather quickly for her. She'd been set up by her personal assistant, and not only did I manage to get all the prints and negatives back for her, but I'd convinced the assistant it was probably a good idea to get as far away from New Orleans as possible. In gratitude, she'd lowered my rent to $100 per month with a permanent lease, and also hired me as a corporate security consultant for Crown Oil, the company she'd inherited from her late husband. The gig with Crown Oil was quite lucrative, required very little work on my part, and not only paid my bills but enabled me to acquire a rather healthy savings account. Barbara is nothing if not a generous and grateful woman. In the years since, she and I had become friends. Barbara was also a great source of information. She knew where all the bodies were buried in New Orleans, from Jackson Avenue to Riverbend. I didn't know how she did it, but she did seem to know everything.

"Chanse!" she answered. "Darling, I am in New Orleans! What excellent timing!"

"Really?" I was a little startled. The last time I'd spoken to her, she was leaving to stay in Paris for a few months. "I thought you were in Paris."

"I changed my mind—I know it's the culture capital of the world and all, but sometimes Paris is just boring—and went to New York instead—shopped, saw some shows, and then decided to get back here and check on things. I got in late last night, and I wanted to give you a call this morning, but you beat me to the punch, as always. Why don't you come by the house? I'm about to make mimosas." Barbara's weakness was champagne. She drank it morning, noon, and night, and never seemed the worse for her intake.

"Let me jump into the shower and I can be there in a little bit."

"Well, don't dawdle. The champagne will go flat. And you know there's nothing I hate more than wasting perfectly good champagne—and I can't drink this entire bottle by myself." She laughed. "Well, of course I could, but I don't want to. You know what they say about women who get drunk before noon ... so hurry, darling."

Half an hour later, I parked in the driveway of Barbara's house on Chestnut Street, between Philip and First Streets. Known to the Garden District tours and the Historic Registry as the Palmer House, it was a huge Italianate monstrosity with black wrought-iron railings on its galleries and was painted a strange deep shade of red with black shutters at every window. Like the Verlaine place, her usually well-tended lawn looked a little unkempt. The first time I'd ever set foot in it, I'd been a little overawed. Barbara had completely redecorated the interior after the death of her second husband—the Palmer who'd left her the house—but now I was used to it. Rather than the traditional Garden District style of antiques, she'd done the entire place with modern stuff. "I like the contrast between the age of the house and the modern look," she told me once, "and it drives the Garden District biddies insane that I did this."

She opened the door before I could even ring the bell. She gave me a big hug and drew me into the house. She smelled, as always, of Chanel. Barbara is one of those women whose age you cannot determine by looking at her. She exercised to keep her figure, and her face showed tell-tale lines she refused to have surgically corrected. She told me once that she had no intention of looking like "one of those frightening old bags with a face pulled so tight her jaw pops open when she crosses her legs." Her blonde hair had traces of gray, and she was still very beautiful. She somehow managed to make fleece sweats look like they came from a designer show in Paris. To me, she was the epitome of elegance and class—although she could swear like a sailor and could, on occasion—usually when she was drinking and bored out of her

mind at a party—be as vulgar and crass as a drag queen. Today, she was wearing a pair of blue jeans, sneakers, and a
black cashmere sweater. Her only jewelry was diamonds at
her ears, and she wasn't wearing any makeup.

She led me to the drawing room and handed me a mimosa before I could sit. "Drink up, darling." She gave me a
big smile. "I'm already two ahead of you." She sat down next
to me on the couch and took a big swallow of her own drink.
"Well, things certainly are different here, aren't they?" She
shook her head. "It breaks my heart to see the city like this."
She waved her hand. "And it simply sickens me that they've
abandoned us." Her face set grimly. "Don't think Crown Oil
won't be throwing its money—and considerable clout—
around to make sure some of those bastards in Congress
don't get re-elected." She sighed. "And so many people are
seriously considering leaving—or not coming back. Isn't that
insane?"

"To say the least." I took a sip. Barbara's idea of a mimosa was to add orange juice for color.

"After living here, how can anyone even consider living
somewhere else? Houston? Atlanta? Dallas?" She went on
as though I hadn't spoken, shuddering at the mention of the
other cities. Barbara was like that. Conversations with her
were generally one-sided—you had to wait until she paused
for breath to get a word, maybe two, if you were lucky—into
the conversation. "I mean, really. How dreadful. We've got to
do something, and if the bastards in Washington aren't going
to help us, well, goddamnit, we have to roll up our sleeves
and get to work."

"Yes." When Barbara was on a roll, it was best to just
listen.

"I have plans. Crown Oil is going to be doing a lot around
here. I've set up a foundation to grant out money, and I'm

going to strong-arm everyone I know to give money. Thank God Crown Oil is *not* responsible for the disappearance of the wetlands. It's criminal, simply criminal what we've all allowed those other bastard oil companies to do to Louisiana. Of course, I've done nothing for years, and look what happens when you just sit around and do nothing." She set her drink down. "So, what's this I hear about you looking for Michael Mercereau? Are you sure it's a good idea to get involved with that whacked-out family?"

I was in the midst of swallowing and almost choked on my mimosa. When I finally managed to get my coughing fit under control, I spluttered, "How did you know that?"

She waved a hand airily. "Darling, when will you learn I know everything? Nothing goes on in this city—and especially not in this neighborhood—without me knowing about it. I have eyes and ears everywhere. The CIA should have as effective a network as me." She grinned at me, her eyes twinkling. "Joshua Verlaine called me to check you out—you know how that goes. Can this Chanse man be trusted?" She rolled her eyes. "Like most men, he gave away more information than I gave him. So, what do you think of the freak-show Verlaines?"

"Well, Joshua seems nice. I like him. He seems like a good guy."

"Certainly not the sharpest knife in the drawer, by any means, but you're right, he is a nice man, and considering that family—that's saying something." She got up to refill her glass, and refilled mine as well. "A shame about Iris, but that girl had some serious problems. But who wouldn't, with a mother like Margot?"

"You didn't like Margot Verlaine?" I asked.

"Honey." She sat down and patted my leg. "*No one* liked Margot Verlaine. One merely tolerated her. Talk about having the personality of a dust mop! How that witch ever landed a man in the first place was always beyond me—and it certainly was no surprise she never remarried. What man would want her? What a cold bitch she was ... we served on several committees together; I remember we did something for the Bridge House, what was it? A concert? A dinner?" She shrugged. "I don't remember exactly what it was, but Verlaine Shipping was one of the bigger donors, so I had no choice but to take her on as a co-chair on whatever the hell it was. What an unpleasant experience that was." She gave me a sharp glance. "She had to have her own way, that's for sure—and she offended everyone. Everyone. I spent most of my time running around behind her apologizing for her sheer bitchery. My God, the sucking up I had to do! And how creepy was it that she never moved out of that house? There was certainly something sick and twisted there, believe you me. She was in her forties and still called him *Daddy.*" She shuddered. "And the old man—Percy. Ugh, what a monster that one is! Mean as a snake, and about as warm as one. . . ."

"Did you know Michael Mercereau?"

"Not well." She looked off into the distance. "I was married to my second husband then." Barbara had never really talked about any of her past marriages to me, other than Charles Castlemaine, her third husband. Paige had done research on her for me, simply because I was curious about her. She'd originally been born in Algiers Point, on the Westbank, to a nice lower-middle-class family. She'd married her first husband at eighteen—they'd apparently been high school sweethearts, but they were divorced before she was nineteen. Her second husband, Roger Palmer, had been thirty years her senior. She was his second wife; his first marriage was childless. They married when she was in her early twenties, and he was the father of her only child,

Brenda. I'd never met Brenda, and Barbara didn't talk about her either. Brenda, I knew, lived in Los Angeles, where she'd moved after graduating from Newcomb. I thought it odd that Barbara never talked about her daughter—and that her daughter never seemed to ever set foot in New Orleans. That kind of thing always made me curious, but I knew better than to ask about it. Obviously, there had been a falling out. Roger had died when Barbara was around thirty, and shortly thereafter she'd married Charles Castlemaine, the heir to the Crown Oil empire out of Tulsa, Oklahoma. Charles had been killed about ten years ago when his private plane went down in the Gulf of Mexico. She narrowed her eyes. "You know I wasn't always the glamorous queen of New Orleans high society I am today, right?"

"Um—"

"You don't have to answer that—obviously, I wasn't born to this." She laughed as she gestured around the room. "No, I married my second husband when I was little more than a child, and he was thirty years older than I. Most people in the Garden District considered it a *mésalliance* on his part; they thought of me as little better than a whore who was after his money. It certainly never occurred to any of them that he was handsome or interesting or charming as well as rich as Midas. I met Michael and Margot at my first Comus Ball, shortly after Roger and I married. Michael was a nice, kind man—Margot was a bitch of the first order. I always figured he married her for her money—why else would anyone marry her? She had to be one cold fish in the sack." She rolled her eyes. "Listen at me! Margot certainly thought I married Roger for his money—but at least Roger was a handsome man with a certain charm. . . . She certainly had nothing to offer but the Verlaine money. I hated Margot on sight—she was so rude and condescending to me, like being born into that family somehow made her better than me. My father might have been an accountant for the Coca-Cola bottling company, but I wouldn't trade him for Percy Verlaine for any amount of money." She shuddered.

"Did you know Cathy Hollis?"

"Ah, Cathy." She smiled. "I adored Cathy Hollis. Now she was a live wire; old Percy didn't know what to do with her. I'll never forget going outside the Comus Ball for a cigarette and there she was, cool as you please, smoking a joint with one of the musicians in the band. She introduced herself to me as a 'poor relation of the Verlaines.' Oh, that girl could make me laugh! Roger didn't want me to have anything to do with her, he thought she was 'fast' and 'trouble,' so of course I sought her out whenever I could get away with it. She liked her scotch, and she liked her men." Barbara scratched her head. "There was a to-do, as I recall. . . . Cathy missed her call outs because she was out partying with the band guys. Percy and Margot were fit to be tied."

"Is it possible that Michael and Cathy were having an affair?"

She frowned. "Well, Cathy was wild ... there was no doubt about that. She liked men ... and she liked to shock the family, but I don't think she would ever go that far. Cathy really liked Michael, but he was more like a brother to her. He used to escort her; chaperone her, if you will, and Margot often stayed home. . . . Margot hated going to things, small wonder. No one would talk to her. You know he was a painter?"

"I'd heard that, yes."

"I went to his last opening." She put her glass down. "It was at this cute little place on Royal Street that isn't there anymore, The owner died from AIDS back in the 80s when everyone was dying. Can you believe not a single member of the Verlaine family went? The old man, of course, was—and still is—a complete Philistine—all of his taste, such as it is, is in his mouth—so it was no surprise he wasn't there. But Margot? Why would any woman not attend her husband's opening? If it was my husband's opening, you couldn't have kept me away from it. But Margot and the old man were two peas in a pod, if you will ... dull as dishwater. Cathy was there, of course, and got drunk. . . . I think she actually passed out ... or was that another party I'm thinking about?" She wrinkled her brow, thinking, and then laughed. "No, it was the opening she passed out at, I believe. I do remember I asked Michael why Margot wasn't there ... he just gave me one of those funny little looks. . . . I got the distinct impression that there was trouble in that marriage ... and then he left, about a month later. And poor Cathy had a breakdown. Although if you ask me, they were just looking for a chance to lock her away somewhere—you know, the old-fashioned way of dealing with a problem—lock it away!" She gestured to a painting hanging between the windows. "I bought that painting at the show. It's a Mercereau."

I'd noticed the painting before, but never really paid a lot of attention to it. I don't know much about painting, and I usually just think of it as wall decoration. I suppose Barbara would consider me a Philistine as well. I like black-and-white photography; paintings have never held much interest for me. I got up and walked over to it. In the lower-right-hand corner was scrawled M. MERCEREAU. The painting seemed innocuous at first from across the room: a simple scene of a man and a woman riding together in a horse-drawn carriage in the Garden District. But up close, you could see that the man's face was tense, his knuckles clutching the reins of the buggy with a death grip. And the expression on the woman's face was disturbing. Her face was cadaverous, the hand clutching at his sleeve claw-like and bony. Her eyes were narrowed, and her exposed teeth looked sharp and predatory. In the background was a house, and as I looked I realized it was the Verlaine mansion, but distorted like in a funhouse mirror. I shivered and turned away from it.

"Disturbing, isn't it?" Barbara said. "It draws you in, though, and you can't really look away. All of Michael's work was like that—beautiful in a glance, but really unsettling the more you looked at it. He was, I think, a genius."

"It seems weird that he would have walked away from everything the way he did."

"We-ell, that's what the family would have you believe." She gave me a sly wink. "Of course, most people whispered that Margot killed him, you know, and Cathy saw it all happen—which is why they locked her up in that mental hospital."

I wasn't sure how to respond to that. "Is that what you believe?"

She shrugged. "All I know is that none of them, other than Cathy, was very upset that he was gone. And his painting career was finally starting to take off; why would he walk away from everything the way he did? If he truly left Margot, and New Orleans, why wouldn't he show his work elsewhere?" She pointed over at the painting. "He was talented. I know art is subjective, and all of that, but he was getting *national* attention for that show. So, he not only left his wife and his children, but his career and his dreams?" She reached for her glass and drained it. "I always thought, you know, that he was dead. But the person you really should talk to is Eric Valmont."

"And who might that be?"

"Eric used to be the art critic for *Crescent City* magazine, and used to write for some national magazines, too." She gave me a sly wink. "He's a little old for you now, but he was quite a hottie in his day."

Barbara had frequently tried to fix me up in the days before I met Paul. "Is he even still in New Orleans?"

"His mother lives in Hammond. Surely you've heard of Joyce Valmont?"

I gave her a blank look. "No."

She rolled her eyes. "I am sure you've met her at one of my parties. Her husband was Congressman Valmont? He served in Congress for about thirty years?" She gave me a disgusted look. "I'll call her and see if I can find out where Eric is. If he isn't in New Orleans, he's at her place." She glanced at her watch. "Now get out of here like a good boy. I've got to meet a contractor at one of my places in the Irish Channel—and the insurance adjustor."

"Thanks, Barbara." I leaned over to kiss her cheek. "You've been an enormous help."

"I'll call you after I talk to Joyce." She blew a kiss at me. "It is nice to see you, Chanse. Are you doing okay?"

I gave her a smile. "One day at a time, Barbara. One day at a time."

CHAPTER ELEVEN

I DECIDED TO SWING BY Phillip Shea's just on the chance he might be home. There had been a car there when I'd driven by before and lights on, so someone was staying at his house. The white Lexus was in the driveway of his house, so I parked in the street and got out of the car. The house was a small Creole cottage, out of place among its huge neighbors in the Garden District across the street. It had probably, at one time, been a part of the grounds of one of its neighbors—maybe a mother-in-law residence or something that had been parceled off and sold years ago. It was a nice house, with a front porch that ran the length of the front, and it looked well-kept. It had been painted recently, and there was a swing at the right end of the porch. The front yard was small, mostly bushes with a brick border around them, and the front walk was red bricks. I climbed the steps and rang the doorbell.

"Yeah?"

Phillip Shea was having a bad morning, apparently. His brown hair looked greasy and unclean, and it could definitely use a comb run through it. He hadn't shaved in days, and his cheeks and chin were covered with black stubble. He had full, thick lips and long eyelashes over gray eyes. He was tall, maybe an inch or so shorter than me, with long limbs and a high waist—he looked like he was almost all legs. He was wearing a food-stained T-shirt with "New Orleans Saints" written across the front with the fleur-de-lis, and a pair of black sweatpants that were also covered with stains, and his feet were bare. His arms were tanned, and his veins were prominent. He looked like he usually kept himself in pretty good shape, despite the condition he was currently in. His eyes were bloodshot, and he reeked of sour alcohol. His eyes weren't even open all the way.

"Maybe I should have called first," I said. "My name's Chanse MacLeod—"

His eyes widened as he cut me off. "Ah, Iris's detective." He smirked. "I was wondering when you were going to show up. Come in." He yawned and stretched, and the dirty T-shirt rode up to show a relatively flat stomach. He ran his fingers through the messy hair. "Come on in. Want something to drink?" He stepped aside and I walked into the hallway of the house. The floors were hardwood and in need of sweeping. There was a thin layer of dust coating them, keeping them from shining.

He walked through a door on the right. I followed him in. "Have a seat." He waved his arm arbitrarily.

I sat down on a green-and-gold-brocade couch that wasn't comfortable in the least. The front room had to be a showroom, even though everything was covered in dust and cobwebs hung from the ceiling. The room didn't look lived-in, and the furniture had been chosen for appearance rather than comfort. There was a baby grand piano in one corner of the room, and Audubon prints hung on the walls. A huge gilt mirror hung on the bricks over the mantelpiece. There were no rugs, just the bare floor. He walked over to the bar and poured himself a glass of gin, and dumped slices of blood-red orange into it. He stirred it for a moment, and took a drink before he came back into the sitting area and plopped down in a chair. He looked over at me and gave me a weak smile. "I look like hell, don't I?" He took another drink. "Don't answer that. I know the answer and I don't need polite social bullshit. I've certainly seen better days. But we've all been through a lot this last month and you know what? I don't give a shit what people think, no offense." He took another drink and looked over at me. "You know, I told Iris not to hire you. Of course she didn't listen to me."

"Why?" I asked. "What harm was there in her trying to find her father?"

"It was a stupid idea. I told her no good would come of it, and I was right—but Iris never listened to anyone once she made up her mind. She was always that way." He shrugged. "I mean, come on. Her fucking dad walked out on her before she was even born, right? If he wanted to know her, he knew where the hell she was—and her brothers. If you ask me, any man who could just walk away from his wife and kids that way doesn't deserve to know them—and it sure seemed like that's how he felt, right?" He barked out a laugh. "And now he'll never know her, right? She's dead." He lifted his glass. "And I doubt if Darrin or Joshua gives a shit. I know Darrin didn't. He had the right attitude, if you ask me."

"You and Darrin talked about it?"

He shrugged. "We all had dinner one night, the week before the storm. Iris brought it up, to feel him out, and he was pretty blunt about it. Said he had no desire to see him, talk to him, anything like that."

"And you didn't think she should look for him either." I crossed my legs. I was feeling a little sorry for him. He looked like hell. He'd lost his fiancée, and who knew what he'd been through with the storm?

"You're quick, aren't you?" He took another swig, finishing off the glass. "So, what are you doing here, anyway?"

"I've been deputized by the police to look into Iris's murder. You probably were closer to Iris than anyone—she might have told you things she might not have told anyone else," I said, trying to pick out my words carefully. "Can you think of anyone who would want her dead?"

"Iris was killed in a robbery." He dismissed the idea with a wave of his hand.

"The police don't think so." I leaned forward. "Nothing was stolen from her house—nothing was missing. The killer even left her purse behind with all of her money and credit cards. Why would he do that, if the point was robbery?"

His eyes bugged out, and he wiped at his forehead. "You're telling me someone deliberately went there to kill her."

I resisted the urge to say, *You're quick, aren't you?* "That's what the police think. So, can you think of anyone who would have wanted to kill Iris? Anyone she pissed off, anyone she might have done something to who may have wanted to get even?"

"Jesus." He closed his eyes and leaned back in his chair. "There was something going on at the company she was worried about, I do know that. She wouldn't tell me anything about it, just said she needed to get some more information, but she was definitely worried about something going on over there." He closed his eyes and thought for a moment. "I know there was a problem with them losing a huge contract—there was even an article in the paper about it—and she was worried."

"She was in charge of public relations, wasn't she?"

"Yeah, but she hated doing that. She wanted to be more involved in the actual decision-making rather than writing press releases and donating money to charity." He opened his eyes. "She went to Harvard Business School, for Christ's sake. Graduated magna cum laude. She was incredibly smart, and she felt like she wasn't given enough responsibility. She could have written her own ticket somewhere else— and there were plenty of places she could have gone to work. But it was a family business, and she felt very strongly about family, if you can believe that—given what a jackass her grandfather is. But Percy was a chauvinist, and as long as he was running things, she never had a chance. She was a woman, and he was willing to let her run public relations, like her mother had—until she started having babies."

"Isn't he too ill to be involved in the company? I thought Joshua was president."

He looked me in the eyes. "Make no mistake, buddy, as long as he can breathe he will run that company. Joshua was president, Darrin was executive vice president—but Percy *owns* the company. *Nothing* can be done without his okay— and he thought all three of them were incompetent. You wouldn't believe the way he talked to them. You'd think they were hired flunkies or something. Man, if my grandfather talked to me the way he talked to them, I wouldn't have anything to do with him." He rubbed his eyes. "I told her, over and over again, with her degree she could get a job anywhere." He got up and refilled his glass. "But no, she couldn't do that. It was the family business and she wouldn't walk away from that. She wanted to run the place—no matter how many times Percy slammed the door in her face, she thought she could prove herself and he'd come around— hope springs eternal."

"How did her brothers feel about that?"

"I think they were all for it, to tell you the truth." He sat back down and stared at the glass. "Josh hated working there. So did Darrin. I always had the impression that once the old man died they'd be more than happy to let her take over. But it was the will, you know. That was the problem."

"Oh?"

"The old man was leaving the majority of the company in the hands of the brothers. I think they were going to wind up with forty percent each with Iris getting twenty percent, so they would always have control, no matter who was actually sitting in the president's chair. Iris wanted. ..." he sighed and looked out the window. "Does any of this really matter any-more?"

"I'm afraid it does."

He took another deep breath. "She told me that without a controlling interest, she would just be a figurehead, a puppet with her brothers pulling the strings. She wanted actual control. I told her Josh and Darrin would probably give it to her—they wanted out as soon as the old man passed, and would be glad to leave that all to her—but she didn't want it that way. She told me she was going to force the old man to change the will."

"Did she say how?"

He shook his head. "No, and I told her she was out of her mind. For God's sake, she grew up in Percy's house. She of all people should know that Percy won't do anything he doesn't want to. You can't force him to do anything." He laughed bitterly. "No, that wasn't good enough for Iris. He'd treated her like crap her whole life—so did her mother—and she was determined to prove herself to him, to show that she was just as tough and driven as he was. No, I don't know what she was going to do. She wouldn't tell me. But there was something—something she found out about the company. She was worried, but she said she knew what she was doing and if everything went the way she thought it was go-

ing to, she'd get control of the company even before the old
man died."

"When did she tell you all of this?"

He shrugged. "That week before the storm? It was
around then, I guess. It was around when she started talking
about finding her father. I don't really remember. Everything
before then is kind of a blur to me now, you know what I
mean?"

I knew exactly what he meant. "Had she ever talked
about her father before?"

He shook his head. "No, and we'd been engaged for over
a year. The wedding—" he hesitated, "was supposed to be
this coming June. And then suddenly, it's all, 'I want to find
my father.' It didn't make any sense to me, but she never
would explain herself to me—and she'd get mad when I
questioned her about it. 'He's my father and I think I should
know him. I want to know him.' And then she would change
the subject."

"How was she the night before she died?"

He thought for a moment. "She got here late. She spent a
lot of time here with me—I rarely went out to Lakeview. She
was in a good mood, a little tired, but she was pretty excited
about something—I hadn't seen her like that in a long time,
you know? She'd taken a trip that day—but wouldn't tell me
anything about it. That's when she told me she was going to
hire you to find her father. I tried to reason with her—I
mean, it's pretty obvious Percy hated her father and so
tracking him down was hardly going to please the old man,
you know? It didn't make any sense to me, but she was up to
something—she'd found out something that day that got her
all amped, you know, like she'd snorted a big line of cocaine
or something. We were supposed to meet some people for

dinner, but she wanted to cancel and stay in. We opened a bottle of champagne and ordered food in." He blinked, and a tear ran down his face. "We made love . . . for the last time." He wiped at his face. "I'm sorry."

"It's all right," I said, "I understand. I lost my lover last year."

"So, you know what it's like." He took a deep breath. "I keep wondering why, you know? Maybe if I'd insisted she stay here that night rather than going out to Lakeview, maybe if I'd done this or that—"

"It gets easier. I know that doesn't really help, but it does. And you can't blame yourself." Which was easier said than done, I knew. How many nights had I lain in bed, staring at the ceiling, missing Paul, and going over it all again in my head? If I'd just done this, if I'd just done that, if I hadn't done this, he'd still be here. I swallowed. *Survivor's guilt,* Paige had called it once when we'd drunk a bottle of wine and smoked a ton of pot and I'd gotten all weepy about Paul.

I gave him a moment to collect himself before I went on. "What about the night she died? If she spent most of her nights here, why was she in Lakeview that night?"

"I left town." He shrugged. "My cousin was getting married in Memphis on Saturday night, and I drove up there Friday morning. She was supposed to fly up on Saturday morning and meet me there. If I'd just decided to stay and fly up with her that morning—" He covered his face in his hands.

"You can't do this to yourself," I said. "Trust me on this, Phillip. You can't beat yourself up over things like this. Yeah, in hindsight it's easy to blame yourself, but you didn't do anything wrong. And she wouldn't want you to blame yourself, would she?"

Yeah, listen to yourself. All you're doing is parroting to him what people said to you—and it's not like you ever listened to them, either. Take your own advice, idiot.

"I know." He wiped his eyes again. "I'm sorry."

"Were your plans for the weekend pretty well known?"

He stared at me. "It's not like we kept it all a secret. And she was taking that Monday off from work so we could drive back down together. We were going to have like a little mini-vacation, you know?"

So, it wasn't a secret or a surprise that she was going to spend the night in Lakeview. Everyone in her family undoubtedly knew Phillip was going to be gone and she would be spending the night in her home out there alone.

"So, you have no idea what was going on at the company?"

He pulled himself together. "No. Iris didn't like to talk about work, frankly, other than to complain about her grandfather and how unfair he was being, you know? It was one of our rules—we didn't talk about work to each other at night." He thought for a minute. "If you want to know anything about what was going on at the company, the only person who would know would be her assistant, Valerie. Valerie Stratton."

"Were they close?"

He shrugged. "As close as Iris was to anyone. They went to school together—you know, not college, but McGehee. I think Valerie wound up going to UNO. Her family didn't have a lot of money—they did at one time, but they went broke when Valerie was a kid." He laughed. "Valerie knew everything that was going on at the company; she was like a ferret, Iris said once, and that she'd be lost without Valerie there. Valerie could find out anything, she told me."

"Did you know her well?"

"Valerie? We didn't socialize, but I talked to her every once in a while, when Iris wasn't in her office or on another call or in a meeting when I called her. I've met her a few times." He made a face. "To be honest, I didn't care much for her. I didn't really trust her."

"But Iris did?"

"Iris swore she would be lost at the office without her." He yawned and stretched his arms up over his head again.

"Well, I should probably get going." I stood up and offered him my hand. "Thank you for your time, and again, my condolences on your loss."

He stood up and shook my hand. "If there's anything I can do, just let me know." He let go of my hand and stretched, catching a glimpse of himself in the mirror. "Christ, I look like hell." He ran a hand over his stubble. "Guess it's time for me to get cleaned up, huh?"

I just smiled. "It might make you feel better." I took a business card out of my wallet, and placed it on the coffee table. "That's my card—it has all of my numbers and my e-mail address on it. If you can think of anything—anything at all, no matter how unimportant it might seem, please give me a call."

"There's going to be a memorial service for Iris this weekend, finally." He walked me to the door. "It's going to be at St. Ann's Church on Prytania Street. You're more than welcome to come, if you'd like." He shook his head. "The coroner apparently finally found her body." His eyes got wet again. "I mean, it's bad enough that she was killed, but then we didn't even know where her body was. . . ."

I put a hand on his shoulder. "It'll be okay, man. Just hang in there."

"Time heals, right?" He gave me a weak smile. "I keep telling myself that, you know?"

I shook his hand at the door again. "You take care of yourself, okay?"

"Yeah. Yeah, I'll do that."

The door shut.

I walked down to the car. I got in, and sat there for a moment, smoking a cigarette.

Something going on at the company had had Iris worried. She was ambitious and wanted to run Verlaine Shipping, and her grandfather wouldn't let her. She decided to look for her father around the same time she told her fiancé that she had found a way to force Percy to give her the president's chair and maybe even change his will.

I decided it would be a good idea to meet Valerie Stratton in person—when you just show up out of the blue, people aren't prepared and let things slip. I decided to stop by the house and change into something more professional before getting up there to see her.

But my plans for the rest of the day changed when I got home to see Paige sitting on my front steps. I parked the car and sat down on the steps next to her.

She looked terrible. Her hair, although she'd dragged a brush through it, was dull and lusterless. The bags under her eyes were thicker and heavier than the last time I'd seen her, and she wasn't wearing makeup. She had on a pair of jeans and a dirty white T-shirt with a blot of mustard just below her right breast. She flicked her cigarette out into the street. "Hey," she said, after giving me a hug.

"How you doing?" I asked, lighting another one of my own.

"Not good." She shrugged. "I just wanted to come by and apologize for my breakdown the other night." She sighed. "I think I need to get away for a while."

"Don't worry about it." I gave her a slight smile. "What are friends for?"

"I'm finding it harder and harder to hold it all together," she went on. "I have some vacation time coming, so I'm going to take a couple of weeks and just get in the car and drive—see where I end up." She ran a hand through her hair. "Get away from all of this ... stay somewhere I don't have to eat off plastic utensils and use paper napkins in a restaurant. Get in the shower and have real water pressure. Walk around where there's no blue tarps hanging on roofs and no refrigerators parked at the curb." She gave me a ghost of a smile. "Have you noticed the refrigerator art?"

"Yeah." I returned her smile. On my way back from Barbara's, I'd seen a refrigerator taped shut on Magazine Street, wrapped in white linen with a tiara on the top; a sign hung on it proclaimed to the world it was POPE FRIDGE II. There had been another covered completely in red and green Christmas foil, with a large card taped to the front: MERRY CHRISTMAS MR. PRESIDENT. Both had made me smile. It was such a New Orleans thing to do. I told her about the ones I'd seen, and she laughed.

"I love this city so much," she said, wiping her eyes. "But I need to get away for a while. I'm drinking way too much, and if I don't stop eating Xanax by the handful I'm going to wind up in rehab."

"Thanks for the ones you gave me, by the way," I replied, and told her about the dream I'd had. "It was amazing—one minute my mind was just racing out of control and then it was like this curtain of calm peace dropped over me and I didn't care about any of it any more."

"Whoever invented Xanax should be given the Nobel Prize." She lit another cigarette. "I mean, really. Solve the

Middle East crisis? Make them all take Xanax. That'd take care of it all in just two seconds."

I laughed. "When are you going to go on your trip?"

"Next week. I got the vacation time approved." She took my hand. "You going to be okay if I'm gone for a while? I don't want to have to worry about you ... although I'll have my cell with me, obviously; you can call me if you need to any time."

"Thanks."

"And thanks for the other night." She shook her head. "Chanse, please, I know I don't have to tell you this, but please don't tell anyone the things I told you. No one knows about any of that, besides me and my mother. And I'd kinda prefer it stayed that way, you know?"

"I'm glad you felt you could tell me," I said, taking her hand.

"Yeah." She blew out a plume of smoke. "I probably should have a long time ago, and I probably never would have if it wasn't for all of this." She gestured with the hand holding the cigarette. "But now that you know, I feel better about it, if that makes any sense. It's all been bottled up inside of me for so long ... and I know it's crazy to think my past had anything to do with Katrina." She laughed. "Yes, it's all about *me*. God destroyed the entire city specifically to punish me. Lord."

"Well, I've kind of felt that way myself from time to time." I squeezed her hand. "But it's funny—how long have we known each other and we've never really talked about our pasts, the time before we knew each other?"

"When I get back, I'll tell you what. We'll smoke a lot of dope and drink a lot of wine and just sit around and tell each other all about our pasts." She winked at me. "Lots of pot and wine, trust me on that one. Oh! I almost forgot." She reached into her purse and handed me an envelope. "I got that information you wanted on Michael Mercereau and Catherine Hollis. There wasn't much—most of it was just stuff from the social pages." She stood up. "Well, I'm going to go start planning my trip."

I gave her a big hug. "Call me if you need anything, or if you just want to talk."

She gripped me tight. "You do the same, Chanse. I love you, you know."

I watched her walk across the park until she was out of sight, then went inside my apartment and smoked some pot before opening the envelope. She was right—there really wasn't anything inside that was of much help, just mentions in the society pages and a big write-up of Michael's opening that Barbara had already told me about. The pictures weren't much help, either. I already knew what Michael and Catherine looked like; but it was strange to look at pictures of her in expensive evening dresses, holding either a cigarette or a cocktail, smiling at the camera and looking like she was having a great time, but knowing she'd been locked up in a rest home for almost thirty years.

I wound up having to change my plans for the Mississippi trip. Jolene McConnell returned my call that night and agreed to see me in Jackson; the problem was she was a nurse and she worked the morning shift. So, I decided to make the long trek to Cortez first and meet her on my way back to New Orleans. I called Joshua—who again sounded a little drunk, and he advised me that since he hadn't known when exactly I'd get to Cortez, he'd called St. Isabelle's and instructed them to let me see Catherine whenever I could make it up there.

I didn't go to the gym either. I spent the rest of the evening smoking pot and drinking.

The next morning I woke up early, drank as much coffee as I could handle without my bladder exploding, and then hit the road heading north. I went back out of the city the same way I'd come home—I-10 West, then caught I-55 north in the swamp. It was a beautiful day, and as I headed toward the Mississippi state line I couldn't help but marvel at the normality of it all—once you got outside the city limits, other than the occasional tree down, snapped in half by the wind, you'd never know a major storm had passed through the area so recently. It was so different when I'd come back to New Orleans. But this time I didn't have a knot of anxiety in my stomach as I drove along I-55, wondering what I was going to find. I crossed the Mississippi state line, stopped in Macomb for gas and to use the bathroom, and kept heading north.

After dealing with traffic and highway construction in Jackson, I found myself in the forests of Mississippi. The sun shone through the pine trees, and the highway was pretty much empty. Every once in a while I had to pass a slow-moving rusted pickup truck, or another car doing about ninety would fly past me on the left, but other than that, there was no one. Mississippi is a beautiful state, with its red dirt and towering primeval pine trees that lined the highway. Most people—myself included—think of Mississippi as a wasteland of ignorance, inbreeding, and intolerance. I always obey speed limits whenever driving through there—I can imagine no worse fate than being pulled over by some rural redneck sheriff on a power trip with mirrored sunglasses and a potbelly, who decides to make an example of the faggot from New Orleans he's pulled over. But it is truly a beautiful drive, and I always wonder at the stunning natural beauty of the state. I found myself singing along with the radio—I'd found a good country station from Jackson whose play-list was heavy with Kenny Chesney, Toby Keith, and Gretchen Wilson. I hate driving in the city—every time I get in the car to drive around New Orleans I'm a bundle of nerves, never sure when some idiot on a cell phone is going to miss a stop sign or run a red light and kill me—but I love highway driving. There's something almost zen about the broken white line down the center of the pavement, the un-broken yellow one on the right, the smooth pavement pass-ing under the tires as the car's odometer clicks off mile after mile. I found myself lost in my thoughts, and wondering what I would find when I finally met Cathy Hollis face to face.

I pulled into the driveway of St. Isabelle's around noon. I showed my ID to the guard at the gate, and he opened it for me and waved me through. St. Isabelle's had to have been a plantation at some point in its past. As I pulled into the park-ing lot in front of the big mansion and parked in a visitor's spot, it wasn't hard to imagine hoop-skirted girls flirting with gentlemen callers on the verandah while slaves toiled in the sun, the overseer's whip cracking from time to time. The power and phone lines, as well as the parking lot, were the only anachronisms in a scene that could have been right out of the 1870s. I got out of the car and lit a cigarette while stretching my legs and cracking my back. There was a line of trees on the right side of the building, and I could see cot-tages back behind them. The lawn was well-manicured and a fountain bubbled in front of the main structure. I tried to figure out how much money it cost to maintain the place while I smoked my cigarette. I stepped on the butt and strolled up the walk past rose gardens to the house.

A man of about fifty in a long white coat over a navy blue suit was waiting for me at the top of the verandah stairs. He was stocky, red-faced, and balding. A veritable forest of hair protruded from his nostrils and ears. "Mr. MacLeod?" His eyebrows were thick and shot through with gray.

I took the hand he reached out and said, "Thank you for allowing me to see Ms. Hollis."

"I'm Dr. Bright." He gave me a weird smile, showing off tobacco-stained teeth. "I've been Miss Hollis's attending doctor for nearly ten years. She doesn't get many visitors. I'm sure she will be delighted to have a guest."

"Doesn't the family come up for visits?"

"About a week before Hurricane Katrina, I don't remember exactly what day, her cousin Iris came to see her. It was quite a surprise; I mean, I periodically make reports to the family, of course, but she was the first member of the family I'd ever met."

"Did she say why she wanted to see Ms. Hollis?"

He shook his head. "No. She only stayed a brief while, and left without speaking to me again."

He opened the front door and we stepped into a grand hallway. The floor was gleaming black-and-white marble; a glittering chandelier hung from the ceiling. There was a bronze plaque on the wall, which I scanned quickly: This historic plantation home had been completely renovated in 1974 thanks to the generosity of Percy Verlaine. I let out a low whistle and pointed at the plaque. "That must have cost a pretty penny."

He gave me that strange smile again as he led me into an office that opened off the inner hallway. He gestured me into a seat, which I took, declining his offer of coffee. He sat down behind the desk. "Percy Verlaine has been very generous with St. Isabelle's over the years, quite generous indeed. Did you notice the cottages outside?" I nodded. "He funded those as well. We are able to take many guests who cannot otherwise afford to stay here, thanks to his generosity."

So, Percy throws his money around up here, where a relative he despises has been locked up for thirty years. Interesting, I thought to myself—almost as interesting as the fact that Iris Verlaine had come all the way up here before hiring me. What kind of game had Iris been playing? "What exactly is wrong with Ms. Hollis?" I asked.

He removed his glasses and wiped them with a handkerchief. "I am not at liberty to discuss her medical condition with you. I was instructed to allow you to see her, but he did not give me permission to discuss anything else with you." He drummed his fingers on his desktop. "I can tell you she is not dangerous. She's very docile, and spends most of her time reading. I've been reducing her medications over the past few years, with no ill effect."

"And when can I see her?"

"She's in her room." He buzzed the intercom next to his phone. "Amanda, you can take Mr. MacLeod to Cathy's room now."

A woman in a nurse's uniform was waiting for me when I left his office. She was not young, probably in her late fifties, with thick red hair shot through with gray and a tall, slender figure. As soon as the door shut behind us, she gestured to me, and I followed her up the stairs. The room was on the second floor, and while it looked comfortable, it was also sparsely furnished. There were bars on the window, and there was a woman sitting at a vanity table brushing bluish black hair that hung halfway to her waist. "Cathy, there's a gentleman to see you."

She didn't stop brushing her hair. "Thank you, nurse," she said in a husky voice.

"If you need anything, let me know." Amanda shut the door softly behind her as she left us alone.

"Hi, Ms. Hollis. My name is Chanse MacLeod."

She turned around and smiled at me. She was still quite beautiful; her heart-shaped face unlined, her gray-blue eyes clear and quite lucid. There was no gray in her thick hair. She extended a hand to me, and I kissed it. She gave a gurgling, girlish laugh. "I can't remember the last time a young man kissed my hand. Thank you for giving an old lady a thrill."

"The pleasure is mine." I pulled up a chair and sat down beside her. "You're a very beautiful woman."

She turned back to the mirror and resumed brushing her hair. "I brush my hair a minimum of a hundred strokes, three times a day. When I get up, once in the afternoon, and before I go to bed. I think that's why it hasn't gone gray on me yet." She laughed again; it was an infectious sound and it made me smile. "Either that or the medication they give me. I'm quite insane, you know."

"You don't seem to be to me," I replied.

"That's because you're not a doctor—or one of my relatives." She gave her hair a final run-through, and set the brush down. "There. Finished. Now we can have a little chat." She turned around on the bench, crossing one leg over the other. "So, what brings you here to see me, Mr. MacLeod?"

"Chanse, please."

"Chanse? Like Paul Newman in *Sweet Bird of Youth*?" She gave another laugh. "I used to love Tennessee Williams's work, until my life became one of his plays."

I smiled at her. "I understand your cousin Iris came to see you about a month or so ago."

A shadow crossed her face. "I don't remember that." A hand went to her throat. "You have to bear in mind, Chanse, they give me drugs that fuck up my memory." She laughed again. "Oops, sorry, pardon moi!"

I gave her a big smile. "Actually, I'm here to ask you about Michael, Iris's father."

"Michael." The shadow crossed her face again, and she looked down at the floor. "Michael is why I'm here, you know." She looked back up at me, and smiled. "They locked me up in here after he went away. They said I had a breakdown, and I had to be put away for my own good because I was a danger to myself and to the children, and of course, Margot's children were more precious than gold to Uncle Percy ... but they also said I'd be able to come home eventually. That was a hundred years ago." She picked up the brush and began plucking hairs from it. "And here I sit ... no closer to home than I was thirty years ago, or however long it's been. . . . I don't really pay much attention to time or dates anymore, there isn't any point ... one day is much like another. . . . I wake up and eat, they give me my pills and I brush my hair. . . ." She broke off and stared at me. "I know better than to talk about Michael. I talked about Michael before and wound up in here. And here I sit, like Mary Queen of Scots waiting for the execution." She leaned forward and whispered, "I wish they would just behead me and get it over with."

"What happened to Michael, Cathy? Where did he go?" I leaned forward and took her hands. "Why did he leave? You can trust me, Cathy. I just want to find him."

She gave me another brilliant smile. "You aren't going to trick me, however handsome you are, young man!" She winked at me. "The days when I can be fooled by a handsome face are far behind me. . . ."

"You know something?" I winked back at her. "I don't think there's anything wrong with you at all. You seem perfectly fine to me."

"Are you a doctor?" She raised her eyebrows.

"No."

"Then you're wrong. Sweet, but wrong. They locked me up in here a million years ago because I was a menace to myself. I didn't used to think I belonged here, either, but after so many years I had to start believing them, you know. I mean, why would they lock me up in here if I didn't belong? I must be crazy . . . you know they say crazy people don't know they're crazy, so that's what I tell myself, and besides . . ." She held her hands out to me and turned them palm up. "See? Scars. I tried to kill myself." She pulled her hands back and tilted her head. "I don't remember why, though . . . and I don't remember doing it." Her eyebrows came together. "I can't trust you. You work for Uncle Percy."

"Actually, I work for his grandson, Joshua. He hired me to find his father."

"Joshua was such a sweet little boy. We used to play cowboys and Indians in the back yard." She looked at me, and suddenly her face changed. When she spoke again, her voice was not in the least bit childlike. "You don't work for Percy? You aren't on his payroll? You really work for Joshua, and are trying to find Michael?"

I nodded. "Iris hired me, but—" I didn't think it was necessarily a good idea to be the one to tell her that Iris was dead. "Now I work for Joshua."

"I won't tell you about Michael." She shook her head. "You'll never find him, no matter how hard you look, so you might as well give up. No one will ever find Michael. . . ."

"Why did he leave? Was he unhappy?"

"He was a bird in a golden cage." She gestured around the room. "Like me. He sold his soul when he married Margot. He didn't love her, you know. He wanted to paint and he married her for her money so he could paint. But he wanted to go, he wanted to escape that house of horror. Like me."

She sighed. "But once you've sold your soul, it's very hard to buy it back, you know. The devil doesn't like to let you go."

"Tell me about Margot."

"Margot." She grinned impishly. "Have you seen *The Wizard of Oz?* She was like the tin woodsman. She didn't have a heart. She was born without one. No, that's not true. She had a heart. After her brother Matthew died, her father stomped her heart right out of her. I grew up with them, you know. Matthew was everything, Margot was nothing. And then Matthew died, and Margot became everything. Sometimes I think Matthew was the lucky one. He escaped his father into the grave and left us behind to pick up the pieces and deal with Uncle Percy." She grimaced.

"And what about you? What did you become?"

"Oh, that didn't change. I was less than nothing when Matthew was alive. After he died, I didn't even move up to nothing." Her laugh this time was brittle. "I was a poor relation, a charity case who was supposed to be grateful for the crumbs from the table. Nobody paid the least bit of attention to me, other than what I cost them to keep me. And then of course, I was wild, you know. I ran after boys and I drank and got into trouble. And they yelled and screamed at me, and told me I was nothing but a whore, a disgrace to the family name. . . ." her voice trailed off. She squared her shoulders and her chin jutted out. "I didn't care. I still don't care. And after Margot married Michael—you know he was just Lower Ninth Ward gutter trash, as Uncle Percy used to say all the time—Michael ... he was *kind* to me."

"Were you in love with him?"

"Michael was my friend."

"Friends can be lovers."

She drew herself up. "Michael and I were never lovers. Never. He protected me from them."

"From who?"

"Uncle Percy. Margot. And then he was gone ..." her eyes glistened with tears, "... and here I am."

"He's dead, isn't he?"

"I won't talk to you about that." She gave me a smile. "But I will tell you the day he left, the day he went away. I bet nobody's been able to tell you that, have they? Uncle Percy certainly wouldn't, and the only one else who knew is Margot, and she's dead." She sat back and smiled. "It was a beautiful day. June 23. A Sunday. That was the day Michael went away."

And then her face changed, became completely blank. Her eyes looked at me without recognition. "I'm sorry, young man, what did you say your name was?"

I stared at her. Amanda said from behind me, "Mr. MacLeod? I'm afraid your time is up."

I stood up, and knelt, kissing her on the cheek. "Thank you for seeing me, Cathy."

She opened her eyes wide. "Will you come see me again?" she asked, in that childish voice she'd used when I first arrived.

"I'd like to."

Amanda crossed over to her, and handed her a cup of water and a small cup with a pill in it. "Time to take your pill, Cathy."

Cathy smiled at her. "Thank you." She placed the pill in her mouth and washed it down with the water.

"That's a good girl." Amanda smiled, patting her on the shoulder. She turned to me. "If you'll come this way, Mr. MacLeod ..."

But as soon she turned her back, I glanced at Cathy. The wide-eyed look was gone. She was smiling, and her right eyelid came down in a slow, knowing wink.

CHAPTER TWELVE

I HELD ONTO THE BANISTER as we walked down the wide hanging stair. The place, I thought as I looked around at the gleaming floors and the seemingly antique furniture, does not look like a mental hospital. But then again, since I'd pulled into the parking lot, I hadn't really seen any other patients, for that matter. I asked Amanda, "How long have you been working with Ms. Hollis?" I didn't figure she'd answer, but it was worth a try.

She pushed a stray wisp of hair out of her face and exhaled, screwing up her face a bit as she remembered back. "Let me think ... Miss Hollis arrived here about a year or two after I came to work here at St. Isabelle's." She shrugged. "She's been here a long time." She gave a bitter laugh. "So have I, for that matter. I've grown old in this place." She scratched her forehead. "It was two years after I started here. My husband was wounded in Vietnam in 1971, and she was admitted almost two years to the day after I started work here."

"And how does she seem to you?" We'd reached the bottom of the staircase.

She stopped and looked at me. Her eyes narrowed. "I can't discuss—"

"You can't discuss her medical history or her medications or her diagnosis, I know that," I interrupted her. "But you can discuss your personal impressions of her, can't you? Or is that a breach of ethics? Surely you have your own opinions."

"Ethics," she snorted. "That's a good one around here." She looked around. Dr. Bright's office door was shut. She gave me a funny look and gestured toward the front door with her head. "I don't want to talk about this inside the building. You never know who's listening."

That was the last thing I'd expected to hear. Curious, I followed her out the front door. Once we were down the front steps, she put a hand on my arm. "You repeat anything I say to you and I will deny every word of it, you understand me? Come on." She walked quickly out into the parking lot, where she stopped and lit a cigarette.

I also lit one. "Well?"

"Look, I've worked at this place a long time. I'm taking early retirement—my husband is sick and I need to take care of him—complications from what happened to him over there and the goddamned government won't do a thing about it, the fucks—and my last day is coming up in a week or so." She flicked ash. "About twenty-five years ago, a nurse decided to talk to Dr. Bright about Miss Hollis, because she didn't think what was going on around here was right— ethics, you understand—and the next day, they found some missing medications in her locker. She was accused of stealing drugs ... like Rose Calloway would ever do such a thing. But she lost her job, and you know damned well she couldn't find work, like they'd give her a reference—they even called the police in and threatened to file charges. I sometimes wonder what ever happened to her. . . . but they have ways around here, Mr. MacLeod, so like I said, I'll tell you a few things I know, but I will deny every word of it if you repeat it." She blew out a plume of smoke. "They don't like any of us to talk to anyone about Catherine Hollis."

"Scout's honor, I won't say a word to anyone," I said, feeling kind of stupid, but it seemed to reassure her. "But Dr. Bright has only been here for ten years—how could ...?"

"His father, the elder Dr. Bright, ran the place then." She gave me a lopsided smile. "When his father died ten years ago, the board hired his son to take his place ... and if anything, the son is worse than the father." She shrugged. "Don't get me wrong; most of our patients here belong here, and they get the best treatment available—therapy, drugs, you name it. But they're allowed visitors and the occasional phone call. Not Catherine. She isn't allowed any freedoms, except once a day she's allowed to walk around the grounds of the place—with two armed security guards, of course. The only time she's ever allowed to be by herself is when she is in her room."

"It sounds like she's a prisoner instead of a patient."

"You're quick, aren't you?" she said mockingly. "When they brought Miss Hollis here originally," she dropped the cigarette and crushed it under her foot, "St. Isabelle's was in financial trouble. Dr. Bright the elder was, well—let's just say he was bad with managing money and leave it at that. Then, about mid-July of 1973, a big black limousine pulls into the drive with Louisiana plates. Percy Verlaine himself. He goes in and meets with Dr. Bright for about an hour ... and our money troubles are over. Percy's 'generosity' lands him a seat on the board, and at the next board election, he's president of the board. . . . We all got huge pay raises, too ... but I'm getting ahead of myself. About a week or so after Percy Verlaine comes calling, his niece is admitted as a patient here—and Dr. Bright's *only* patient, just like the

younger Dr. Bright only sees her now. They passed her from
father to son ... no other doctor has seen her in all the time
she's been here."

"That's odd," I replied.

She rolled her eyes. "Your damned straight it's odd. Every
other patient in St. Isabelle's sees several doctors, you know.
But not Catherine Hollis. She belongs to Dr. Bright, and Dr.
Bright alone ... and the other doctors know better than to
even suggest they see her for any reason. He says she's uncomfortable around strangers, that another doctor might
cause a psychotic break. I think that's bullshit, but I'm not a
doctor. My opinion isn't worth two cents around here. And I
need my paycheck, so I just keep my mouth shut and do my
job."

"You think Percy had her committed here, and she
doesn't belong here?"

"She thinks she belongs here now, whether she really
does or not." She stared at me. "She didn't when she was
brought in." She clicked her tongue. "Let me put it to you
this way. Have you ever seen one of those movies where
someone who's not insane is put in a mental hospital? You
know how they always manage to get out at the end, and ex-
pose the horrors they experienced inside? Well, St. Isabelle's
isn't one of those places—we take very good care of our patients here—but if someone sane is kept in a place long
enough, given enough drugs, and told on a daily basis they
aren't sane, *you can drive them insane.*"

"My God."

"When she first came here, she was disturbed, all right,"
Amanda went on. "She had terrible mood swings; she was
real manic—hysteria one minute, deep morbid depression
the next, and you never had any idea when the change was
coming. She fought the nurses, she fought Dr. Bright, she

tried to escape—they had to put her in a straightjacket a few times, or strap her to her bed to sedate her. But you know something? If you were sane, wouldn't you fight at first? Try to escape?"

"Yeah." For a moment, I tried to think about what that would be like. It made the gooseflesh stand up on my arms.

"And when you slowly begin to realize you're never going to escape? That there's no way out? She isn't allowed calls. She's allowed to write letters, but Dr. Bright doesn't mail them. She is completely isolated here." She paused to give her words greater emphasis. *"For thirty-two years."*

My God. I couldn't even begin to imagine it.

"And of course, at first she used to want to call the police. … Then she would get hysterical, and fight. She used to scream she would see them all in jail, every last one of them." She shrugged. "Then of course they'd sedate her."

"So, you think Dr. Bright—staying here—drove her insane?"

"I don't know whether she's in her right mind or not, but I can assure you, Dr. Bright doesn't know either—and besides, I wouldn't take his word for anything." She spat contemptuously. She shrugged her shoulders. "You saw her. She has some lucid moments, when she's flirtatious and acts like she's the belle of the ball, and then she'll lapse into childlike speech and behavior. Sometimes I wonder if it's all an act— the way she copes with everything. I don't know. I don't think even she knows herself anymore." She shrugged. "And I'll deny every last bit of this if you repeat it to anyone. As far as I'm concerned, we've never met." She turned on her heel and walked back into the house.

I watched her, and once the door shut behind her, got into my car, and drove off the grounds.

My mind was racing.

Percy Verlaine had locked his niece away in a mental hospital shortly after his son-in-law vanished without a trace.

It didn't take quantum physics to connect those dots.

Percy Verlaine had killed Michael Mercereau, and Catherine Hollis knew it—might even have been a witness. And what better way to get rid of the only witness to your crime than to have her declared mentally incompetent and have her locked away for the rest of her life in a mental hospital?

It was so perfect it made my blood run cold. Who would listen to her, in a mental hospital? It would all be dismissed as part of her delusions. And Percy could walk away from a crime scot-free, without a care in the world.

It would take a lot of money and power, but Percy Verlaine had both. To spare, and then some.

But then Iris decides she wants to find her father—and Percy can't have that either. She'd even made the trek up to Cortez to see Cathy. What had Cathy told her? Had Cathy told her the truth … and was that why she'd hired me? To find the *proof* that her grandfather had killed her father, and finally get some justice for the father she never knew?

Only Iris knew for sure, and she too was dead.

But would I be able to prove it? What evidence existed besides what possibly was locked inside Cathy's head—and after thirty-two years at St. Isabelle's, she wouldn't exactly make a credible witness.

I glanced at my watch. I wasn't going to have time to stop to eat anywhere if I was going to make it to Jolene Mc-Connell's on time, so I drove out onto I-55, barely avoiding being crushed by a speeding eighteen-wheeler who didn't slow or even attempt to change lanes. I flipped him the bird and started heading south.

As the countryside sped past my windows, I couldn't stop wondering about how to proceed with my investigation. Iris must have believed there was a way to prove that Percy had killed Michael, but without being able to question her, I had no idea where to start looking. And even if I might not ever be able to prove Percy had killed Michael, it might be possible to prove Percy had killed Iris. It was difficult to wrap my mind around the notion that he'd killed his own granddaughter—but then again, he couldn't have. He wasn't physically capable of it—there was no way he could have gotten himself in that wheelchair up the stairs at her home. He must have hired someone to kill her—and that person wasn't exactly going to confess.

This case was now growing beyond my abilities and access to information. I was going to have to give it all back to Venus, who'd have to go to the district attorney to get subpoenas for financial records, phone records, and so forth, to try to locate the money trail murder for hire always left behind in its wake. No matter how careful someone might be, there's always some kind of paper trail. Even the wealthy and powerful can't completely disguise moving money around, and most killers for hire don't take checks; so there was evidence of unexplained cash somewhere ... but again, it could take auditors and forensic accountants months, if not years, of searching through Percy's accounts, and those of the company, to turn something up. And even to get that ball rolling, I was going to have to give Venus probable cause, and without some evidence as to *why* Percy had Iris killed, no district attorney in his right mind was going to take on Verlaine Shipping's wealth and power—and battery of attorneys.

Maybe Jolene McConnell somehow held the key.

I was about an hour north of Jackson and the highway

was deserted when I noticed a green pickup truck—one of those gigantic monsters with double wheels in the back on both sides—coming up rather quickly behind me. I was plugging along at a respectable eighty miles an hour, so he had to be going about a hundred, minimum. I watched as he got closer and closer—with no indication of either slowing down or changing lanes.

"Slow down, buddy," I muttered as my heart rate started to increase. If he didn't slow down …

The green truck slammed into the back of my Cavalier.

I was thrown forward by the impact, and my head exploded with pain as it hit the steering wheel. Dazed, I screamed a few incoherent obscenities as my car started swerving out of control, onto the shoulder on the right side of the road. I could feel the dirt beyond the pavement starting to give way just as the back of my car reconnected with the highway. Out of my peripheral vision I saw the truck go past on the shoulder, but the windows were tinted dark, so I couldn't see the driver in that split second before the truck was speeding away down the open road. My heart racing, I kept fighting the wheel, reacting solely by instinct, my foot stabbing at the brakes as the back of the car kept fishtailing, hoping against hope that it wouldn't go off the road and flip over, and then it swooped around and came to a stop. The engine stalled.

I sat there, hyperventilating and trying to catch my breath while I listened to the engine tick. After a few seconds I started the car and pulled over to the shoulder, black spots still dancing before my eyes, and shut the engine off again.

I don't know how long I sat there. Finally, I opened the car door and got out onto shaky legs, holding the side of the car for support as I shook a cigarette out and managed to light it. Two puffs later, I walked around to the back of the car and took a look.

One of my rear taillights was broken, and the trunk had crumpled a little bit, but that was it.

I was lucky not to have been killed.

I leaned back against the trunk and took another drag on my cigarette. My heart rate was slowing down, and my mind was starting to clear. I pulled my cell phone out, but didn't open it. I was a gay man out in the middle of nowhere, Mississippi—did I really want to call a county sheriff? Granted, there were no rainbow stickers, pink triangles, or SILENCE EQUALS DEATH bumper stickers on my car shouting to the world, HEY I'M A GREAT BIG HOMO, but nevertheless, my standard rule of thumb is never to deal with Southern county sheriffs if it can be at all avoided. Besides, all I knew for sure was that it had been a big green truck—I didn't get the plate number, or even know if it was a Mississippi truck, nor had I seen the driver. And big green trucks were hardly rare in Mississippi—every other Jim Bob probably had one. Without a police report, my insurance company wouldn't pay for the repairs, but again, I could just pay for it myself and my rates wouldn't go up.

Still, it was incredibly unnerving.

"Another random highway incident," I said out loud as I got back into the car, but froze as I placed the keys into the ignition.

Now, what were the odds of me almost being killed by a hit-and-run driver on my way back from seeing Catherine Hollis?

Iris had been killed the day after she'd gone to Cortez to see Cathy. I was almost killed on my way back from seeing her.

Like Venus, I don't like coincidences, but as I started back out onto the highway, I couldn't connect the accident to my visit. No one had known I'd gone up to Cortez other than Joshua Verlaine, and I doubted that he'd told anyone or that Dr. Bright was somehow behind it—since he, according to Nurse Amanda, was part of the cover-up of Michael Mercereau's murder—no, that didn't make sense either. If Nurse Amanda was right, and Catherine was being kept there as a prisoner, Dr. Bright had to know what I'd been told. And if by going there, Iris had signed her death warrant as well, how had anyone known what Catherine had told her?

You never know who's listening, Amanda had said in the empty hallway before she'd led me outside. I hadn't given that a second thought when she'd said it, but now. . . .

Jolene McConnell lived in a neighborhood that looked like it had been built in the big boom of the 1950s, when every new housing development seemed to think that the ranch house style was the greatest thing to hit architecture since the pyramids. Although the houses had been maintained and the lawns kept up, there was a sense of tiredness to the neighborhood—a feeling that its best days were past and decline had set in. When I pulled up to the curb in front of her address, her house was like every other one on the block—other than the statue of the Blessed Virgin Mary in the front yard. I got out of the car and walked up to the house, ringing the doorbell. I heard movement inside, and then the door opened.

"Mrs. McConnell?" I asked.

She nodded, and held the door open so I could come inside. She was still in her white nurse's uniform, and the tired sense I'd gotten from the neighborhood was heightened by the décor of her living room. The white sofa and matching reclining chair were covered in plastic. The walls were painted a dull beige, and a brown shag carpet covered the floor. A dusty upright piano was shoved into a corner, and photographs in cheap frames lined its top. There was a painting of Jesus with a halo on the walls; other than that, they were bare. "You want some tea?" she asked in a quiet voice with a slight echo of the Lower Ninth Ward to it. "I just made some. It's sweetened, though."

"That would be nice, thank you."

"Have a seat," she said before walking into the kitchen. I sat down on the sofa, plastic squeaking underneath me. She came back in with two tall glasses of iced tea, handed me one, and sat down in the recliner. "You know, I don't know what you think I can tell you. My brother's been gone for over thirty years. If he wanted to be found, he'da been found by now."

"Were you close to him, Mrs. McConnell?"

"Call me Jolene." She reached up and removed her cap, letting her shoulder-length gray-streaked black hair fall. "No, I wasn't close to my brother Michael." She looked up at Jesus on the wall. "He was about five years older than me, and he never had much time for me growing up. After he got married, none of us saw him much, really. He sure never talked to us much. . . . I think we embarrassed him, after he got used to bein' around those fine high-falutin' Uptown society folks. His wife, though, Margot—" her lined face creased into a smile, "I always liked Margot. She was always real nice to me."

"Really?" No one yet had said a kind word about Margot, so I was a little surprised.

"Really." She took a sip of her tea. "Margot paid for me to go to nursing school, and she was always giving me a call, meeting me for lunch, buying me things, you know. Michael was lucky to marry her—though you'd never know it from the way he acted."

"They weren't happily married?"

"Margot was miserable being married to him, but she loved him, God rest her soul, and did what she could to make the marriage work." She looked up at Jesus again. "My brother was one of those men who should never get married, you know." She shrugged.

"Meaning exactly what?" I asked, but even as the words came out of my mouth I knew exactly what she meant.

"I guess there's no shame in telling you now, since Margot's passed on, and can't be shamed by it anymore. He liked men." She shook her head. "The way the Lord intended for a man to like women. Oh, it was horrible, just horrible. I remember this one time, when he was seventeen, Mama caught him with another boy, out in the back yard, and she screamed so loud she liked to brought the house down or wake the dead or both. When Daddy got home he beat Michael almost to death, and then he had to go see the priest. Father Darrin was such a good man … and Michael, I'll never forget how Michael told Mama and Daddy he'd see them in hell one day." She shuddered. "It made my blood run cold the way he talked to Mama and Daddy—until Daddy threw him out of the house. Why he couldn't understand they were trying to save him from his own sin, I'll never know."

I didn't answer. The house was still and quiet. I could hear my own heart beating, my breathing uneven and ragged. It was like being a little boy again and listening to my grandmother, who'd been a member of the Church of Christ back in Cottonwood Falls, lecturing me about sin and salvation.

"I told Margot about him, you know," she went on. "Before they got married, and she just smiled and told me that all it took was the love of a good woman, and she was going to love him enough so he'd forget all about that. I prayed for her. She was such a good woman."

"But if Michael liked, um, liked men, why did he marry her?"

"My brother was a terrible sinner, Mr. MacLeod. He married Margot for her money, of course." She sighed. "I just pray he's repented of his sinful ways, wherever he is, but I rather doubt it, don't you? I mean, what kind of man would run off with another man, and never see his wife or his own children again?"

"Michael ran away with another man?" I repeated, thinking maybe I hadn't heard her correctly.

She nodded. "Margot told me herself. The night before he left, he told her he was leaving her and going off with some man. It crushed her. . . . I'll never forget how she looked when she told me about it. The look on her face, well, it would have broke your heart right in two to see a woman look like that. I know it broke my heart."

"It's the first I've heard of this." I stared at her.

She laughed. "Do you think Margot went around bragging about it? She didn't tell anyone, besides me. . . . I guess she didn't want me to worry about Michael since he was gone." She shook her head again. "Poor, poor Margot. She never married again, you know—and she was never the same after he left. How a man could do that to a woman, the mother of his children, is beyond me." She gave Jesus another look. "I pray for him, you know. Every morning and every night, I pray that he's repented and asked God for forgiveness for what he did to his wife and children."

"Thank you." I stood up. "For the tea, and for talking to me."

"Well, if you ever do find Michael," she said, getting to her feet to the squawk of plastic, "let him know I've forgiven him, but he needs to make his peace with God."

I forced a smile onto my face, said, "I'll do that," and walked out to my car. My cell phone went off before I could put the keys in the ignition. I checked the caller ID; it was Venus.

"I've been trying to get you for hours," she snapped as soon I answered.

"I'm in Mississippi, about to head home now . . . probably couldn't get a signal," I said, starting the car. "What's so important?"

"Joshua Verlaine is dead."

CHAPTER THIRTEEN

IT USUALLY TAKES ABOUT three hours, give or take, to drive
from Jackson to New Orleans. After getting Venus's call, I
made it in just over two hours by breaking every speed law
under the sun. I was able to maintain a good ninety-mile-
per-hour pace once I got outside Jackson. There was little to
no traffic, other than the occasional moving truck or eighteen-wheeler. I was able to weave around the slower-moving
traffic without problems or having to even slow down. I kept
an eye out for the big green pickup truck—I couldn't help
but feel there was a connection between the hit-and-run and
everything that was going on. I may not be the sharpest private eye around, but I don't believe in coincidences.

Venus hadn't been willing to share a lot of information
about Joshua Verlaine's death; she merely told me he'd apparently fallen to his death from the roof of the Verlaine
house sometime during the night. He'd been found in the
morning when the housekeeper had gone outside to shake
out a kitchen rug, and saw his broken body lying there. She
didn't answer any of the questions I'd asked, and I finally
gave up. She'd agreed to meet me back at my apartment
later on that evening, and she'd also stopped me from telling
her anything I'd learned. "We can discuss that when you get

back to town," she'd said in a tone I'd been used to before, but hadn't heard since I'd returned. In fact, she'd sounded like the pre-Katrina Venus throughout the entire phone call—which made me feel better about things. She'd always been one of the best cops on the NOPD; the shell of her former self she'd been since I'd gotten back was unsettling for me.

I was just making the long swooping turn from the I-55 off-ramp to I-10 when my cell phone rang again. I grabbed it off the passenger seat and looked at the little screen. The caller ID read BODYTECH. *Allen.* I reached down and turned down the car stereo before flipping it open. "Hello?"

"Chanse?" His voice was tentative. "Hey."

"Hey, Allen, what's going on?" I tried to put some warmth into my voice.

"Um, I was wondering—" he paused. After a few moments, he said, "You didn't come by the gym yesterday or today. Um, I—" Again he stopped.

"Allen, I'm on I-10 heading back into the city," I said, slowing down behind a U-Haul before swinging out past it into the left lane. "I, uh..." I didn't know what to say, and I cursed at myself inwardly. I've never been good in these situations. "I went out of town today, and yesterday I had some stuff to take care of, so..." I ran out of words and racked my brain for something, *anything*, to say.

"Oh." There was more silence. "Chanse, about the other night ..." His voice trailed off.

"Allen—"

"I don't want things to be weird," he interrupted me, and now that he'd gotten past the awkwardness, the words came out in a rush. "I mean, it was great, don't get me wrong, but I don't want you to feel like I think you owe me something or anything, it just kind of happened, I didn't mean for it to happen, you know, that wasn't what I was thinking when I invited you out for dinner and I don't want you to think that I'm trying to push myself on you or anything ... oh, hell." His voice cracked in despair. "I've been in a relationship for eighteen goddamned years, Chanse. I don't know how to deal with this kind of thing anymore! I'm out of practice!"

I couldn't help myself. I laughed. "Allen, Allen, please—just slow down a minute." I took a deep breath. "I seriously wasn't avoiding you. I just didn't have time to come by yesterday or today, and I really am on I-10, out over the lake marsh"—I swerved around an eighteen wheeler—"and no, I never for one minute thought you were just trying to get laid the other night. We've known each other for a long time—I think I know you better than that. I mean, things just kind of happened, you know?"

"I'm just confused," he replied in a low voice. "I mean, with everything that's going on with me and Greg—you know, I've never ever done that, in all the years we've been together."

"Really?" I was startled. I'd always believed all the sanctimonious preaching about gay monogamy was pretty much a big load of crap. It always seemed that the guys in long-term relationships, who always talked about love and commitment and how monogamous relationships were the only *real* ones, were always the ones who tried to put their hands down my pants after a drink or two—or once their other half was out of sight. "Now I feel like a real shit." And I did. How could I have been so stupid?

"Don't. You didn't do anything wrong. If anyone was at fault, it was me." He sighed. "Look, I don't want to talk about this with you in your car. Do you mind if I stop by later so we can talk a bit?"

"Well—" I thought for a moment. "No, not tonight. I've got an appointment later and I don't know how long it'll take, and it's important. I'll come by the gym in the morning and we can talk then, okay?"

"Okay." He breathed out a sigh of relief. "You'll definitely come by?"

"Yes. I'll see you in the morning. 'Night, Allen." I closed my phone and tossed it into the passenger seat just as I passed the airport exit. Christ, this was all I needed, but despite my initial instinct—which was to just blow it off and find another gym—I knew that I couldn't just do the usual Chanse MacLeod patented avoidance routine. Allen was a friend and I'd known him for too long to blow him off. He was hurting, he was confused, and what kind of person would I be to just walk away from the whole thing? Besides, I wasn't looking for a boyfriend, and who knew what his future with Greg would be? I found it hard to believe they'd just walk away from eighteen years together. All we had to do was keep our mouths shut, and everything would be fine. There was no need for Greg to know anything about it. I didn't know him that well, but we'd always gotten along fine. Back when Blaine and I were doing our "hey its just sex and no one is going to get hurt" thing, I'd always felt incredibly uncomfortable around his partner, no matter how much Blaine insisted they had an open relationship and everything was just fine. His partner was always distantly polite to me— still was, to this day—and while it was just possible it was my own guilt fueling that feeling, it bothered me.

And I didn't want to be uncomfortable around Greg Buchmaier.

It was just after six when I pulled into the driveway leading to the parking area alongside my house. The gate was open, and I clicked the remote to see if it would close after I passed through. Nothing. I sighed. I turned off the car and went inside, kicked off my shoes inside the back door, and walked into the kitchen. I got a soda out of the refrigerator, popped the tab—and that was when I noticed the living room.

"Jesus." I breathed out, walking to the big double pocket doors that separated the living room from the rest of the apartment. I stood there for a moment, the can of soda in my hand, surveying the disaster area that was my living room. Every one of my desk drawers had been dumped out on the floor. My filing cabinet drawers were also hanging open, and had been emptied out. There was paper scattered everywhere, empty manila file folders tossed around, and even the couch cushions had been tossed aside. I set my soda down on the counter and took a deep breath.

I could feel my mind starting to race, and my hands started to shake.

I felt violated, unsafe.

Anger started to build inside me. My home had made it through a fucking Category 3 hurricane intact. The city had flooded when the levees failed, but my house was on high ground, so no water had destroyed it. My apartment survived all of that and now some miserable son of a bitch had broken in and trashed it? "Mother fuck!" I shouted and my entire body began shaking from the massive adrenalin rush. I wanted to smash something, get my hands on someone, and throttle him to death. I wanted to kill. The fury was white-hot and swept through my consciousness, and as my eyes began to tint everything slightly red, I was aware in a small corner of my mind that I was overreacting. I needed to stay calm, to relax; this didn't matter as much as I was making it matter. My breathing was coming faster and faster. *Calm down,* that tiny voice in the back of my mind whispered, but that voice of reason was being swallowed by rage. Uncontrollable rage. I picked up my soda can and threw it against the kitchen wall, where foaming soda exploded out of the sides and splattered all over the wall, but that wasn't enough. I wanted to destroy things. I was furious and I couldn't control it, and as the rage continued to build I realized I was out of control but could do nothing about it. I couldn't stop. I was giving in to the fury.

I couldn't control myself.

My breaths were coming so fast now that I wasn't getting enough oxygen. I knew it, but couldn't control my breathing.

Just as quickly as it had come the anger was gone.

And my mind began to spiral down into a horrible depression.

It's pointless. It's all pointless. New Orleans will never come back. The city is gone, gone forever and no one cares. Look at this! My home isn't safe, nothing here is safe. What if another storm comes? The season isn't over yet. Best to just pack what I can and get the hell out of here, find another place to live in that's safe. Safe. It's not safe here. It's never going to be safe here. This city reeks of death and destruction. Maybe they're right. Maybe we should abandon the city.

And the most horrible part was I knew I was thinking crazy thoughts. I knew the depression was chemical in nature, not what I really felt or believed. But I couldn't stop it.

I couldn't stop myself.

I couldn't control my mind.

I'd learned early in life that out-of-control emotion was a bad thing. My father had been prone to sudden blinding rages—rages that terrified all of us. We never knew what would trigger one. Something innocuous, something that just the day before had meant nothing, would one day fire a synapse in his brain and he would rage out of control. In the grips of his raging fury, he became violent. He would destroy things, beat me or my brother or my sister or my mother. He would throw things. He would scream horribly vile and hurtful things at us, things that stuck in my mind, that no matter how hard I tried I couldn't forget. Ever, no matter how hard I tried. My earliest memories of my father were of his rages. And I hated him—how I'd hated him, and hate him still. It was genetic, too—his brothers were the same way, as was his horrible mother. It was why my mother drank, and why I couldn't get away from Cottonwood Wells fast enough when I got my scholarship to LSU. It was why I never went back there after I did get away. It was why I never called. It was why my parents didn't have my address or phone number. I had always sworn I would never be like my father, that I would rather die than be like that, be that kind of person. And even though my entire life, I knew the rage was there, buried deep inside my head, I was always able when it tried to emerge to fight it down, take deep breaths, get control of myself.

And his rages were always followed by a horrible depression he also couldn't control.

And that was what I was going through.

I couldn't get control of myself.

I need a Xanax, I thought as my legs became rubbery as the horrible depression washed over me, as my carefully constructed mental defenses against emotion crumbled beneath the weight of the depression.

They were in the medicine cabinet.

I had to get there. I had to get there fast.

My hands were shaking so badly by the time I got to the bathroom I could barely hold the small pill bottle containing the Xanax that Paige had given me. I finally managed to get the cap off and shook one out, threw it in my mouth, and gulped down a handful of water. I sat down on the toilet and took some deep breaths. I could hear my heart pounding in my ears, my entire body was shaking, and my breath was coming in horrible gasps. Spots danced before my eyes. *Get a grip, Chanse, get a hold of yourself, don't go into that dark place.* I got to my feet and staggered back into the kitchen. I was able to breathe somewhat normally, but still too fast. *Focus, Chanse, focus.* I grabbed my phone out of my pocket and called Venus.

"Hey, Chanse," she said. "Blaine and I are about two seconds from your front door. . . . We just turned onto Camp Street."

"Someone broke into my apartment," I said. "You need to call the lab and get a team over here. The whole place has been tossed." My voice didn't shake, and I closed my eyes. *Stay calm, stay calm, don't go there, Chanse, don't go there. . . .*

"Jesus!" she hissed. "Are you alone?"

"Yes."

"Get out of there, don't touch anything, and meet us out front on the sidewalk." She hung up.

I walked out the back door and around the side of the house. The Xanax kicked in just as I got to the gate to the front walk, and once again, it was like a curtain of calm coming down over me. I was definitely going to get my own prescription. Blaine and Venus drove up and parked right in front of me. I lit a cigarette as they got out of the car. "Lab on the way?" I asked.

"Things aren't like they were before, bud." Blaine shook his head. "We called, but there's no telling when they'll be here—and they're just as short-staffed as the rest of the force. But at least they don't have as much work—crime's pretty much a thing of the past here now." He shrugged. He looked tired. The circles under his eyes were more pronounced, his eyes more bloodshot than I'd ever seen them. There was bluish black stubble all over his chin, neck, and cheeks. Even his curly black hair didn't look as shiny and alive as it usually did, and he looked pale beneath his tan. His voice had a lackluster, lifeless tone to it.

"Did you touch anything?" Venus asked as we walked up the front steps.

"I went in through the back like I always do," I replied, suppressing the sarcastic urge to remind her I'd been a cop and wasn't some stupid moron—apparently the drug hadn't completely kicked in. "I took my shoes off in the bedroom, walked into the kitchen for a soda, and that's when I noticed the living room, and called you right away"—there was certainly no need to tell them about the Xanax and the near-breakdown I was still fighting off—"so, no, I didn't really touch anything." I pulled my keys out, and then groaned. Whoever had broken in had done so by simply removing the deadbolt. The deadbolt was lying on the porch in pieces, carefully lined up together and ready to be reassembled. *Nice,* I thought, *a thoughtful burglar.* I suppressed a rueful laugh. In the pre-Katrina world, someone with a screwdriver wouldn't have been able to just walk up on a porch and remove a deadbolt. But in the ghost town New Orleans had turned into. . . . I shook my head again. Better not go there right now—at least until I was sure my mood had stabilized. "Jesus fucking Christ."

Blaine took out his cell phone and took a picture of the door, then another of the dismantled deadbolt. He put on a pair of gloves and placed the deadbolt into an evidence bag, which he labeled. "Doesn't look like it'll be safe to stay here till you can get another deadbolt, buddy." He gave me a little smile. "You can always stay with us, if you want. Still plenty of habitable rooms in the big house." He looked at his watch.

"I don't even know where you can get another deadbolt—the Ace Hardware on Magazine hasn't reopened. Maybe you can find one on the Westbank or in Metairie."

Venus slipped on a pair of gloves and turned the knob, whistling as she surveyed the mess inside. "Well, your electronics are all still here." She gave me a half-smile. "Can you tell if anything is missing?"

"The only thing of value in the whole place is the electronics, and all of that is still here," I replied, pointing to my computer, the DVD player, and the television. "Damn, what a fucking mess."

"Well..." Venus closed the door again, and motioned for us all to sit on the stoop. "No point in going in there until they dust for prints and things." She whistled. "Now, I don't know what to think."

"What do you mean?"

"Well—" Blaine looked at Venus, and she nodded slowly. "We were thinking about a whole new direction on the Verlaine case, but if someone tossed your place. . . . I don't know."

"New direction?" I looked at both of them. "What the hell—"

"Chance, you know as well as I do when someone is murdered, unless it was a random thing, most times the killer is someone close to the victim—and most likely very close. A spouse, a parent, a sibling." Venus reached into my shirt pocket and removed my cigarette pack, shook one out, and lit up. "One thing we didn't think about—mainly because we didn't have time—was who benefited from Iris's death? What were her financials like, who inherited her money?" She inhaled, coughed, made a face, and flicked the cigarette out into the street. "And we leaped to the conclusion that since she'd hired you the morning she was killed, that it

might have something to do with her trying to find her father—we just never thought about the financial angle. . . ."
She sighed. "And part of it is this post-Katrina malaise or
whatever the fuck you want to call it. My mind just isn't as
sharp as it was before, you know? I'm kind of pissed at myself for not thinking about that. But now with Joshua Verlaine dead ... who benefits if both Joshua and Iris die?"

"Darrin Verlaine," I replied. "The old man is in poor
health and won't last much longer. With Iris and Joshua out
of the way, Darrin stands to inherit everything. He's all that's
left."

"Bingo." Venus gave me a wink. "There's no one else.
They are the last of the family—Margot's children. And now
two of them are gone ... hundreds of millions of dollars,
Chanse. Hundreds of millions of motives."

"So you think Joshua was murdered?" Much as I hated to
admit it, it made the most sense. But it also meant that everything else was coincidence—both Iris and Joshua hiring me,
the hit-and-run, and the tossing of my office. But then again,
they could all be related to the financial gain motive. Darrin
Verlaine might not know why they'd hired me; Iris hadn't told
Joshua; why would she tell Darrin? In his mind, I was a com-
plication that might need to be taken care of.

"And just what the hell was he doing up on the roof of the
house in the middle of the night? I can't believe he was just
up there for the hell of it—so I doubt it was an accidental
fall. And I don't believe it was suicide, either." Venus
shrugged. "Not the way he landed. People who jump off
roofs don't fall backward." She rolled her eyes. "I hate dealing with rich people, you know? The old man was sedated—
the doctor wouldn't let me anywhere near him, and the only
other people who live in the house are Darrin and that bodyguard—what's his name?"

"Lenny Pousson," Blaine replied. "Both he and Darrin claim they were in their rooms all night and heard nothing. But Darrin's suite of rooms is right next to Joshua's on the second floor—and he could easily have knocked his brother unconscious, carried him up to the roof, and just pitched him over. He's in pretty good shape."

"I don't know—why would he do it himself?" I replied. "What about Lenny Pousson? He could have done it as well as Darrin."

"You got a motive?" Venus raised an eyebrow. "He's just a longtime employee—why would he suddenly start knocking off the Verlaine heirs? I seriously doubt he's in the old man's will."

I shrugged. "Look, Iris hired me to find her father—the same day, she's shot. Then Joshua hires me to find their father, and now he's dead. If it was just one victim, I'd be more inclined to believe it's just a coincidence—but both of them? No, I can't prove anything—but listen to this." I laid out everything I'd learned and what I'd been thinking since leaving Cortez. I also told them about the hit-and-run, and showed them the back of the car. "Now, don't you both think that's odd? I'm telling you, all of this has something to do with Michael Mercereau."

"You seriously think the old man killed his son-in-law?" Blaine shook his head.

"The old man is a serious homophobe." I shrugged. "And so is Lenny Pousson. Think about it, Blaine. His only son is killed in a car accident. All he has left is his daughter, and he focuses all his energies on her. She marries, not some Garden District prince, but some poor kid from the Lower Ninth Ward who wants to be a painter. I am sure he approved of *that*. And then he finds out the son-in-law, who he's never approved of, is gay."

"I don't know, Chanse." Venus shook her head. "It seems a bit of a stretch."

"Have you ever actually met the old man, talked to him?" I lit a cigarette. "Trust me, he's capable of it, all right. So he has the son-in-law killed—no body is ever found; they spread the story that he just abandoned the family. Whether Margot ever knew the truth, I'm not sure. And then Iris decides she wants to find her dad, and hires me."

"And so he has her killed?" Now Blaine shook his head. "And then his other grandson? He's just mowing down his family to cover up a thirty-year-old crime? It doesn't wash for me, Chanse. No one has found the body for over thirty years. Thirty years. After all this time—there's no way there's any evidence to be found. You don't even know for a fact that Michael is dead."

He had a point. "The key to all this is Cathy Hollis. I'm telling you. She knows the truth and they've had her locked up for years to keep this secret."

"I need more than that," Venus replied.

"She knows more than she was willing to tell me," I insisted. "I mean, she told me the date he disappeared … that's a place to start. And that date means something…." I drove my fist down onto my knee. "I just can't figure out why."

"What was the date?" Venus asked.

"June 23, 1973," I replied.

"Oh my God." Blaine paled. Venus just shrugged again. "You two don't know that date?"

"Should we?" Venus asked.

Blaine shook his head. "That was the date of the Upstairs Lounge fire."

CHAPTER FOURTEEN

I HAVE AN ABSOLUTELY terrible memory—I always have.

As a result, I was not a good student. I never made the honor roll, and often I was lucky to squeak by with a passing grade. I could study my ass off, trying to commit things to memory, and then on test day my mind would be a complete blank. I graduated from LSU with one-tenth of a grade point over what was required to get my diploma. I barely kept my head above water in grade school and junior high, but once I got to high school and became a standout on the football field my grades inexplicably became better—I'm sure my success as an athlete had *nothing* to do with that.

My strength is the security end of my business. It's very easy for me to look at a system and determine where it is vulnerable, which is why Crown Oil pays me such a huge sum of money. I'm also good at proving insurance fraud and adultery. I'm terrible at murders, though. I just can't wrap my mind around them; I can't seem to get inside the heads of people who would actually kill another human being. Granted, there were times when I personally wanted to kill someone else, but my own morality always kicked in—it's usually just a fleeting thought in a moment of anger, like when some idiot cuts me off in traffic. I don't understand people who don't have the mental block to actually taking another life. To me, there's never enough justification to take another life. Trying to understand someone who is cold enough to commit murder just doesn't work for me. So I generally don't like to get involved in homicide investigations more complicated than someone snapping in a moment of rage. *That* I can understand; I can't understand people who can plan a murder in cold blood.

I'd killed a man once—and his death haunted me for quite some time. I wasn't even completely sure I was over it yet. And it wasn't cold-blooded; it was self-defense and had I not killed him, he certainly would have killed me.

Life is just too sacred to me—and Paul's death had brought that belief home to me even more forcefully.

That was one of the reasons I left the New Orleans police department. I knew I didn't have what it took to make detective grade, and the thought of spending the rest of my life punching a time card and riding in patrol cars terrified me. I also knew that at some point I was going to have to use my gun, and the thought of even shooting another human being, as my two years passed, became even more unappealing to me. I also had to take into consideration the toll on my body from years of bad coffee and junk food, one I could see every time I looked at a twenty-year veteran of car patrol. I couldn't ride a horse, so the mounted duty in the Quarter was also out. The only other option for me would be a desk job—and I couldn't see myself sitting at a desk pushing paper forty hours a week either.

I also have never been a huge fan of taking orders without question.

I couldn't believe I'd forgotten the date of the fire at the Upstairs Lounge.

What made it worse was that I'd actually attended the

ceremony where a memorial plaque commemorating the victims was placed in the sidewalk at the corner where the bar used to be. Paige had been assigned to cover it for the *Times-Picayune,* and had asked me to come along. When she mentioned it to me, I didn't even know what she was talking about. I'd never heard of the Upstairs Lounge fire, which resulted in my receiving a lecture as well as copies of all the articles from the newspaper morgue about it.

Reading them made me sick to my stomach.

The Upstairs Lounge was a gay bar located in the French Quarter at the corner of Iberville and Chartres Streets. Fairly popular back in the days when almost every gay man or lesbian in New Orleans was deeply closeted, before there was a gay pride celebration or a gay paper, it was one of the few havens in the city where gays could gather and be themselves. It still boggled my mind that as recently as thirty years ago it was dangerous to be openly gay in New Orleans. It was a completely different time, a different mentality. Homosexuality was still considered a mental disorder—one that could get a queer locked up in a mental hospital and given electric shock treatments. Not only were queers deep in the closet, many of them got married and had children—satisfying their true sexual needs on the side, always afraid of the ruin that would follow upon being found out. The Upstairs Lounge was one of the few havens they had—and while everyone in the Quarter knew it was a queer bar, most people simply looked the other way. The existence of queers wasn't a secret, but as long as it was kept quiet and no one had to really be confronted with it, an uneasy coexistence was possible.

On that fateful Sunday afternoon in June, over twenty people were gathered in the bar, relaxing and enjoying themselves. They had a beer bust every Sunday afternoon:

one dollar and all the beer you could drink. There was a piano, and often the people in the bar would gather around it and sing along with whoever was there and could play. The bar was on the second floor, accessed by a staircase. There was a buzzer installed at the bottom of the stairs for identity protection—if you called a cab, they would buzz to let you know to come down. That way no one ever had to hang around on the corner waiting … and thus run the risk of being exposed as a queer.

That afternoon, someone opened the door at the foot of the stairs and threw a Molotov cocktail. As soon as the stairs were engulfed in flame, the arsonist rang the buzzer. The bartender asked if anyone had called a cab—and since no one had, he went over to the big steel door to shout down to the cabbie it was a mistake. The back draft created by opening the door sucked the flames into the bar, where they fed on the air and the flammable decorations. Within seconds, the bar became an inferno. Most of the windows had burglar bars on them, and there was only one way out. Only a few of the patrons managed to escape. Almost everyone who was inside the bar either died there or in the hospital. It was one of the most fatal fires in the history of a city known for fires. Many of the victims' families turned their backs on them and refused to claim the bodies. One, a teacher, was fired while lying on his deathbed. Some bodies were never identified.

The heat was so intense some of the bodies fused together.

And the arsonist was never caught.

It was without question one of the most horrible moments in the history of the city of New Orleans. Churches refused to have memorial services for the victims. The governor, who would eventually go to jail for accepting bribes, never made an announcement about one of the most fatal fires in Louisiana history.

But out of the horror, the queer community of New Orleans was born. The reaction of city and state officials—or their lack of reaction—made people angry. People started coming out. Activism began in an indolent city where most people couldn't be bothered to get involved. Within a few years, New Orleans became a haven of tolerance for gays and lesbians throughout the South. And although homophobia was never completely eradicated, the city no longer tolerated it in an official capacity. New Orleans was one of the first cities in the country to recognize gay couples and offer partner benefits. And despite the heavily conservative beliefs of the rest of the state, New Orleans refused to give in. New Orleans welcomed gay tourism, encouraged gay businesses, and was proud of its open-minded reputation. Sure, every once in a while there might be a gay bashing, but it wasn't locals committing hate crimes—there's a *live and let live* mentality in the city. Those kinds of crimes were committed by homophobic thugs coming in from one of the outer parishes around the city. You know, the dopes who sit around drinking beer and then go hunting gays for sport, as if we were deer or ducks, not human beings.

"Oh my God," I said in response to Blaine, lighting another cigarette. "Michael Mercereau could easily have been one of the unidentified bodies." Despite the slight fog of the Xanax, my mind raced ahead. "Obviously, the Verlaines would have never claimed the body—let alone even *admitted* there was a possibility he could be there. And so Michael just vanished. would"

"That's a possibility," Blaine said with a shudder, and ran a hand through his curls.

"I wonder ..." Possibilities were whirling around in my head. "Maybe Percy hired someone to get rid of Michael, and ..."

"But don't you think that's a bit of overkill? Are you thinking that Percy Verlaine hired an arsonist and killed all those people to get at his son-in-law? I mean, Percy's a mean old bastard, but—"

"And what guarantee did he have that Michael would even be there that afternoon?" Venus finished for him. "No, Chanse, I don't believe it. I can believe Michael Mercereau was one of the unidentified victims, but I don't believe Percy Verlaine was behind the fire." She shook her head. "It's possible, of course, but it's really a bit of a reach. You think the killer just walked around for weeks waiting for a chance, carrying a Molotov cocktail with him, in case Mercereau went into that bar? That doesn't work for me … it seems like a really sloppy way for a hired killer to work. It would be much more likely he'd have shot Mercereau and dumped the body somewhere. And besides, there's no physical evidence, for one thing—and it would be pretty damned hard to find any after all this time. And I seriously doubt that Percy would have his own grandchildren knocked off on the off-chance that you'd find out their father died in that fire. You might have been able to prove Mercereau was one of the unidentified victims, but no offense, babe, you'd never be able to connect Percy Verlaine to the arson."

Put that way, my theory went down in flames. But I grasped at a straw. "Then why did they lock Catherine Hollis away all these years?"

"Chanse," Venus patted my leg. "Maybe she is mentally unbalanced."

There was nothing to say to that. All I had was my gut feeling, and I didn't have a medical degree. Just because she seemed rational and in control to me didn't mean she was.

The lab techs pulled up a few moments later, ending the conversation. It took them about an hour to photograph everything, dust for prints, and do all the things they had to do—which meant making a big mess even bigger. When they finally finished, both Venus and Blaine offered to help me clean up. I turned down the offer—I hate having other people go through my stuff—as well as an offer for a place to spend the night. I got them to help me push my loveseat over to block the door, and then sent them home. I put the rest of the furniture back where it belonged, picked up all the paper and made stacks on my desk, and wiped down every surface before giving in to exhaustion and going to bed.

I didn't sleep well, not that I expected to. I kept waking up throughout the night, and never really went into a deep sleep. I tossed and turned, thinking maybe that if I found a really comfortable position I'd finally lose myself in sleep. It never happened. It seemed like I was looking at the clock every five minutes, and every so often I'd hear a noise in the front of the house that would make me sit bolt upright in bed, my ears cocked, listening. It was a mistake not to stay over at Blaine's. My house had already been violated once, and without the ability to lock the front door, I didn't feel safe. And considering how much death was hovering over this investigation, even having my gun on the nightstand didn't make me feel safer.

Finally, at seven in the morning I gave up on sleep and got out of bed. I took a shower, drank some coffee, and went into the living room and started reorganizing all my files.

The Xanax had worn off during the night, but I didn't feel the need to take another. I was a little foggy from lack of sleep and probably a residual drug hangover, so it was nice to have something to keep my mind occupied and off other things. Filing requires some focus and concentration, but not a great degree of analytical thinking. Well, that was the theory at least. I started sorting papers and refiling them into the folders they originally came from, and once everything was in its proper file, I organized each file before putting it back into the cabinet.

Nothing was missing, which I didn't understand. Everything I had in my file for Iris was still there. What the hell had they been looking for?

What nerve had my investigation touched?

Venus had made a pretty convincing argument that Percy Verlaine had not been behind the Upstairs Lounge fire. I had no evidence—only a gut feeling based on nothing more than the fact that Catherine was certain the day Michael disappeared was also the day of the fire. It was just hard for me to believe a gay man could disappear so completely off the face of the earth on that very day and not have the two events be connected. Two plus two equals four. But I also had no proof that any of the Verlaines had known that Michael was even gay—other than Margot. Did it stand to reason that Margot would have confided the truth about her husband to her father—a man who obviously did not approve of her marriage? Venus was probably right; I was trying to connect Percy Verlaine to the fire because I didn't like the wretched old homophobic bastard. And while it stood to reason Michael was one of the unidentified victims, it was unlikely I'd ever be able to prove it. And that was that.

But I couldn't get it out of my mind. Call it instinct, gut feeling, whatever—I was *certain* I was right. Catherine Hollis was the key. I was also positive if I could just get her to open up to me, she'd be able to tell me the truth. She'd been locked up in that mental hospital for over thirty years— Venus was right, she wouldn't make a credible witness unless I could somehow prove she had never belonged there, which again would be impossible. Surely, though, if there truly wasn't anything wrong with her, why would they lock her up? It might have been *embarrassing* to the family to admit that Michael had been gay, but if anything, Margot would have seen herself as a victim of a fortune hunter who'd lied to her.

Unless somehow Catherine knew Percy was behind the fire.

But that would be next to impossible to prove. She was under lock and key and watched; she certainly hadn't been willing to tell me any of her secrets. Why would she tell anyone else?

I finished reorganizing the files and had just put the last one back into the cabinet when there was a knock on my front door. "Hang on a minute," I shouted, "who's there?"

"It's me, Allen."

I muscled the couch away from the front door. I glanced through the blinds, and opened the door.

"Hey." Allen smiled weakly at me. He looked like he'd slept about as well as I had. He looked around. "Do you always keep your couch in front of the door?"

"I had a break-in yesterday. I was just straightening up. Whoever did it took out my deadbolt." I shrugged. "So I put the couch there."

"Oh man, that sucks." He shifted his weight from one foot to the other.

"Have a seat. You want anything to drink? I can make coffee or something."

He plopped down on the couch, spreading his legs wide. "No, if I drink any more coffee I'll turn into Juan Valdez. Thanks, though."

An awkward silence fell over both of us. I didn't know what to say to him. As the silence lengthened, I finally said, "Are you okay?"

"No." He gave me a weak grin. "No, I'm not okay. I talked

to Greg last night—oh, don't worry, I didn't tell him about the other night. No, Greg called to tell me that he'd made up his mind. He's moving the business to Atlanta permanently."

"I'm sorry," I replied, feeling like an idiot. "Are you going to move?"

"I told Greg my business—and my life—were here, so no, I am not moving to Atlanta." He buried his face in his hands. "We pretty much decided to, um, end things between us. So much for eighteen years together."

I put my hand on his shoulder, and he took it with one of his. "Don't worry," he went on with a slight laugh. "I'm not going to start blubbering or anything like that. I mean, the truth is our relationship was pretty much over for a while now, and neither one of us wanted to admit it, you know what I mean? It was *comfortable,* but we weren't getting what we needed from each other anymore."

"Where are you going to live?"

"Well, Greg can't sell the house—it's a living trust. And he'd already talked to his sister; she doesn't want it either. So, I get to keep living there."

"That's pretty nice of him."

"He's not an asshole, Chanse," he replied sharply. "He's not going to throw me out and leave me without a place to live."

"I didn't—"

"I'm sorry." He interrupted me with a sigh. "I know you didn't. I'm a little off this morning—it's a bit much to take."

"It's okay."

"I didn't sleep well. . . . Of course, with this new storm out there, it's no wonder." He ran his hands through his hair. "Is this fucking season ever going to end?"

I felt a knot forming in my stomach. "There's another storm out there?"

He nodded. "Yeah, they're saying it could be Katrina-sized. It's going to turn into a hurricane in a day or two—Wilma. And she's going to head into the Gulf most likely."

"It won't come here," I said, my hands starting to tremble. Jesus *fucking* Christ. The levees were only patched, not repaired—and there was no way the patch job would hold if another major storm came onto the lake or, God forbid, up the river and overtopped those levees. If that happened, that would be it. The 10 percent of the city that didn't flood was on the high ground along the river. If the river levees went—that would be it for New Orleans. "It can't come here."

"Yeah, well." He stood up, wiping his palms on his knees. "I guess I'll head back to the gym. I just wanted to stop by and let you know—about me and Greg." He awkwardly reached out his hand. "I also wanted to let you know that I—um, I don't have any expectations of anything from you. We can just go back to being friends, if that's okay with you."

I looked at him, then at his outstretched hand. His lower lip was quivering, just a bit, and his eyes were glistening. He looked like he was holding himself together with baling wire and duct tape. I stepped close to him and gave him a big hug. He stiffened for a moment, and then he put his arms around me and started to cry.

Sometimes it's a good thing when you can't think of anything to say. I just stood there and held him while his body shuddered with his sobs and his grief. I felt my own eyes starting to fill, as I thought about everything I too had lost over the last year. Even though I knew in my gut the city would recover, that New Orleans would again be the city it once was, it was hard sometimes when faced with the everyday horror that life in the city had become. And even if this Wilma went somewhere else, if the city continued to rebuild and find its way back to its former self, Paul was still gone.

After a few minutes, Allen pulled away from me and wiped at his face. "Sorry. I didn't mean to break down."

I wiped at my own face and laughed. "Dude, it's okay."

"Well, thanks." He stroked my arm. "Take it easy, okay?"

"Can I call you later?"

"Yeah." He smiled at me. "Yeah. I'd like that."

He walked out of the apartment and I watched him get into his car and drive away. I went back inside and was just about to get on my computer and do a search for information on the Upstairs Lounge fire when my cell phone rang.

"Chanse!" It was Barbara. "I just heard. Are you all right, dear? Did they take anything?"

"I'm fine. And no, they didn't steal anything. I don't know what they were looking for."

"Well, I have a locksmith coming over to put in a new deadbolt. He should be there in about an hour or so. But I have some good news for you."

"I could use some."

"I tracked down Eric Valmont." She laughed.

"Who?"

"Chanse, really. You need to stop smoking pot. Your memory is atrocious. He was a friend of Michael's, remember? I told you about him ... he was an art critic."

"Oh. Sorry about that."

"I had to listen to his mother go on and on for about an hour about how worried she's been about him—but he's back in New Orleans. He lives down in the Marigny, and I gave him a call. He said he'd be happy to talk to you about Michael Mercereau." She inhaled sharply. "The problem is he's planning to head back up to Hammond later this afternoon to stay with his mother a few days."

"I'll head right over there. What's the address?" She gave it to me, and I wrote it down. "But what if the locksmith comes while I'm gone? I don't really feel comfortable leaving the apartment open."

"Oh, I'll send Jasper over." Jasper was her driver. "He'll wait there for the locksmith—and if you aren't back before the locksmith is finished, he can just leave the new keys for the front door for you on the kitchen counter."

"You are way too good to me, Barbara."

"Yes, I am, aren't I?" She laughed. "And don't ever forget it." She hung up.

I went outside to wait for Jasper.

CHAPTER FIFTEEN

ERIC VALMONT'S HOUSE was in the last block of Dauphine Street before Frenchmen, in what was called the Marigny triangle—a name that's never really made a lot of sense to me.

The Marigny district, on the lake side of Elysian Fields, had not gotten water; I'd been told that the flood stopped at Elysian Fields. I was pleased to see that the little Frenchmen Deli's OPEN sign was lit up, even though everything else on Frenchmen was dark. Frenchmen Street in the time before the storm had been going through a Renaissance—turning itself into a smaller version of Bourbon Street with bars, restaurants, and music venues. There was also a tattoo parlor and a bike shop. Even with the renewal, the area still seemed a little derelict in the daylight. There weren't any real trees on Frenchmen Street, just a lot of pavement, and telephone wires seemed to hang low over the street. Some of the buildings remained vacant. Regardless, at any time of night or day, there were always people milling about on its dirty sidewalks, and finding a place to park was next to impossible. Now, there was no one around and there was parking everywhere. There were piles of debris almost everywhere I looked, along with the occasional refrigerator with a nasty message for the federal government written in magic marker on the front.

Paige was right. Refrigerator art was the new art form of the city.

I pulled up in front of Washington Square and gawked at what was going on at the park. There were at least twenty, maybe thirty people inside the black wrought-iron fence that circled the park. There were tents set up everywhere, and in one place a huge vat of something was cooking over an open fire. I got out of my car and locked it, taking a closer look at the crowd. It looked like a makeshift soup kitchen—or the parking lot at a Grateful Dead concert. I wasn't sure what to make of the crowd inside—they all appeared to be relatively young. The average age of the people apparently camping out there seemed to be about twenty-three—and they were the kind of kids we used to refer to before the storm as the gutter punks. They were all white kids, their arms, necks, and bare legs covered with tattoos and piercings. Most of them had their hair in dreadlocks, and they all looked like they hadn't bathed in weeks. Some were playing Frisbee with equally ratty looking dogs. *Maybe they're here to help out,* I thought for a moment, *in that way that kids do—not wanting to deal with an organized group like the Red Cross, just rolling up their sleeves and getting to work.*

But they didn't seem to be doing anything other than hanging out.

I stood there for a moment, watching them, before heading around the corner and finding Eric Valmont's address.

There were trees on Dauphine Street, so it didn't look as bare as Frenchmen. The houses were closer together, the way they are in the Quarter, with narrow passages guarded by gates between them. Dauphine was one of the first streets in the Marigny to get the "extreme makeover" treatment, and even though there was still a house here and there that looked like it might be blighted or a haven for crackheads, overall the street had come back nicely. It looked deserted now, and some of the houses had those horrible painted crosses on them, but I was also pleased to see that no bodies—human or animal—had been found on the street.

Eric's house was a single shotgun on the uptown side of the street, about four houses down from the corner. Ironically, it was one of the houses I would have picked as blighted. It was badly in need of paint, having once been painted that orange-coral shade that was fairly prevalent in the Quarter, which helped give the city a Caribbean flavor. The front porch sagged a bit to the left where a wheelchair lift had been mounted. There was a wooden gate on the right of the house with razor wire looped over the top of it. There was a beat-up blue Toyota Corolla parked in front, behind the HANDICAPPED PARKING sign mounted beside a towering oak tree. I climbed the steps, which groaned under my weight, and rang the bell. I heard footsteps inside, and then the door opened.

"Yes?"

I stood there and gaped for a few moments. The man who'd opened the door was one of the most gorgeous young men I'd ever laid eyes on. He was about five-ten, maybe one hundred and fifty pounds of lean muscle. He had short black hair with blond highlights, green eyes, and perfectly white even teeth showing in a wide smile in his tanned face. He was wearing a sleeveless white T-shirt reading *I stayed for Katrina and all I got was this lousy T-shirt ... and a plasma TV ... and a Cadillac ... and a new computer. . . .* There was a tattoo of St. Sebastian pierced by arrows on his right bicep. Veins bulged out on his tan arms. He was wearing a loose-fitting pair of jeans that hung low enough on his hips to reveal not only the trail of curly black hairs disappearing down into the red waistband of his Calvin Klein underwear, but the flat defined muscle of his lower abs. He looked like he was barely out of high school. His face was open and friendly.

I laughed. "That's a great shirt. Where did you get it?"

His smile widened. "I know, huh? I got it at this little shop on Magazine Street near Aiden Gill. It might be in bad taste, but I thought it was funny."

"It is."

"You must be Chanse MacLeod." He stuck out his right hand for me to shake. "I'm Devon; I work for Eric. We've been expecting you. Do come in. Can I get something for you to drink?" His voice was deep with a friendly lilt to it, with just a smidgen of the outer parish accent.

"Um, I'm fine." I finally managed to get the words out somehow. "Thanks." I stepped past him into the dim interior. He flicked a light switch and the room filled with light from a dusty chandelier hung in the center of the room, suspended from a fourteen-foot ceiling, which bore more than a few water stains. It was a large room, with a comfortable-look-ing worn sofa and some reclining chairs arranged around a coffee table piled high with magazines and art books. None of the furniture matched, which seemed a little odd to me. The bare floor was covered with a worn and dusty Oriental rug. A cat yawned and stretched from atop a pile of books on a dusty end table. A plasma TV hung on the wall over the mantelpiece. I couldn't tell what color the room was painted because every inch of the walls was covered with framed artwork. Paintings, black-and-white photography, and litho-graphs hung everywhere the eye could see. The pocket doors opposite were pulled open. The next room was much the same—spare furnishings, but the walls were covered with art.

"Make yourself comfortable." Devon shut the front door behind him. "I'll see what's keeping Eric." He gave me that wide smile again, and I watched him walk through the next room to the back of the house. He walked lightly on the balls of his feet, and on his way through the room he picked up the cat and carried it out with him.

I glanced over the books on the huge coffee table: Bruce Webber, Greg Gorman, Tom Bianchi, and a bunch of other names I didn't recognize. The magazines ran the full range from *Louisiana Cultural Vistas* to *New Orleans* to *Modern Photography,* the *New Yorker,* and various other publications I'd never heard of. A half-empty water bottle sat on a mosaic-tiled coaster, and on the other side of the table a huge mug of coffee looked like it had been sitting there for a day or two. I was more than a little surprised. It wasn't like any home of an elder gay man with money I'd ever been in— those usually are decorated in what I call *gay museum* style and looked like no one ever lived in them. This place, on the other hand, looked comfortable and lived-in. I smiled to myself. Obviously, Eric Valmont was not a neat freak.

I liked him already.

I sat back and crossed my legs, and then I heard a rolling sound. I looked up and saw an elderly gentleman in a wheelchair rolling through the other room. He was completely bald, with a salt-and-pepper goatee, a wide smile, and pince-nez-style glasses perched on his nose. His eyes flashed with intelligence and warmth. A knit comforter covered his legs, but his broad shoulders and thick arms were evident beneath the red-and-black flannel shirt he was wearing. He maneuvered himself into the living room and held out his hand. "Don't get up—I'm sitting so it would be rude for me to expect you to get up." He laughed. "And besides, you look like a rather tall one. I don't want to get neck strain looking up at you."

His grip was strong, and I smiled back at him. "It's a pleasure to meet you, Mr. Valmont. Thanks for agreeing to see me—especially on such short notice."

"The pleasure is all mine." He smiled back at me. "I don't get many visitors, you know. Most people seem to have forgotten my existence—though to tell you the truth, in most cases I'm relieved." He rolled his eyes. "Most people are such insufferable bores that it's all I can do to stay awake, let alone engage in conversation." He shook his head, then winked at me. "Being a crip comes in handy, you know. All I have to do to get rid of someone is just say, 'I'm tired' and then they are out of here like lightning."

I couldn't help it. I laughed. "Well, that's a good thing. Although now if you tell me you're tired, I won't know if you really are or just want me to leave."

He let out a shout of laughter. "Oh, no worries on that score. I like you already."

"Do you need anything, Eric?" Devon asked from the other room. He was holding a dish towel.

"I'll call you if we do, thanks, Devon." He turned a bit in his chair and watched Devon walk to the back of the house. "Isn't he a find?" he turned back to me. "That one should be a model, don't you think?" He winked. "That face and body belong on the covers of magazines, don't you think?"

"Um, yeah, he's gorgeous." Which was putting it mildly.

"Don't get any ideas, now." He wagged a finger at me. "Alas, Devon is a straight boy and has a girlfriend." He shook his head. "Devon is a good soul with a good heart, an absolute sweetheart of a boy, but he has the most unimaginably bad taste in women. He likes those slutty types with the ratted bleached blonde hair and the long red fingernails and the silicone tits." He rolled his eyes. "It makes me so glad to be gay when I meet those horrible women. And he has absolutely no idea how beautiful he is—which, of course, to me makes him even more beautiful. Nothing is quite so ugly as a beautiful boy who knows he's beautiful, and uses that to manipulate people. No, Devon isn't one of those, bless his heart."

I smiled, not sure what to say.

"I met him through a photographer friend of mine—do you know Davis Rochelle?"

I thought for a minute but drew a blank. "The name's familiar—"

"He teaches photography at UNO. Devon was one of his models—a student who answered an ad in the school paper because he needed money." He gestured behind him with his head. "I bought two of Davis's shots of Devon—if you have to avail yourself of the facilities, they're hanging in there. They're definitely worth the look"—he winked at me again—"but alas, Devon had to drop out of college—money problems again—he comes from an unimaginably poor family out in Chalmette, and they lost everything in the flood on top of that. It's so awful, his family is out in Lake Charles with relatives now. . . . Anyway, I hired him to work with me. As you can see, I have some difficulties getting around, and Devon has been a dream. He's been wonderful since the storm, you know. He made sure I got to the north shore safely, and then he stayed with my mother and I, and was just absolutely wonderful. When UNO reopens, my mother is going to pay his tuition for him—she's fallen as madly in love with him as most people do when they meet him. Bright and beautiful, it would be a shame for all that potential to go to waste. If only I could wean him off those horrible women. . . . They'll wind up being his downfall eventually." He shook his head. "Anyway, you didn't come here to find out about Devon. Barbara said you were looking for people who knew Michael Mercereau." He shrugged. "There aren't many of us left who knew him, you know. But she didn't give me any particulars. Why do you want to know about him?"

"I was hired by Iris Verlaine to find him, before the storm," I said. "She was getting married and wanted to find him."

"Ah, the Verlaine snake pit." He folded his arms. "She wanted you to find him?" He stroked his chin for a while. "Well, I wish I had better news for you—but since she's now dead, I suppose it doesn't really matter. He's buried out in a pauper's grave somewhere—wherever they put them here. I'm afraid I can't help you with that; I have no idea where they buried him. No, I'm afraid looking for Michael was nothing more than a wild goose chase for you, son." He sighed. "Poor Iris. It must have been awful for her to grow up without knowing her father. Even a dreadful father is better than none at all."

"How did he die?" I asked, even though I was certain I knew the answer.

"He died in the Upstairs Lounge fire." His voice cracked for a moment, and he took a deep breath, removed his glasses, and wiped his eyes. "That was such a horrible day. ... Would you like me to start at the beginning?"

"Please." It was hard not to smile. I was right.

"I met Michael a few years earlier, at a show for a mutual friend of mine." He slapped his legs. "I wasn't in this chair then, Chanse, and believe it or not, I was a rather decent-looking young man. I knew the Verlaine family—we didn't really travel in the same social circles, but you know how New Orleans is ... you can't help meeting people and knowing more about them then you'd care to, if you know what I mean. I never much cared for Percy Verlaine, and I know my parents detested him. My father—did Barbara tell you anything about my family?"

"I know your father was a congressman."

"He fought very hard for civil rights—which didn't really make him terribly popular in the state, but my father, bless him, believed that *every* American was entitled to the same basic rights. Percy was a racist, among other things, and he often tried to finance my father out of office. My parents believed in the basic dignity of every human—not just the white men. So, I didn't really come into contact with the Verlaines very often, but I knew them." He sighed. "But I'm off topic, aren't I? Don't be afraid to point that out to me, Chanse."

"All right."

"Anyway, I don't remember whose show it was, and I suppose that doesn't really matter, but I was introduced to Michael and Margot—that I do remember. And as we talked, I began to get the feeling that Michael was flirting with me—in front of his wife!" He wiped his glasses again, replaced them on his nose, and grinned at me. "You have to remember, it was a different time back then, Chanse. We weren't quite so public about our sexuality in those days as you boys can be today—but then, weren't you the private eye who solved the Mike Hansen murder a few years back?" He shuddered. "That was a terrible thing—it brought back all those horrible memories of the fire. . . ."

"Yes, that was me," I replied. "Did you know Mike Hansen?"

"He modeled for Davis—I think I have a photograph of him hanging somewhere in the house. He was a beautiful young man ... such a waste. Anyway, Michael asked me for my card at the end of that evening and called me a few days later. We became lovers, although it was more of a sex thing than anything else. It was a dangerous time … that monster Jim Garrison had just destroyed Clay Shaw, you know … but then again, no one thought it odd if two men had dinner together at Galatoire's or spent a great deal of time together—people didn't automatically suspect anything in those days." He smiled. "It just never entered people's minds that someone might be gay, you know, especially if there was a wife and children—which is why so many of us had them, you know. I never did … it didn't seem right to me."

"But it was okay to sleep with a man with a wife and children?" I shook my own head with a smile at his logic.

"Does that shock you?" He raised an eyebrow and smiled at me. "I know today 'married men' are the forbidden fruit—if you pardon the dreadful pun—for gay men. But you have to remember, at that time most gay men and lesbians *got* married and hid who they were. Marriages were a wonderful smoke screen—and Margot knew all about Michael's 'little quirk,' as she called it." He coughed. "I know a lot of people didn't like Margot, but she was a remarkable woman. She loved Michael—and figured his men weren't a threat to her or her family. And they weren't. Michael knew where his bread was buttered, if you'll pardon the cliché. I seem to be speaking in puns and clichés today."

"So Margot knew?"

"Of course she knew! She may have been a lot of things, but a fool wasn't one of them. They had a very nice little arrangement, and it worked for everyone. I certainly didn't want Michael for anything other than an afternoon in bed in my home." He shrugged.

"You didn't love him?"

"Have I shocked you? Surely people today don't only have sexual relations with people they love?" He threw back his head and laughed. "No, I didn't like Michael very much as a person. Michael was certainly charming, and he was a very talented painter, and he was wonderful as a lover, but other than that? He was very unemotional, very cold. He was like biting into tinfoil. Have you ever done that?" When I nodded, he went on, "I don't think Michael was capable of feeling or caring about anyone rather than himself. It was unfortunate, but there you have it. So, no, I didn't fall in love with Michael. I wasn't that stupid. No, I thought Michael had a great deal of talent, and I thought he was a beautiful man, and a wonderful lay, to be crude—but other than that, no. I didn't want to see him waste his talent, so I pushed him to paint, to show his work—and he was remarkable—but no, I didn't love him. In fact, by the time he died, our little arrangement had been over for quite some time. No, he called me that morning and wanted me to meet him at the Upstairs Lounge, to talk about a gallery owner in Palm Springs I was going to introduce him to—it wasn't an assignation or anything. It was purely business, and Michael did like to go there every once in a while to relax and maybe pick up a boy. And I wasn't averse to going there—it was quite fun on a Sunday afternoon." He closed his eyes. "My mother called me just as I was leaving the house, and would *not* get off the phone—although as it turned out, she may have saved my life. I was furious with her, and I remember having to walk very quickly. I was a few blocks away when I saw the smoke and the flames." He closed his eyes for a few moments, and then he opened them. "I lost several wonderful, irreplaceable friends that day," he said softly. "And afterward, it wasn't too hard to figure out, was it? Michael was supposed to meet me there, and he disappeared without a trace. Margot wouldn't return my calls. I talked to the police, but they didn't care. He was just another dead fag to them." His eyes narrowed. "And that was when I realized things had to change. They were *people,* not garbage, and that was how everyone was acting. I thought about going to the papers with it, but my mother convinced me not too—my father was a congressman, and she was afraid it might harm his career." He wiped at his eyes again. "So, no, I kept my mouth shut. I never told anyone else. And so. There you have it. I'm not proud I kept my mouth shut, that I didn't raise a fuss."

"Do you think it's possible that Percy Verlaine—" I stopped myself. I was beginning to doubt the theory myself.

"Percy Verlaine." He laughed bitterly. "A monster of a man. Inhuman. Do you know when the Metropolitan Community Church tried to get the plaque laid commemorating the tragedy a few years back, he tried to get it stopped? He's been one of the biggest enemies of the gay community—behind the scenes, of course, always behind the scenes—this city has ever seen. He hates everyone except white men, you know. I've always thought it the greatest irony that the father of his grandchildren was a gay man."

"Do you think it's possible that Percy Verlaine was behind the fire?"

He inhaled with a hiss. He leaned his head back and closed his eyes. After a few moments, he opened them and looked at me. "Let's just say it wouldn't surprise me." He tapped his fingers on his knees. "You know, they never did find who set the fire—not that they looked too damned hard, if you ask me."

"You're sure Percy didn't know Michael was gay?"

"If he knew, I—" His eyes got wide. "Oh, good lord," he whispered. "I almost said that if Percy knew he would have killed Michael. You don't think—"

"I don't know." It was my turn to shrug. "It's an interesting theory I'm kicking around."

He glanced at his watch. His face had gone pale, and his hands were shaking a little. "Um, Chanse, would you mind terribly if I terminated this interview?" He gave me a weak smile. "I truly am getting tired, and Devon is driving me to Hammond in a little while, and I'd like to get some rest."

I rose. "Well, I thank you for your time, Eric." I smiled at him. "I enjoyed talking to you. Maybe we could have lunch or something sometime?"

He smiled. "I'd like that—as long as you aren't just trying to use me to get to Devon."

I laughed as I walked over to the door, and was about to walk out when he called my name. I turned around. "Yes?"

He rolled his chair across the room to me. He pointed an index finger at me. "Find out if that old fuck did this. If he did this"—his voice shook with emotion—"he needs to fry for it." He swallowed. "Like they did."

CHAPTER SIXTEEN

JUST OUTSIDE MY CAR, a kid with blond dreadlocks who smelled like he hadn't bathed since New Year's asked for spare change.

"Sorry," I said as I unlocked the driver's side door.

"Come on, man," he whined. "I need something to eat."

I stopped getting into my car and looked at him, trying to control my rising temper. "Why don't you get a job? There are help wanted signs everywhere."

"A job?" He looked at me as if I'd sprouted a second head. "Why would I want to do that?"

"You know, panhandlers who aren't willing to work aren't what we need in this fucking city right now," I snapped, getting into my car and starting the ignition. My hands were shaking as I felt the rage continue to build. *No*, I said to myself, *I am not going to lose it, I can get this under control, I don't need to take a Xanax.*

The last thing in the world I needed was to become chemically dependent.

Fortunately there was no traffic on the roads as I headed Uptown, which helped me to calm down.

All the possibilities were swirling around in my head. I started to make the turn at Race to head home, and then swerved back onto Magazine as another possibility hit me in the forehead like a brick. I'd been going about this entire case all wrong. Sure, Michael Mercereau's death had something to do with it—I was sure of that—but I needed to take a look at things more current. Iris was murdered—and it didn't make sense that she'd been killed simply because she'd hired me to find her father. The likelihood that I'd be able to dig up anything about the fire was pretty low. I didn't think it was a coincidence she'd been killed the very day she'd hired me—but it was also likely there was another reason, a more pressing one, that the killer had wanted her out of the way.

What did Iris know that made her a threat?

Phillip had said she'd found out something—something that would put her in the driver's seat at Verlaine Shipping.

The major flaw in the case I was building against Percy Verlaine was the consideration that no grandparent would have his grandchildren killed. It was unnatural, against every conceivable law of nature. The truth is that parents and grandparents behave unnaturally all the time. I saw that when I was a cop. Most people can't wrap their heads around it—so juries are loathe to convict on that kind of crime unless the evidence is so damning and concrete they have no other choice. Family members kill each other all the time, but we are so socialized to hold familial bonds as sacred that when it does happen, it comes as a complete shock to our systems and we don't want to believe it. Part of that comes from the fear that perhaps *we* might wind up being capable of doing such a thing—or that a relative could be. I could recognize the weakness of my logic. Percy Verlaine was a monster—every single person I'd talked to agreed on that point—but they still couldn't believe that he would have his grandchildren killed. Even I had some trouble with it, myself. The Upstairs Lounge fire was a horrible tragedy, but would he have Iris and Joshua killed to cover it up after all this time? Just hiring me to find Michael wasn't even motivation enough, to be perfectly honest. What were the odds I'd find out Michael had died in the fire, had been a gay man who'd married Margot as a blind? There had to be more; it had to go deeper than that.

And I also couldn't rule out the possibility that Darrin Verlaine was behind the deaths of his siblings. He was, as Venus had pointed out, now the sole heir to the company and the family fortune. It was possible there was no connection to the fire, no connection to Michael's disappearance. Much as I hate them, coincidences do happen.

It was time to have a sit down with Iris's assistant. I drove over to where the company headquarters were located on Poydras Street and parked. It wasn't hard to find Iris's office. I knocked on the door and walked in. There was no one seated at the outer desk, and the inner office door was open. Various generic-looking paintings of popular New Orleans tourist spots were placed at even intervals on the walls— Jackson Square, the Huey P. Long bridge, Bourbon Street at night, and the city skyline as seen from the West Bank.

A woman I assumed to be Valerie Stratton was seated behind Iris' desk. Her blonde-highlighted dark hair was pulled back into a bun. She was in her early thirties and just missed being pretty by the hard set to her jaw and eyes. She was wearing dark red lipstick that matched the polish on her long nails, and I could catch a hint of her perfume—something that vaguely smelled of roses and lavender. On her left hand was a silver ring, and her watch looked expensive. She was wearing a powder blue business suit over a salmon silk shirt. "May I help you?" she asked with a smile.

"Ms. Stratton?" I asked as I sat down in one of the chairs

facing the desk. When she nodded, I went on, "I'm Chanse MacLeod. We spoke on the phone the other day. You weren't completely honest with me, were you?"

She started tapping a pencil on her blotter. Her eyes narrowed. "I don't know what you mean, Mr. MacLeod." She gave me a frosty smile. "As I recall our conversation, I answered your questions."

"Ms. Stratton, there were several things you didn't tell me." I crossed my legs. "For example, you acted as though you and Iris weren't close—her fiancée tells me differently."

"Perhaps Phillip and I have a different definition of *close*. It's not like I was going to be a bridesmaid in her wedding or anything. We talked sometimes about personal stuff, or her plans—well, she talked; I mostly listened. That was how she was. She made it very clear to me I was her employee." She said it with just a bit of venom, and shrugged. "She didn't tell me everything." Again the frosty smile. "Whatever Phillip might have told you, Iris liked to keep things pretty close. I don't really think she confided much in anyone, to tell you the truth. She didn't have a lot of friends. She was all about the job, you know. She lived and breathed Verlaine Shipping." She tilted her head to one side. "She could be quite tedious about it."

"He also told me that you knew everything that goes on in this company." I wanted to slap the smile off her face. "And I need to know some things."

"Company business is confidential information."

"Even when it might have something to do with the reason why Iris—and Joshua—were murdered?" I gave her my own version of a frosty smile. "I'm here as a representative of the New Orleans Police Department. I've been deputized to look into Iris's murder."

She had the decency to color a little. "I thought Iris was

killed by a burglar, and Mr. Verlaine's death was an accident."

"The police don't think so." I leaned forward in my chair. "And soon enough, they'll be wanting to know everything that I want to know—and they can force you to tell them things. You know, subpoenas and all that." I raised my eyebrows. "I could call them and have them take you down to the precinct to answer questions—and you know, it will look pretty odd to your co-workers if the police come in and drag you out. That would make for talk at the water-cooler for days, I would think."

"Then I should probably wait for them, shouldn't I?" She regained her composure, smoothing her hair. "I could be fired for telling you anything. Confidentiality, you know. I had to sign a legal document barring me from talking to anyone about what goes on around here."

"You know, if you tell me what you know," I smiled at her, "maybe you won't have to talk to the police officially at all."

She wanted to tell me everything. I could read it in her body language. She was, as Phillip had said—and Iris herself had told me—a gossip. People like her, once they opened up, wouldn't shut up until they told you not only everything you wanted to know but also a bunch of stuff that didn't matter—they just liked to talk to hear themselves talk. And whatever she had to say, it would be colored by her own perceptions and innuendoes. She was the kind of person who made a terrible witness, the kind whose testimony district attorneys hate to build a case around. I sized her up again. Threats wouldn't work with her—if anything, she'd shut down completely and refuse to answer any questions. No, the way to get her to open up would be to be friendly, make her feel like she was privy to inside information—and that anything she might know could be really important. People who gossip do it, I think, to make themselves feel more important. Phillip had said she came from a family that had gone broke when she was young, but they'd managed to keep her in McGehee. Then she'd had to go to college at UNO, which had to have stung. If she and Iris had been friends when they were young, she also had to resent working for her on some level. I smiled to myself. *Play on her bitterness toward Iris. She resented not being asked to be in the wedding—otherwise she wouldn't have mentioned it. It's a sore spot.* I gave her a wide smile. "You could really help me out here, Valerie. You probably knew Iris just as well as anyone, working closely with her every day, right? She wanted to run the company, didn't she?"

"Oh, that was hardly a secret." She laughed. "She let everyone around here know that." She leaned forward. "It was all she ever talked about, you know. And she'd tell anyone who'd listen. Even the lowest clerk in the mailroom knew that. You couldn't work here and not be aware. She would rant and rave about how unfair it was that her grandfather thought she couldn't handle the job because she was a woman, that he was positively medieval, someone needed to drag him into the twenty-first century, on and on and on. I could quote her, chapter and verse. It got so whenever she'd go off on it, I just tuned her out, you know? It was *boring.* I just wanted to tell her to get over herself and do her damned job—public relations isn't exactly *beneath* her, which is how she acted. She'd work herself up into quite a frenzy, you know. If he wasn't her grandfather, she probably would have sued for sexual discrimination or something. But as long as he had control over the will, she couldn't do anything. He could cut her off without a cent. Hell, he could fire her at will—and she sure as hell didn't trust him not to do that very thing."

"Do you think she could have run the company?"

She took a drink out of her coffee mug, and thought for a moment. "Yes, I think she could have. Of course she could have. She certainly couldn't have done a worse job than Joshua." She smothered a laugh. "I could have run the company better than Joshua. A five-year-old probably could have. He didn't know what he was doing, and anyone could see that."

"Joshua was screwing up?"

"Calling it *screwing up* is the understatement of the day." She leaned back in her chair. "We lost a five-hundred-million-dollar contract last summer when a boat we built for an oil company sank within three days of launching. The verdict was shoddy construction—and you can imagine how well *that* played with our other customers. Didn't you see the article? It made the front page of the business section in the paper. Iris was livid, absolutely livid. She couldn't put a positive spin on that no matter how hard she tried." She took another drink. "And several of our other customers were threatening to go elsewhere. You can't lose contracts of that size and stay in business. So, yeah, we were in trouble. A great deal of trouble. Of course the hurricane helped out a lot." She shrugged. "It was a godsend, in a way. The damage to the yards, the damage to some of the ships—our clients couldn't very well go elsewhere without looking like complete assholes ... and the insurance settlement sure came in handy."

"So why was he still running things? That doesn't make a lot of sense to me." I leaned back in my chair. "Percy Verlaine doesn't strike me as a particularly stupid man—why would he let his grandson run his company into the ground? I don't follow."

"Changes were in the air, Mr. MacLeod." She gave me a

superior, knowing smile. "Mr. Percy was not happy. And Darrin didn't want the responsibility." She gave a disdainful sniff. "He's more interested in going to the casinos then doing any work."

"That left Iris," I answered. "A magna cum laude graduate of the Harvard Business School. Why wouldn't he give her a chance?"

"Iris was living in a dream world. Mr. Percy was never going to let her run this company—and she finally realized that when he didn't fire Mr. Joshua. Rumor was Mr. Percy was thinking about bringing someone else in—a co-president to ride herd on Mr. Joshua. I don't know how true that was—it was just gossip." Her smile faded. "The meeting was the Monday before the hurricane. Old Mr. Percy actually came into the office, you know—oxygen tanks and all."

"Were you in the meeting?"

"I took the minutes, like I always do." She paused, and then her face hardened into an angry mask. "Yeah, Iris graduated *magna cum laude* from the Harvard Business School all right—try to get her to shut up about it. Her brothers barely made it through Vanderbilt, and I am sure the Verlaine money had something to do with that. I'm sure the old man had to build a library wing or something to get them their diplomas. She had offers from companies all over the world—and instead she chose to come back here to work for the family business." She sniffed. "Vice president of public relations? That was her *mother's* job. Margot stepped aside and retired so Iris could have her job. Iris thought it was just a matter of time before her grandfather realized she was the most qualified of them all to run the whole company. At that meeting, she presented her case. And you know what Mr. Percy said?"

"What?"

"A woman couldn't run this business, and what she really needed to do was think about her wedding, and having babies, because that's what she was *meant* to do—like her mother." She hissed the words at me. "The old pig. Iris was humiliated in front of all the other vice presidents, and then the old man gives Joshua a vote of confidence. I thought Iris was going to kill the old man, she was so angry. And after we came back here and had a drink, she decided that the only way she was ever going to get her due around here was to *force* the old man to make her president." She shook her head angrily. "Why anyone would humiliate his own granddaughter like that in front of every executive in the company is beyond me. My grandfather would certainly never treat me that way."

"How was she going to do that?" I prodded. "How could she force him to do anything?"

"Have you met Lenny Pousson?" One of her plucked eyebrows went up, and she gave me a slight smile.

"Yes." I nodded. "What does he have to do with anything?"

"He's been on the company payroll for years, only nobody really knows what he does." She shrugged. "Iris was certain something was not quite right there, and she started digging around in the old financial records."

"What did she find?"

"She wouldn't tell me—but she found something, all right. The Wednesday before the storm she was excited, but all she would tell me was she was onto something, but she needed the final proof, and she knew exactly where to get that." She got up and refilled her coffee mug. "She went up to Cortez, Mississippi, on Thursday to visit some relative, and Friday afternoon she told me she had everything she needed."

"But she didn't tell you what?"

She shook her head. "She wouldn't tell me—all she would say was on Monday morning everything was going to be different around here." She shrugged. "But all her files are gone, you know. Before I came back here to work, someone went through and took everything out of her office—even her computer's hard drive had been wiped clean." She sat back down. "You know, I'm the acting vice president of public relations—they're letting me fill in for her. You have no idea how hard it's been to do my job without any of her records—but I muddle through. The other day, though, we had something come up, and I went to Mr. Joshua to tell him I needed access to one of the old files. He looked at me like I was crazy. He had no idea the files were gone. He didn't even know her hard drive had been wiped." She shivered. "It was kind of creepy. I mean, things have been a lot more loose around here since the storm, you know, but I just figured"—she bit her lip—"I just figured, you know, that they did that kind of thing as routine, you know, in case there was sensitive information in her files and computer, you know—a security precaution—although it seemed kind of stupid to me, I mean, how the hell was I supposed to do the damned job without access to her files—but he had no idea what I was talking about. And he wasn't making it up either. He had no idea, no idea at all." She snorted. "And he's the president of the company?" She rolled her eyes. "He said he'd find out what happened to her files and then would get back to me."

I sat up. "When did you have this conversation with him?"

"Three days ago."

And two days later he was dead.

"He had no idea what happened to her files?"

"He said he didn't, but he'd find out." She shrugged. "I

was able to solve the problem without them, so in the end it didn't matter, but how am I supposed to do my job?" She sighed. "Mr. Joshua, though, was very understanding about it, and he kind of promised me Iris's job." Her face became radiant. "Me, a vice president! I couldn't believe it—but then, now that he's gone, that's probably not going to happen." She started drumming her fingers on her desk again. "But it won't be that easy for them to get rid of me. I know things." She gave me that smile again.

"You know things."

"Yes." She leaned back in her chair. "I *will* be vice president of public relations. Or they will regret it."

She knew what Iris knew. There was no doubt in my mind. "Valerie ... if you know what Iris discovered, you need to tell me."

"I don't know what you're talking about."

"Iris wasn't killed by a burglar. And Joshua Verlaine didn't accidentally fall off that roof either." I leaned forward. "Think about it, Valerie. You're not a fool. Iris was determined to force her grandfather to make her president of the company. You know Percy Verlaine. In order to do that, she had to have something big to make him knuckle under to her. She told you the day she died she had everything she needed. And that night she was murdered. Someone came in here and took her files and wiped her hard drive. When you mentioned it to Joshua, he said he'd look for her files—and then he falls off a roof." I paused for a few beats, watching the color drain out of her face. "Do you think any of that could be coincidence? And if you try to use that same information ..." I let my voice trail off.

She sat there quietly for a moment. She bit her lower lip. "The Wednesday afternoon before the storm, she sent me to Office Depot to get her a digital voice recorder. She said she needed it for her trip on Thursday."

I tried to keep my voice casual. "Do you know what happened to it?" It wasn't in the inventory of Iris's purse that was in the police report. *Please God, don't let it have been in her purse that night, don't let it have fallen into the hands of the thief. . . .*

She took a deep breath. "I have it."

I could barely control my own excitement. "Where is it, Valerie?"

She opened a drawer and pulled out her own purse. "Iris gave it to me that Friday afternoon." She started rummaging through it. "After she came back from meeting with her grandfather." She held it in her hand, and stared at it.

"Did you listen to what's on it?"

She nodded. "I can't believe ..." she whispered, her face pale. "I was going to use it. I was going to make them give me the promotion. How could I have been so stupid?"

I chose not to answer that. "Ms. Stratton, can you hand that to me, please? It's evidence in a police investigation." I held out my hand, which was shaking just a little bit. *This was it, the evidence I needed.*

She handed it to me. "Here. Take it." She wiped her hands. "I don't ever want to see that thing again." Her voice shook. "They would have *killed* me. I just never thought—"

"Valerie, you didn't know this was why someone killed Iris—how could you have known? You're not a psychic, nor are you a cop." I held it in my hand. It was tiny; it would easily fit in a shirt pocket and be completely unseen. I had one myself, the exact same make and model. I bought it because it was much easier than taking notes. I could simply record my interviews and then download them into my computer and listen to them again later, even have them transcribed word for word. It seemed hot in my hand. "Are you okay?"

Now that the recorder was out of her hands, her color was coming back. "Yeah—yeah, I guess." She took another swig of her coffee. "I think I'm going to take the rest of the day off, though."

"So what do you think Lenny Pousson's job is?" I asked casually, slipping the recorder into my pants pocket.

"We-ell—" she made a production of looking around to ensure no one was listening. "Like I said, no one really knows, and his job description is listed on the books as 'assistant to Mr. Percy,' but most people think he's a thug. Hired muscle. He does the old man's dirty work for him. No one's really sure what that means, but rumor has it he was instrumental in breaking the workers' strike back in the 1980s, when the yard workers went out on strike." She shuddered. "He kind of gives me the creeps, you know what I mean? He used to always look at me like he was imagining what I looked like naked—and he was that way with Iris too. She couldn't stand him." She sighed. "Once she was running things, he was going to be the first change she was going to make. She told me so that Friday morning, you know, before she left to go meet with you."

That was one thing I still didn't understand—why had Iris felt the need to hire an outside investigator? She seemed to have been doing quite well on her own.

"Did she tell you why she was hiring me?"

"All she said was she wanted to hire a private eye to find her dad." She shrugged. "It was weird. You know, in all the time I knew her, she never once talked about her father until that morning. But then, like I said, she liked to keep things close."

"Yes, apparently she did." I started to stand up. "Can you think of anything else that might help me out here? Anything else she might have said or done that last week—no matter how unimportant it might seem? You never know when something might be important."

"No, not really." She stared at me. "Do you think I've been helpful?"

"You never know." I handed her a business card. "If you think of anything else Iris might have said or done that last week—about Lenny, her grandfather, anything—call me. Anything. It might seem like nothing, but again, you never know."

"Well—" She looked at my card like it was a poisonous snake, then slipped it into her purse. "All right." She pulled her purse out of her desk drawer and stood up. "I'll walk out with you."

"You listened to the recording," I said as we walked to the elevator. "What does it say?"

Her eyes got wide. "No. I never heard anything, I never listened to anything, I don't know what you're talking about." She gave me a brittle smile. "And if anyone asks me, I never spoke to you." The elevator doors opened and she stepped in. She held up a hand as I started to walk in. "Do you mind waiting for the next one?"

I was itching to get out of there and get home, but I could understand her caution. If two people had been killed because of what was on that recorder... "You might want to think about getting out of town for a while, " I said casually. "Is there somewhere you could go?"

She smiled as the elevator doors started to close. "I'll find somewhere."

It took another couple of minutes before another elevator came, and I could feel my own nerves starting to get the better of me as I waited. In the elevator on the way down, I pulled out the recorder. It was the same make and model as mine, which was good—I already had the software I needed loaded in my computer, and I didn't need an instruction manual.

The sky was overcast as I got into my car—roiling black clouds moving in fast from the river, and lightning flashed over the west bank of the river as I started it up. My cell phone rang. It was Allen. I debated for a moment taking it, but the recorder was too important. Allen could wait.

I put the car into drive and headed home.

CHAPTER SEVENTEEN

I COULDN'T GET HOME fast enough. The digital recorder felt
like it was burning a hole in my shirt pocket. Iris had been a
good detective—hell, she'd been a better one than I'd been
thus far, but on the other hand, she'd had access to financial
records at Verlaine Shipping that I hadn't—and she'd had
some idea of what she was looking for. I could guess what
was on this digital file. It was the evidence she needed to
force her grandfather to make her president of the company—whatever that might be. It was also the reason she'd
been killed.

I parked in the lot beside the house and went inside as
fast as I could. I switched on lights as I went—the storm was
rolling in and the entire house was dark. I turned on my
computer and while it booted up, I dug out the connection
cable for my digital recorder. I downloaded the file into my
computer and turned up the volume. My finger trembling, I
pressed the play key.

The first few seconds were silence, and then it began
with Iris talking.

*"Hello, Aunt Cathy. Thanks for agreeing to see me. How
are you?"*

"I don't know you. They said you were my cousin, but I don't have any women cousins other than Margot, and they told me she died. But you kind of look like her, only you're prettier."

"I'm Margot's daughter, Iris."

"Margot didn't have a daughter. She had two boys, Joshua and Darrin. They were sweet boys, but they never come to see me. Family doesn't mean what it used to, I guess."

"Well, I'm here to see you now. You don't know me because I was born after you came to stay here. Aren't you glad to see me?"

"I don't know you. Why have you come?"

"I'm Margot and Michael's youngest child. Iris Verlaine. You remember my father, don't you? You remember surely that my mother was pregnant before you went away? Well, I'm their daughter. My father went away before I was born, too. I want to talk to you about him."

"I don't want to talk about your father. I won't talk about him."

"But I want to talk about him. I never knew him, and you're one of the few people left who knew him who is still alive. My mother would never talk about him—and neither will my grandfather."

"Then why should I? I have nothing to say about Michael, not now, not ever."

"Please, Aunt Cathy, won't you tell me about my father? Please?"

"Talking about your father is what got me locked up in this place, and I am never ever going to talk about him again."

There was silence, and then Iris tried again.

"Well, can you tell me if my parents loved each other? Can you tell me at least that much?"

"Margot loved Michael very much. Almost too much, if you ask me. It wasn't a healthy kind of love. Margot never understood that love sometimes means letting go. She always wanted to hold on to everything she loved." Cathy laughed. "Margot wasn't nearly as pretty as you are. There weren't many men interested in her—I used to think Margot would marry the first man who paid any attention to her at all. And then your father came around. He was handsome, he was charming ... and Margot fell for him very hard. She loved him, all right. She loved him far too much for it to be healthy." More laughter. "But what do I know about it? What do I know about what's right and what's good and what's healthy? Look where I am!"

"So she didn't want my father to leave her?"

"Does any woman want to be left? I'm sure it destroyed her, made her bitter and angry—more so than she already was."

"Did you like my mother? It doesn't sound like you did very much."

"I liked her well enough; she tried to be as nice to me as she could, given I was just a poor relation ... she was always kind to me, but no one in that house could ever let me forget I was just there on their charity. It's a terrible thing, you know, to always be made to feel like you should be grateful for the least little kindness ... but Margot did her best to make me feel like I was really her sister, not some poor cousin they'd taken in because it was either that or foster care. . . . It was her father that was cruel. But his cruelty wasn't just for me, it was for everyone ... he enjoyed being cruel for the sake of cruelty. He was cruel to Margot, he was cruel to your Uncle Matthew while he was alive—I always thought it was a merciful release when Matthew got himself killed in that accident—just as Margot thought having children would change the way he treated her. It didn't. Every-one was beneath Percy ... and he thought Margot married beneath her. He hated Michael, because Michael just laughed at him, wouldn't listen ... he couldn't get under Michael's skin, and he knew it ... he couldn't control Michael the way he could control us. . . ."

"He hasn't changed. He's still trying to control all of us."

"Leopards don't change their spots, do they? I hate Uncle Percy. I always have."

"There are times when I almost hate him myself. If he weren't my grandfather. . . ."

"You want to know about your father? That wouldn't please Uncle Percy, you know. He would hate that."

"Yes, yes, I want to know. Please, won't you reconsider and tell me? I've come a long, long way to hear what you know—no one has to know. It's just for me. I want to know about my father."

"You have to promise you won't tell. I'll get in trouble."

"I won't tell anyone. I swear to you."

"I tried, you know. I tried to tell everyone, and all it got me was locked up in here. So I decided I wouldn't talk about it anymore. Nobody wants to know the truth when it's incon-venient, you know. It's only when the truth is what they want to hear. You may not like it when you hear it. Do you promise not to tell anyone? You must promise!"

"It'll be just between us, Aunt Cathy."

"Your father was a wonderful man. He could make me laugh like no one else, and he was always up for a good time. And your mother, she didn't mind. She had the boys to take care of, so she didn't mind if he and I went out clubbing or to parties. She was very kind to me in that regard. Other people talked—thought I was sleeping with your father, of course. I had a terrible reputation; although if they really *knew what I was doing it would have been much worse. Your father covered for me. He made it possible for me to do what I wanted by being my escort. Back then a woman's reputation meant a lot, and I liked men."*

"Why didn't you sleep with Dad?"

"I wasn't his type." Hysterical laughter. "But then neither was your mother."

"What was his type?"

"I don't want to say."

"Please tell me."

"You don't want to know."

"I'd rather know. Now I don't know anything, please tell me."

"Your father liked other men."

Silence. "I suspected as much."

"Your mother didn't care as long as he was discreet. Discretion was everything in those days, Irene."

"Iris."

"So, I covered for him and he covered for me. We would go to clubs together, where I would meet men, where he would meet men, and we lived as we pleased, and it worked. I had an escort, so it was okay for me to go out, which I couldn't do alone. . . . Back then the only women who went anywhere alone were whores, and I was a Verlaine—a poor relation, but still a member of the family, and so I couldn't risk a lot of talk. . . . It would have gotten back to your grandfather, and then there would have been hell to pay. He was such a monster ... but it was a good arrangement, and it would have gone on forever until I married—which I never wanted to do. I was not the marrying kind. Tie myself down to a man and lose all of my freedom, become one of those dreadfully dull Uptown women with no life other than her husband and her children? No, thank you, that wasn't for me. I didn't want

anything to do with that, you can be sure of that. Your grandfather was desperate for me to marry; he wanted me to find a rich husband so he wouldn't have to go on supporting me, but he couldn't very well throw me out into the streets. He even tried to get me to marry that horrible Lenny Pousson ... if you can believe that. How desperate would I have had to be to marry that son of a bitch?"

"You knew Lenny Pousson?"

"Oh, yes, I knew Lenny. Lenny was always around. You know, Lenny was in love with your mother, but he would have settled for me." More laughter. "Poor Lenny. Since your father was a nobody from the Lower Ninth Ward, he thought he was good enough for your mother, too. He didn't understand that your father was smart, handsome, and charming. So what if he was white trash? No one would ever talk to him and know it. . . . Lenny was a yat, and would always be a yat. He thought he could marry into the Verlaine family and become a gentleman, as if that would be all it would take! But Percy was willing enough to let him marry me ... as if I ever would. And then I found exactly what kind of a monster Lenny was ... and even then Uncle Percy wanted me to marry him! He was perfectly willing to let me marry a monster, may he rot in hell for eternity."

"What are you talking about?"

"There was a horrible fight that night. That Saturday night before."

"Before?"

"Before everything went to hell."

"What was the fight about?"

"It was at the dinner table. Your father and I were going out to a party. Your mother was pregnant—that's right, she must have been carrying you, you're the one I never met, Irene—and Uncle Percy was angry about something, and

*made some horrible remark about me being a tramp or
something, and your father got angry and they started
shouting at each other, and then Uncle Percy said something
like, 'You think I don't know what you are, Michael, but I do
know. . . . Everyone knows and everyone pities your wife and
your children, who will have to grow up knowing their father
was a pervert, how does that make you feel?' and Margot
got upset and ran out of the room, and Michael told Uncle
Percy, 'Better a pervert than a bigoted old monster incapable
of love—and don't act so high and mighty with me, old
man—why don't you ask your precious daughter who got
her pregnant THIS time?' and he grabbed me and pulled me
out of the room, and we went to that party—I think it was at
Barbara Palmer's, I don't remember whose party it was, and
we got stinking drunk and then we went down to the Quarter, and we both picked up men and went to a nasty little
motel on Esplanade Avenue. . . . We drank some more and
smoked some pot and your father took his boy to a room and
I took mine to one and before dawn we snuck back into the
house ... and he invited me to meet him for a drink that Sunday afternoon at a bar on Chartres Street—we met there
every Sunday to sing along with the piano player and drink
beer with the other gay men and just get stinking drunk and
then we would go to a little Greek diner just up the street
and eat gyros to soak up the liquor before heading home. It
was always a lot of fun. By the time I woke up that Sunday
afternoon your father had already left the house. No one was
around, not even your mother ... so I had breakfast and
drank mimosas and then got dressed and called a cab to go
down to the Quarter. . . . It was such a warm, beautiful day
for late June ... sunny and the sky was blue, but it wasn't really humid like it usually is. . . . I remember thinking what a
beautiful day it was. I was wearing a white sundress and I*

thought I looked beautiful. I had the cab driver drop me on Canal Street and decided to walk the rest of the way in. . . . On the next block from the bar where we would go to the diner for gyros was some bars that the sailors liked to go to, and I always liked to walk by there when I looked pretty. . . . I remember that day there was this gorgeous sailor from Italy, he was so beautiful but a little shy and he wanted to buy me a drink, so I thought why not and I went in and had my dirty martini and then told him I had to go, and then I walked out into the sunshine and started down the street, and that's when I saw. . . ."

Silence.

"Aunt Cathy?"

No response.

"What did you see?"

"I don't want to talk about it."

"Please, Aunt Cathy."

"No, no, every time I've talked about it I've gotten into trouble. You know what they did to me when they first brought me here? They strapped electrodes to my forehead and ran shocks through my brain to try to make me forget what I saw, and all the time they kept telling me that I was imagining it all, that none of it ever happened, that I was delusional ... so I decided that I'd never talk about it again. I won't. You can't make me."

"But you've already told me so much!"

"You have to forget everything I've said, and you must swear to me you will never repeat anything I've said."

"I already promised you I wouldn't. Please tell me, Aunt Cathy. My father would want me to know!"

"Maybe he would at that. . . ."

"Please!"

"I walked down the street. It was so pretty out, and I was

in a good mood and I was a little buzzed, and then I saw Lenny Pousson, standing outside the door to the stairs. I remember thinking, 'What the hell is Lenny doing there?' He was holding a bottle, and I couldn't figure it out, why was he there and why did he have his own liquor, the Upstairs Lounge has a full bar, and surely Lenny isn't queer, and then he shoved a cloth into the mouth of the bottle, lit a book of matches, and set it on fire ... then he threw it inside, and shut the door... and then as I stood there staring, he rang the buzzer, the one the cabbies always used to let the bartender know there was a cab waiting, and I just stood there and it happened so fast I couldn't think what to do, I could hear people screaming, and the flames were everywhere and I started screaming and I ran down there because I knew your father was inside waiting for me ... and then I don't remember anything else until I woke up in the hospital ... and I kept trying to tell them, but they just said I was hysterical and kept drugging me, and I kept on and on and then they brought me here. And I've been here ever since."

"You're telling me that Lenny Pousson set a fire that killed my father?"

"Not just your father, Irene. Not just your father. . . . A lot of people died in there. And then I woke up in the hospital and I tried to tell them, but they told me I'd imagined the whole thing, and I tried to convince them that Lenny had started the fire, and then Percy himself came to see me, and he told me I needed to shut my mouth or I would be sorry."

"He threatened you?"

"I wanted to talk to Margot, I wanted to talk to the police, I wanted to talk to anyone who would listen—but they kept drugging me. And then I woke up here, and they kept telling me I was crazy."

"So, my grandfather knew."

"Of course he knew! Lenny never had an original thought in his mind. He would have never thought to set a fire, he would have never thought to murder your father and a bunch of innocent people. . . . Of course it was your grandfather's idea. Lenny always did his dirty work; he was happy to do anything for money ... he was like a lapdog with your grandfather. Anything the great Percy Verlaine wanted, Lenny was only too happy to do for him."

"Who was my father, Aunt Cathy?"

Laughter. "I don't know. Michael suspected, but he never told me. And you promised me you wouldn't tell anyone about the fire. You mustn't, because then they would come after me. Lenny would come up here and take care of me—or they'll shock me again. You know they threatened me with a lobotomy once. . . . It's where they stick an ice pick through your eye socket and scramble your brains so you can't really think anymore. Every once in a while when I don't do what they want me to, they threaten me with that again. . . . Can you imagine how horrible it would be to have an ice pick stuck into your brain?"

"I'm so sorry, Aunt Cathy. Thank you for telling me. And I am going to try to get you out of here."

"I will never leave here alive, Irene. They've told me that. I will never leave here alive. . . ."

The recording ended.

I felt sick to my stomach, like I was going to throw up. I could hear my heart pounding.

Catherine Hollis had been an eyewitness to the setting of the Upstairs Lounge fire.

For thirty-two years, she'd been locked up in mental hospital to keep that secret.

Lenny Pousson had set the fire that had killed over

twenty people, just to kill Michael Mercereau—because he had become dangerous to the Verlaine family.

Michael Mercereau wasn't Iris's father.

And the day after Catherine had finally told Iris her secrets, Iris had been shot and killed.

In my mind, I could hear Nurse Amanda saying again, *You never know who might be listening.*

I heard Valerie: *I told Joshua that someone had cleaned out Iris's files and wiped her hard drive, how am I supposed to do my job without that information? He said he'd see what he could find out. . . .*

And two days later, he was dead.

On my way back from Cortez, someone had tried to run me off the road—and while I was gone, my apartment had been broken into and searched.

If my life had been in danger before, now that I'd listened to this recording—it wasn't worth two cents.

My hands shook as I slid a CD into my computer and burned a copy of the recording onto it. I ejected the CD and slid another in. While the second one burned, I wrote *Venus* on the first one and slipped it into a jewel case. The second one was for Blaine, and I made a third for Paige. Once the three CDs were ready and labeled, I put them in envelopes and addressed them. I leaned back in my chair.

I could feel something inside me, but I didn't really know what it was. Fear? Horror? Something like that.

I pulled out my cell phone. My hands were shaking so badly I could barely hold it, let alone hit my first speed dial number. I held it up to my ear. Nothing. It just rang and rang ... and then I got that horrible recording, *We're sorry, all circuits are busy, please hang up and try again.* I tried three times more before I gave up—I was ready to throw the phone across the room.

I had to do something.

I walked out my front door, checked to see if anyone was around, sprinted across the park, and slid the envelopes marked *Blaine* and *Venus* into the mail slot at Blaine's house. There were no cars around, so no one was home. The wind was blowing, the branches of the park's oak trees waving lazily, leaves shivering. I then hurried over to Paige's, and put one in her mail slot. I felt a little better. If anything happened to me ... the truth would come out.

If anything happened to me.

My mind was spinning. I didn't know what to do, or where to go.

Somehow I managed to find my way back to my apartment.

I sat there for a moment, and then felt the anger starting to rise inside of me.

Twenty-four people had died in that fire. Been murdered in the most horrible way imaginable—incinerated to death for no reason other than being gay and in the wrong bar at the wrong time. They'd been exterminated like vermin, burned to death.

The heat was so intense in some cases the bodies fused together.

For thirty-two years, Percy Verlaine and Lenny Pousson had gotten away with it.

Percy had had his own grandchildren murdered to cover it up.

He doesn't deserve to live.

I got my gun out of the safe under my bed, and loaded it. I kept it clean and well-oiled. I don't like to carry it, and I certainly don't like to use it, but I go out for target practice once a month, just to be on the safe side.

Destiny is a funny thing. I'd never really believed in it. I was raised in the Church of Christ, and the most important tenet of that incredibly intolerant sect was *free will*. We choose our paths, we make decisions, and we must suffer the consequences of our actions. The notion of *destiny* denies free will. And even though I'd shaken off the outer trappings of my religious upbringing, at the root of my being my early training was still there, controlling what I thought and what I believed and what I did. I thought Paul's death was a punishment for killing a man—the consequences of my taking a life.

Now, as I sat there holding my gun, I believed differently.

It was my destiny to punish Percy Verlaine and Lenny Pousson for their crimes.

It was destiny that had brought Iris Verlaine to me. It was destiny that had sent me to see Catherine Hollis, to get the recorder from Valerie Stratton. It was destiny that had led me into law enforcement, so I would learn how to shoot a gun. It was destiny that had made me go into private investigation. All those years of training, all those hours spent at the shooting range perfecting my ability to handle a gun—it was all preparation for what I was about to do, what I had to do.

The anger that had been building inside me cooled. I felt calm, and at peace. Now that the decision had been made, there was no turning back. They had to pay for their crimes. Percy Verlaine would never have been brought to justice in our courts—he had too much money and too much power. He would get away with it—and he would protect Lenny Pousson as well. He had covered for Lenny for thirty-two years—at the cost of losing two of his only grandchildren.

He was old and he was sick, but he didn't deserve to draw another breath.

I had always held life to be a sacred thing, and had never

understood how one person could knowingly and willingly take another life.

Now, I completely understood.

I put on my leather jacket, put the gun in my pocket, and walked out the back door.

CHAPTER EIGHTEEN

IT STARTED TO RAIN almost at the exact same moment I started the car. I turned the wipers on as I backed out of my spot and switched on the lights. The sun was just setting, but the sky was covered with dark clouds. Lightning forked nearby and the thunder that followed almost immediately was loud enough to shake my car. I drove down the drive and pulled out onto Camp Street. The streetlights weren't working, and all of the houses were dark. The darkness was almost absolute; it was like being in the country. I circled the park—still no cars over at Blaine's, which wasn't a good thing—and swung back down to Magazine Street and headed for the Garden District.

Confronting a killer is generally not a smart thing to do. I had done it once before in the past, armed with nothing more than a pocket tape recorder. It had never occurred to me that day as I went over there that he was a hardened killer, that he'd be willing to kill me as well. Live and learn. Once I confronted him with what I knew, he'd first tried to talk me into not going to the police, to let him get away. I couldn't do it, and so he'd tried to kill me. He came after me with a knife, and we'd fought—and it was the first time in my life I ever feared I was going to die, faced my own mortality. In the ensuing struggle I'd wound up punching him and knocking him backward. He had crashed through a glass door, hit a railing, and gone over—breaking his neck when he landed on the cement courtyard below. I hadn't meant for him to die—I was just trying to save myself—but he died anyway. I hadn't been charged—the knife was still in his hands and there was a matching cut on my arm from when he'd come at me with it—and I'd had the tape recording of our conversation. It was open-and-shut, but nevertheless his death had haunted me in the ensuing months. I'd relived it in my dreams over and over again, waking up covered in sweat and sometimes screaming. Paul had always been there to hold me and comfort me, to make me feel safe and better.

When Paul had been murdered, a part of me had honestly believed it was divine retribution. I had sinned by taking a life, and God was punishing me by taking the life of someone close to me, to make me suffer. There had even been a little voice whispering in my mind that the hurricane and ensuing flood was also a part of my punishment. But now I knew better. That had been self-absorption. I was not the center of the universe. Paul did not die because I loved him. A mentally disturbed man obsessed with Paul had kidnapped and killed him. That would have happened to Paul whether he knew me or not. God had not sent Hurricane Katrina to punish me. It was simply nature, the randomness of the world. Was I really so worthy of divine punishment that the city had to be destroyed and hundreds of thousands of people forced to suffer? No, I wasn't. I knew that now.

The recording was certainly more than enough evidence to send Lenny Pousson to death row. Whether he had set the fire at the Upstairs Lounge on Percy Verlaine's orders—that would be up to the district attorney's office to prove at some point. They would have to go through the financial records of Verlaine Shipping to find whatever Iris had dug up, if that evidence hadn't already been destroyed. Percy was certainly wealthy enough to hire a battalion of lawyers to fight any charges, and given the state of his health, he'd probably die before going to trial.

Sometimes, justice needs a little help.

It was pouring when I got to the Verlaine house; the windshield wipers were unable to keep up with the onslaught of water. I wondered briefly if the patches on the levees would hold, or if the pumps had been repaired enough to empty the streets of the gathering water, but dismissed the thought. It was just a heavy storm—we'd gotten through those plenty of times before. The deep gutters dug around the Garden District streets were already filled with water. I parked, got out of the car, and ran down to the driveway, where the gate was open. I headed up the driveway and had just climbed the front steps when the front door opened.

Emily Hunter stood there with a box in her hands. She gave me a wry smile. Her blouse was splotched with wet marks, and her hair looked bedraggled. "Well, well, well. Look who's here."

"Hello," I replied. "I need to see Percy."

"Be my guest." She stepped aside. "He's in his room—third door on the left at the top of the stairs." She smiled. "Give the old bastard my regards, will you? I don't trust myself to go in there myself. I might just smother him with a pillow."

"What?" It was so close to what I was thinking about, it threw me a little.

"Oh, I've been fired." She gave me a nasty smile. "After twenty-odd years working here, I've been informed my services are no longer necessary or wanted, and told to get off the premises immediately and to never darken the door of

the Verlaine home ever again. Nice, huh? Two months sever-
ance."

"Why?"

"No explanation—but around here that's no surprise."
She shrugged. "Go on in. And tell the old man to go to hell
for me, will you?"

I stepped inside and shut the door behind me. There were
no lights on in the downstairs, and the staircase was dark,
and I didn't know where the light switch was. I started up
the stairs. The second-floor hallway was lit up, and in just a
few moments I was standing in the third doorway on the left.
I felt the gun in my pocket and looked in.

Percy Verlaine was lying in his bed, the oxygen mask over
his withered face. A single light burned on his nightstand.
The curtains to the big windows were open, and the rain
was pelting the glass. I could barely make out the branches
of a huge oak tree bending in the wind outside. "Who's
there?" he called out. He reached over to the nightstand and
put on a pair of glasses. His eyes focused on me. "How did
you get in?"

"Emily let me in." I walked into the room and pulled up a
chair next to the bed. I sat down. "Why did you fire her?"

He closed his eyes. "I don't have to explain my dealings
with my staff to you."

"We need to have a talk, old man."

He opened his eyes. "I have nothing to say to you."

"Then you can listen." I leaned in close. "Do you remember Cathy Hollis? The niece you locked away in a mental
hospital thirty years ago?"

"I raised her like my own daughter." He glared at me.

"And that only makes me feel even sorrier for Margot
than I already do—and believe me, I felt pretty bad for her
already."

"Get to your point, and spare me your lectures about things you know nothing about—and then get out." He spat the words at me.

"I don't know why you hated your son-in-law so much," I went on. "Whatever the reason, you hated him and wanted him gone—out of your daughter's life and out of this house—for good, didn't you?"

"She deserved better. He only married her for her money."

"Did he make her happy?"

"He made her miserable!" The eyes flashed open and glared at me again. "Anyone could see she was suffering!"

"And so that made it all right to have him killed?"

Lightning flashed right outside the window. He didn't answer for a moment, and I was about to ask him again when he said, his voice so low I could barely hear him, "I didn't have him killed. You're wrong about that."

"Did you know that Iris went to see your niece before she was killed? And they had a rather interesting conversation—which Iris recorded." I smiled at him. "I have a copy of the recording—and the police have it now as well."

He turned his head slowly to look at me. "You don't understand anything. Have you ever heard the story of Henry II and Thomas a Becket?"

"What?" I stared at him. "What the hell are you talking about?"

"Becket and the King were great friends, and then the King came up with this great idea—he was having problems with the church, and decided to make Becket the new Archbishop of Canterbury—a great idea, because then his best friend would be running the organization he was having trouble with. It was a big mistake, because Becket took to the job with a vengeance. He was a bigger thorn in the

King's side than his predecessor—he gave Henry fits. One evening he cried out in irritation, 'Is there no one who will rid me of this troublesome priest?' A group of his knights set out that very evening and murdered Becket."

"You've got to be kidding me." I stared at him. "You don't expect me to believe—"

"I didn't order Lenny to do anything. I never asked him to kill anyone." He blinked his eyes at me. "There was a big fight at dinner the Saturday night before it happened. Catherine and I started shouting at each other, and then Michael got involved—and then after dinner he came into my library and threatened me. He *threatened* me. He was going to take the children and go—told me my daughter was a whore, was carrying some other man's child. I would never see them again if I didn't start treating them all better. Pfah!" He spat. "What did that Ninth Ward yat trash know about family? Afterward, as Lenny and I shared a brandy, I made the horrible mistake of wishing Michael was gone and out of my hair forever. The next day, Lenny set that horrible fire." His eyes glinted. "Did I tell him to do it? No, I didn't." He licked his lips. "But if you ask me if I am sorry he died, I won't lie and say yes. I wasn't sorry he was dead. And I'm still not."

"I don't believe you," I replied. "It's a good try, though. How did Lenny know where Michael would be? How did he know to have a Molotov cocktail ready? How did he even know it would work? This was planned. . . ."

"I don't know what you mean." He turned his head away from me.

"*You* hated Michael. *You* didn't think he was good enough for your daughter or to father your grandchildren. When exactly did you find out he was gay?"

"I always knew. Do you think I would have allowed him to

marry my daughter without having him checked out first?" He spat the words at me. "She married him anyway. She didn't care. She loved him despite his perversions. Even though she knew he only wanted her money. She didn't care. She was a fool. She had no pride." He looked at me again. "Sometimes I find it hard to believe—even now—that she was my daughter."

"She *was* your daughter, and he made her happy. That should have been enough for you." My voice shook. I put my hand in my pocket and felt the gun. *Use me,* it seemed to whisper in my head, *this miserable old man deserves to die.*

"Pfah." He waved a hand in dismissal. "How could she be happy married to a pervert?"

"He wasn't the only person who died in that fire."

The lights flickered. "A bunch of perverts got what they deserved."

Kill him, just do it. Stop talking and do it!

"Why did you lock Cathy up in that mental hospital? Why didn't you just let Lenny kill her too?"

"I put her there to protect her from Lenny, you jackass." He glared at me. "You don't understand anything, do you? I was trying to protect her! She *saw* him do it! How much do you think her life was worth after that?"

"You were protecting your own ass. As long as she was locked up and people thought she was unbalanced, no one would listen to her story." I struggled to keep my voice from shaking. I could feel the anger starting to rise inside me. "Why not just turn him in? You could afford enough lawyers to keep your own sorry ass out of jail."

"It was a huge mess." He closed his eyes. "We couldn't risk the scandal. Lenny was more than willing to turn me over to the police if he went down as well. And then he started blackmailing me. I've paid him a lot of money over the years. . . ." There was a roar of thunder and the lights flickered again. "I thought it was best this way. Maybe I was wrong."

"And so you allowed him to kill your grandchildren. What kind of monster are you?" I gritted my teeth. "That's the one thing I can't understand. Why would you condone that? Your life is almost over. Why did you let him kill Iris and Joshua?"

He gaped at me. "What are you talking about?"

"Do you mean to sit there and tell me you don't know he killed Iris and Joshua? To continue covering up your crimes? You don't think I'm that stupid." I laughed. "And surely you don't expect me to think you didn't know about that?"

"Iris ... was ... killed ... by ... a ... burglar." He was struggling to breathe, and his face began to flush. "And Joshua ... fell ... he was a drunken fool. It was just a matter of time before he did something stupid."

I stared at him. "You *didn't* know. Iris found out, you know—"

"She threatened, she threatened me." He closed his eyes, his chest rising and falling. "She had a recording, she had records of the payments I made. . . ."

"And Lenny killed her. He took all the files from her office, erased her hard drive. Joshua was looking for them—and then he fell." I leaned forward and hissed at him, "And the fall was no accident—the way the body landed, there's no way he fell on his own or jumped. He was *thrown* from the roof, Percy. Who do you suppose would want to do that?"

Percy started gasping for breath. "Are ... you ... saying ... that ... Iris ... and ..."

"The cover-up you started thirty-two years ago, old man, cost your grandchildren their lives. How does that make you feel?" I snapped.

"What's going on in here?"

I turned around and faced a man of about thirty-five. He was about five-nine, wearing a Tulane sweatshirt and a loose-fitting pair of jeans. He had the same color hair as Iris, the same coloring, almost the exact same features.

"Who are you and why are you upsetting my grand-father? I think you'd better leave."

"You must be Darrin Verlaine. I'm Chanse MacLeod. I was hired by your sister, and then again by your brother, to find your father." I stood up. "And I found lots of other things as well."

"My grandfather is not well." He walked into the room and went to the other side of the bed. "And you're upsetting him. I'm going to have to ask you to leave."

I stood up. "May I speak to you privately?"

"NO!" the old man gasped out. "I forbid it!"

"You don't want your only remaining grandchild to know you were responsible for murdering his father?"

"What?" Darrin looked at me, then back at the old man. "What are you talking about?"

"Are you going to tell him, or should I?"

"Get out!" The old man gasped. "I ... can't ... breathe ..."

"What's going on?" Darrin stood up. "You can't come in here and make wild accusations. I've already asked you to leave. If you don't, I'll have you thrown out."

"By Lenny Pousson? The man who killed your father? And your brother and sister?"

"Lenny?" Darrin's face went white. "What are you talking about? This can't be true!"

"Lies!" the old man wheezed out. He gasped and clutched at his heart. "My God ... my God ... my heart!"

"Grandpa!" Darrin picked up the phone and started dial-ing.

"Put the phone down."

The voice came from the doorway. We both turned. Lenny was standing in the doorway, and he was holding a gun. His eyes were wild, his hair and clothes were soaking wet. The gun moved back and forth from me to Darrin.

"Lenny?" Darrin stared at him, the phone in his hand. "What are you doing? Have you lost your mind?"

"I said put the phone down!" Lenny half-shouted.

Darrin replaced the phone slowly. "I have to call the doctor. He needs a doctor, Lenny, please."

"No." He took a step into the room. "No doctors, no phone calls. I don't care if he dies."

"It's all over, Lenny," I said, keeping my voice calm while tightening my grip on my own gun. *If I could get it out without him seeing me...* "Cathy told Iris everything—but you already knew that, right? You knew that as soon as Iris left St. Isabelle's, because her room was bugged, but Iris recorded the conversation. I found it ... and the police have it now."

"I should have killed that bitch thirty years ago." His gun swept from me to Darrin. "She was always nothing but trouble for everyone."

"You can't kill both of us," I went on. "And for what reason? The police already know, Lenny. You won't be able to get away with it. They're probably looking for you already. You can't just shoot us both and walk away from this. It's too late."

"Let me call the doctor," Darrin pleaded. "He's dying. *Please.*"

"It's good enough for him!" Lenny shouted. "It was all his idea! He told me how to do it! To set the fire!"

"Lenny—"

"I loved her." He went on as though I hadn't said a word. "I wanted to marry her. Michael was making a fool of her, and I hated to see it. She cried all the time, every night when he was with one of his men. And *he* knew it. He worked on me … all the time insinuating how much Michael was hurting her, making her life a living hell. If only Michael were out of the way, then I could have her. So I did it, yes, I did it. I set the fire. *On his orders.*"

"And you got her pregnant." It started all falling into place now.

He stared at me. "What?"

"Iris was your daughter," I went on. "Michael and Margot stopped having sex after Darrin was born."

"No." His eyes grew wilder.

"What—what are you talking about?" Darrin demanded. "None of this makes any sense!"

"He's … lying. . . ." Percy's face was turning a strange shade of pale blue.

"You killed a bunch of innocent people in the process." I kept my eyes on the gun. It was wavering.

"They were perverts who didn't deserve to live." He was perspiring. "No one would suspect, he said. If it looked like arson, no one would care, no one would care about a bunch of dead faggots … and no one would ever suspect that it was really a murder. . . . The more who died, the better it would be. And so I did it. I followed him every Sunday when he left the house. I went up there the day before and checked around, saw what a firetrap it was. . . . It was easy enough. And I'm not sorry. He made her suffer."

"But she didn't want you again, did she?" I said. "She made a mistake with you once, right? And then she never stopped mourning him, hoping he'd come home one day. She never knew he was dead—you put her into hell, didn't you?"

"I wanted to tell her. *He* wouldn't let me."

"And then Iris found out," I went on. "And so she had to die, too, right?"

"Is this true?" Darrin's face went pale. "Oh my God, this can't be true."

"And Joshua too. He found out, didn't he? So he had to die as well." I went on. "But the police know. And they're going to arrest you."

He pointed the gun at me. "I'm not going to jail!"

My entire body went cold. Everything seemed to slow down. I had my hand on my own gun, but if I fired it, I couldn't be sure I would actually hit him. *So this is how it ends,* I thought to myself, *shot to death by a sociopath during a thunderstorm.* The lights flickered again. I watched him. His hand was shaking. Maybe I could talk my way out of this. . . . "Lenny, you don't want to do this," I heard myself saying. I heard Darrin say something and Lenny turned, pointing the gun at him. I pulled my gun out, spread my legs wide, and gripped the gun with both hands. Without hesitation, I pulled the trigger and watched as Lenny fell backward, still in slow motion. He fell backward. "Call the doctor!" I shouted at Darrin as I reached for my own cell phone. I dialed Venus's number as I ran over to where Lenny fell.

I could hear Darrin talking to the doctor as I leaned down and felt for a pulse. There was none. He was still holding his gun.

"Casanova."

"Venus, this is Chanse. You need to get over to the Verlaine house," I said, my voice starting to shake. "I've got a dead body and a story to tell you."

"I'm on my way."

I got up, walked back over to the bed, and reached down, putting my hand on Percy's carotid artery. There was a slight heartbeat—weak, but still there. I leaned down and started doing CPR.

I had gone to the Verlaine house with my mind made up. I was going to kill Percy Verlaine, to avenge the innocents who'd died in the fire, to avenge the deaths of his grandchildren.

And now I was performing CPR, trying to keep him alive before the paramedics came.

As I breathed into his mouth, I kind of hoped he would live.

Wouldn't it be the greatest irony of all time for Percy Verlaine to realize that not only had a pervert saved his life, but I had put my mouth on his in order to do it?

Call it poetic justice.

CHAPTER NINETEEN

"I don't know whether to thank you or beat you to death," Venus said.

Venus, Paige, Blaine, and I were at our usual table at the Avenue Pub. There was no one else in the place, and I was glad of that. The big-screen televisions were tuned in to some poker show and the jukebox was silent. The bartender was wiping down the counter, and the girl working the grill was sitting on a barstool drinking a Coke and reading a Nora Roberts novel. It was almost eleven; the curfew was less than an hour away, but we were with cops—so I didn't think we had anything to worry about, should we get stopped on our way home.

Percy Verlaine didn't make it. When the paramedics arrived, they tried to save him, but he was too far gone. And Lenny never had a chance. I'd shot him in the chest—didn't get him directly in the heart, but he was dead. And unlike the first man I'd killed, I didn't think I was going to lose any sleep over killing Lenny Pousson.

"I feel kind of sorry for Darrin Verlaine," Blaine said, taking a swig from his beer. "Man, how do you deal with all of this? His brother and sister are dead, his grandfather's dead, his grandfather was responsible for killing them—and his father." He shook his head. "That's a lot to handle."

"Darrin is now worth many millions of dollars," Paige said. She had a glass of red wine in front of her, which was nice to see. Maybe she was coping better now. "He can afford the best therapists in the world—and the best drugs. He'll be fine—eventually. Is he going to get Cathy Hollis out of St. Isabelle's?"

"She's already been released," I replied. "Darrin took care of it."

"What were you thinking, going over there like that?" Venus whacked me in the arm. "You almost got yourself killed, jackass. And then I'd have to explain to the commissioner why the man I deputized was in the morgue." She sighed. "Although it's just as well—that they both are dead, I mean, not that you almost got yourself killed. We probably would have never been able to bring them to trial."

"What do you think, Chanse?" Paige asked. She hadn't touched the glass of wine. It was just as full as when it was brought to the table. "Do you think Percy ordered Lenny to set the fire?"

"We'll never really know—although even if they were still alive, we'd never know for sure." I shrugged. "They were too busy playing 'my word against yours.' Deep down, there's no doubt in my mind that Percy ordered him to do it. But to give the old bastard credit, his surprise when I told him about Iris and Joshua was genuine. I don't think he knew about that—although ..." I hesitated, then shook my head and changed my mind. "No, he did know. He wasn't a stupid man, and there's no way he could have ever thought it was just a lucky coincidence Iris was killed by a burglar on the same day she confronted him with everything. He might not have known about Joshua, though."

"Well, it's never a smart idea to blackmail a killer—I guess they didn't teach Iris that at Harvard." Venus finished her drink and set it down. She laughed. "I'm done. Long day, and I should already be in bed."

"Yeah." Blaine yawned and stretched. "And we gotta be in early tomorrow."

"Can everyone just wait a second?" Paige said. She cleared her throat. "Um, I just wanted to let you all know that I'm leaving tomorrow."

"Leaving? For good?" Blaine asked.

Paige threw her arms up. "I don't know. I doubt it. I've got a lot of vacation time saved up, and I'm taking all five weeks of it. A guy at the office has a cabin up in the mountains in Tennessee, and he's letting me use it." She bit her lower lip. "I'm going to go up there and get away. I'm going to finish my book." Paige had been working on a historical romance novel set in New Orleans during the War of 1812 for at least five years. "I'm never going to finish the damned thing working on it in bits and pieces here and there around my job, you know? There's always going to be something else more important for me to do here. And I do want to finish it. I can't keep putting it off. And I think the peace and quiet would do me a lot of good."

There was silence. Blaine was playing with his cocktail napkin. Venus just looked at Paige; her mouth opened and closed without saying anything. I took a deep breath and said, "I think that's great, Paige." Everyone turned and looked at me. "Really. The one thing we should all learn from what we've all been through is we need to stop putting off the things we want to do. Life is short, and we don't know how much time we have. We've got to make the best of it while we can."

"Thank you, Chanse." Paige gave me a weak smile.

"Don't get me wrong—I'm happy for you, but I want you to come back." Losing Paige permanently would be like losing a limb. "What about you, Venus?"

"I'll miss you, Paige," she replied. "But he's right. Go for it." She looked at me. "All right, I know what you meant. No, I'm not going to retire. I'm not leaving New Orleans. This is home. If I ever get my insurance settlement on the house, I'll start looking for another place, or start paying rent for the carriage house." She playfully punched Blaine in the shoulder. "I can't mooch off these guys forever."

"You know you're welcome to the carriage house as long as you want it." Blaine played with the label of his empty beer bottle. "And you don't have to pay rent."

"No, I *need* to," she smiled. "As long as I stay there for free, it won't feel like it's my home. And I need that, you know? I need to feel like the place I'm living is my home, not some transitional place." She gave me a sidelong look. "And what about you, Chanse? You going to stay or move on?"

I didn't answer for a moment. They were all looking at me. "I'm staying."

Once I said the words, I felt a sense of relief. It was as though saying it out loud made it real somehow.

New Orleans was home, in a way Cottonwood Wells and Baton Rouge never had been. I'd known that the first time I'd driven down I-10 to come to the Quarter when I was in college. The city was part of me now. I couldn't even imagine living anywhere else. No matter how many frustrations and irritations the city had thrown at me in the years since I'd moved down after college, it had never once occurred to me to move away, to leave and never come back. The best memories of my life were in this city. Yes, of course, there were bad memories as well, but that would be the case anywhere I chose to live. Even during the worst days, when the city was under water and people were dying, trapped with no way out, as I watched the city die on national television, as my heart was ripped out and all I could do was cry, all I could think was *I want to go home.* And I'd finally been able to do just that. So many people couldn't, might not ever be able to. Their jobs were gone, their homes were gone, and if they had children, they couldn't come back until the schools were open again. And so many had nothing to come home to—so would they? Or would they just choose to stay wherever they'd relocated to, rebuild their lives somewhere else?

Even if I never got another job on the investigation side of my business, my contract with Crown Oil enabled me to live anywhere I chose. I couldn't just abandon the city simply because it was no longer *convenient* to live there.

New Orleans deserved better than that from me.

I looked around the table at the faces of my friends. Sure, Paige was going away for a while to get her head together and chase her own dream. But there was no doubt in my mind she would come back. New Orleans was a part of her as well. The city had that kind of effect on people. It gets into your head, your heart, and your blood. It becomes a part of your soul, your very being.

With no offense intended to Dallas, the weeks I'd stayed there had hammered that very point into my brain. Dallas was not my home. Dallas could never be that for me. I would miss New Orleans too much.

I could never live without being able to walk into a dive of a place and get a shrimp po'boy that tasted better than anything I could get in a chain restaurant.

I could never give up the beauty of the swamp oaks on St. Charles Avenue.

I could never give up walking two blocks to watch a Mardi Gras parade and catch beads.

I could never give up that sense of community that everyone in New Orleans shared.

The old New Orleans might be gone, but the city was still here. And no matter what changes were to come in the future, it would always be New Orleans.

Another hurricane could come. The levees could fail again. The next one could be even worse. But as long as there was a New Orleans, I was staying.

It wouldn't be easy, but life in New Orleans had never been easy.

Our little get-together broke up, and we walked Paige back home. We said our goodbyes, shed a few tears, and then Blaine and Venus drove me back home.

I walked into my apartment and turned on the lights. I sat down on the sofa and picked up my pipe. As I took a hit, I looked up at the print of Paul on the wall.

We hadn't had a lot of time together, but we were really happy during that time. I'd been happier than I'd ever thought I would be, happier than I'd ever imagined in my wildest dreams. Maybe I didn't realize or appreciate it at the time, but it was true. And I appreciated it now. I'd been too hung up on my own issues while he was alive to truly recognize what I'd had, and that had been a waste.

There are no guarantees in life. You don't get a warranty when you are born. Things happen. Hurricanes come in, levees fail, people die. You never know when your own number is going to come up. There might be an afterlife; reincarnation might be true—no one really knows. But the one thing certain is you get one shot at your life, and it is what you make it. You can spend the rest of your life bitter over not having the kind of parents or background you think you should have had. You can bitch about growing up in a trailer with a drunk mother and an abusive father. You can close yourself off from other people because your partner was murdered. You can allow that to twist your perspective, make you think you don't deserve good things from life. You can stop trying to be happy because it seems like life is always right there, ready to kick you in the teeth and knock you down.

We like to think we have control. We build our lives and we pretend we have security. But security is a myth. It doesn't really exist. It's an illusion we create to protect ourselves from the realization that so many things are random, out of our control. So we soldier on, pretending that it can't all be taken away from us at any moment, but the major drawback of that mental insulation is it makes us less appreciative of what we have. We don't live in the moment; we don't take time every day to enjoy life and savor the great gift of being alive.

I stood up and walked over to the wall. I reached up and took the print down.

It was time to let go and start living again.

It didn't mean I loved him less. It didn't mean I'd stopped missing him and wishing he was still here with me. But it was time to stop hurting. It was time to appreciate what we'd had and move on.

Fee was right. Paul wouldn't have wanted me to mourn him for the rest of my life. That wasn't who he was. He would want me to be happy.

Maybe things with Jude would have worked out—but I didn't see how they could have. I would never move to Dallas; I couldn't expect him to give up his job and move to New Orleans. My only regret was that I'd hurt him, but I was hopeful we were getting past that now and could be friends.

Maybe something would develop with Allen. Maybe not, but if I didn't give it a try I'd never know. Yet if I spent the rest of my life inside my own walls, afraid to live and take risks, I'd only be a shell of a person.

That wasn't living.

New Orleans would endure. She had survived plague, pestilence, war, fire, flood, death, and destruction in her almost three hundred years of existence. She always came back defiantly, ready for more. She never became bitter; she didn't live in the past. She lived in the moment and tried to make us all understand how important that was. So many of us failed to listen and to learn from her example.

Laissez le bon temps roulez.

ACKNOWLEDGMENTS

THIS BOOK was written over a period of time from early October 2005 through December 2006, in the wake of Hurricane Katrina and the devastating flood that followed.

I would be remiss if I didn't take this opportunity to thank my editor, Joe Pittman, for his incredible patience, his insight, and his kindness. It was he who pushed for this book to be done at all, at a time when I had long since given up on there ever being a third Chanse MacLeod book. His support at a time when I was probably at one of the lowest points of my life is something for which I will always be grateful.

In those horrible weeks after the evacuation, when I had no idea when I would be able to come home, or even if I had a home to come back to or if New Orleans was gone forever, the incredible love and kindness of so many friends and strangers from all over the country made the misery almost bearable. Thank all of you for your big hearts.

My co-workers at the NO/AIDS Task Force are a great bunch of people who do amazing work for the New Orleans community. They've also been good friends and a valuable base of emotional support for me: J. M. Redmann, Noel Twilbeck, Mark Drake, Joshua Fegley, Allison Vertovec, Ked Dixon, Seema Gai, and Darrin Harris. Bless you all.

This book began while I was staying in Hammond, Louisiana, a wonderful little college town on the north shore of Lake Pontchartrain. Hammond has become a second home to me, and the folks I always associate with Hammond (even though some of them are from New Orleans) are very dear to me: Bev and Butch Marshall, Michael Ledet and Patricia Brady, Elizabeth Schmidt and her husband Norman, Bev's writing classes at Southeastern Louisiana University, and many others.

Julie Smith and Lee Pryor are two of my biggest cheerleaders. Love to you both.

A special thanks to John Pope of the *New Orleans Times-Picayune,* for sharing his experiences and that of other reporters in the wake of the disaster. An entire book could be written about the courage of the *Times-Picayune* staff, who did their jobs so that those of us scattered to the four corners of the country could know what was really going on in our beloved home city. Any errors of fact in Paige's experiences after the hurricane are completely my fault.

Poppy Z. Brite and her husband, Chris Debarr, are also worthy of mention, for their support, their friendship, and their ability to make me laugh no matter what else is going on around me.

Becky Cochrane, Timothy J. Lambert, and Tom Wocken deserve mention for making Houston another safe haven for me.

Marika Christian is a good friend who supports me no matter what.

And of course, Paul J. Willis, my life partner, makes everything worthwhile. We've survived a lot together, and I thank God for him every day for always loving me, supporting me in my endeavors, and loving me when I am not very lovable.